E.D.F Chronicles – The Cyberian menace

It is a period of peace and stability in the galaxy, all the major races E.O.C.A, Solarian, Krenaran and Dracos have largely kept to their own affairs. All this is shattered however when a new threat looms on the fringes of the galaxy, one like no other, only by working together can the peoples of the galaxy hope to prevail against this ancient enemy. Can the major powers put aside old hatreds and past injustices and unite against this greater foe that threatens them all. Because if they fail, all will burn.

First published in Great Britain in 2015.
ISBN#978-0-9574705-3-8

Typeset in Garamond by the author.

By Ian J. Smethurst

E.D.F Chronicles : The Krenaran massacre.
E.D.F Chronicles : E.D.F Resurgent.
E.D.F Chronicles : Eye of the Dracos.
E.D.F Chronicles : The Cyberian menace

E.D.F Chronicles – The Cyberian menace

Ian J. Smethurst

For Steven

For being a true and caring brother, always there when most needed, and despite how our lives have changed us, when it comes down to it, you are still my dear little brother, and when times are tough you are there by my side.

Contents

Tears of Orialis	1
Fealty lost	9
Flight of the Faeriath	15
Exodus	22
Revelations	33
Pilgrim's journey	41
The drawing of the lines	62
Against the tide	80
Re-emergence	91
Return of a legend	101
The re-grouping	124
The search	133
The great battle for E.O.C.A	140
Storming the command ship	162
Epilogue	171

1. Tears of Orialis

November 2081
Orialis
Inside Solarian space.

It was once called Arcanthis, that far away world on the north eastern fringe of Solarian space, a world of joy, of wonder. A thriving technological and cultural jewel in the crown of the powerful Solarian empire.

Abruptly that all changed three weeks ago. Overnight all contact with this world, home to some seven billion of their kin, was lost. A complete blackout, the Solarian empire, the most technologically gifted, most powerful race in the known galaxy had lost a world: Unthinkable.

Televis, former second officer aboard the Liberty, now commander of the Solarian battlecruiser Faeriath, dropped the ship quietly and neatly out of plasma drive on the far reaches of the system.

"Give me a full multi-spectral analysis of the system, I want to know the instant anything is out there." His hairless blue tinged face flushed a shade of purple, revealing his consternation.

"Understood Comraa." Another junior officer replied back from the periphery of his bridge. After some time checking through the findings, the answer came back "I'm not picking up a single object, it is as if the entire system is empty, barren."

Televis stroked his chin, deep in contemplation. A habit picked up whilst spending time with humans. Where were all the supply ships? The streams of transports and civilian tourist pleasure cruisers that went to and from this place all the time. Something was very wrong here. Well he knew that anyway his people had never lost a world in this fashion before, it had come as a bolt from the blue, to coin a phrase the Earth people would often say.

"Order alert status, and raise all shield grids, I want continuous scans, head toward the fourth planet; cautiously." Televis spoke his orders rather than barked them out like the humans tended to do. He simply put it down to the fact that his people were much longer lived than humans, and therefore much more patient. He was after all, approaching his two hundredth birthday though had only commanded the Faeriath for the past ten years. A virtual blip on his lifepath, although he was not about to let his people be caught napping a second time.

The four hundred metre long, silver, crescent shaped Solarian battlecruiser, the pride of his people, and a technological masterpiece in its own right, slowly, carefully picked its way through the system, now fully alert to the merest hint of danger. And, should it come, more than capable of dealing with it, with that femay powerful Solarian fusion cannon mounted beneath its, sharp, raised, beak-like command structure, looking from a distance like a thin tusk of death jutting out from the fore of the ship.

As the hours passed by and the lone ship neared the isolated world, the crew stared wide eyed in shock, their mouths agape at what they were witnessing, every single person on the bridge took in a sharp intake of breath. The crystal blue haze of the atmosphere of that world, once thought akin to the tears of an Acara, the Solarian angel, had changed. It was sullen and black, clouded by ash and thick dense fumes, who could do this to a world? One of their worlds?

Startled by the sheer scale of the destruction, Televis did bark out his orders this time. "I want a full geo-spacial scan of the surface, I want to know what in the name of Acraa happened down there!"

"Working on it," one of the scientists replied. "I am picking up extensive signs of a battle having been fought on the surface, scorch patterns, blast marks, but so far only minimal damage to the infrastructure. All the buildings are more or less intact. I am picking up intermittent energy signatures though and movement on the surface, but still no life signs."

Televis stroked his chin for a second time as he mulled over this new information, "what kinds of energy signatures?"

"Unknown at this time, it is not like anything we have previously encountered, it is like some form of tri-fusion.

"Tri-fusion? What like three reactions all occurring simultaneously around one another?"

"Exactly."

Televis raised an eyebrow at the revelation. "Astounding, how do they contain that kind of power?"

"Again, that is unknown." The scientist replied, his gentle blue brows furrowed in concentration.

"You said there was movement, but no lifesigns. What kind of movement?"

"Metallic, either drones or machines of some description."

"A mechanised civilisation," Televis whispered in awe.

"Quite possibly, they seem to be centred around a gigantic unknown complex, definitely not Solarian in origin. It could be some sort of production facility for the machines? Judging by the soil displacement around it, it has only been there about two weeks."

"Built right after we lost contact with the planet," Televis finished for him. "Prepare a landing party, we need to capture a specimen for further study. If they are self-replicating this could prove to be a threat to more than just this one planet." He briefly wondered if they had stumbled upon something far more serious than they had first thought. "Pilot, bring the ship in low over the atmosphere." He turned back toward the science officer, "once in place we will activate the teleporters and transport you to the surface."

The pilot gently eased forward on the shining chrome arms of the augmented chair, and the ship immediately complied, pitching downward into the ash strewn miasma that was the atmosphere of Arcanthis until it came to within fifty thousand feet of the surface.

The assembled science team strode onto the teleporter array, all donning white environment suits to protect them from the devastated atmosphere, their features masked by the reflectiveness of their helmets, and armed with pulse laser blasters and magnetic grappling equipment to subdue their prey for transport.

"Now!" Barked Televis.

The science team began to gradually de-materialise, and for a brief instant existed as pure energy, it was a cold, dark, strange and nerve racking experience, hence why so few actually liked to be teleported. Although just as quickly they re-materialised on the surface of the planet.

The tall slender spires of the native Solarian architecture were indeed intact, but instead of the resplendent chrome of the surrounding buildings, they were now dulled, covered in a film of black ash partly from the attack and partly from the immense clouds being spewed into the atmosphere by that alien production facility far off in the distance.

The thing looked like some sort of gigantic metallic pyramid, cut in half along the centre, so that it had a flat roof. Numerous chimneys and flare stacks rose up from within it, each pouring out black ash and a plethora of noxious fumes high into the atmosphere, like a great black miasma.

The science team hurriedly pressed on, nervous, not wanting to linger a second longer in this place than they had to. As they passed empty building after empty building, they noticed dark shapes scorched into the sides where the structure met the ground, as if someone had painted a mural of Solarian shadows upon the walls. In places there were only a few shapes, others were almost completely blackened with them.

It took some time for the team to realise what this meant, but soon the awful realisation of what these shapes really were hit home to all of them. They were bodies, charred remains literally melted into the sides of the buildings themselves. The whole team felt a cold chill run up their spines.

One of the group noticed a faint metallic glint about fifty metres distant, and pointed it out to the others. It was moving, emerging out of the caldera of a blast crater, a lone, damaged robotic creature no doubt hit by Solarian weapons fire when the attack took place and left to crawl around all this time.

E.D.F Chronicles – The Cyberian menace

As they neared, they saw that the robotic warrior's legs had been blown apart, it was meant to be bi-pedal just like they were. Although these robotic creatures were shorter at only six feet and had no discernable means of communication. It had no mouth to speak through, its cranium resembled an elongated skull with its jawline extended and narrowed where its mouth should have been, and bright scarlet sensor palettes that resembled the compound eye of a housefly. It was completely artificial, there were no organic parts of any kind. Upon detecting the approach of the science team it crawled toward them, even in this badly damaged state it still wanted to kill them.

The scientists fanned out, quickly forming surrounding this damaged warrior, keeping a safe distance until they managed to attach the magnetic clamps to it, effectively paralysing the construct and rendering it safe for travel.

As they had finished restraining their subject they noticed something else in the distance, a single solid mass of metal moving straight toward them, at least that was how it appeared. Although it wasn't a solid mass at all but thousands upon thousands of individual units, like a gigantic swarm, a living tidal wave sweeping everything before it in its effort to get to them. Yet completely silent, all that could be heard was the faint metallic crump of robotic feet upon the soft ground, menacing in their inexorable march.

The science team looked on in horror at the massed swarm of metallic creatures approaching, threatening to wash over and consume them all.

Then the dematerialisation began, and soon they were back aboard the Faeriath and safety.

The Solarian battlecruiser began its rapid ascent until it escaped the tainted atmosphere of that world entirely. Now they had a bigger problem however, a massive unknown ship had entered the system blocking off their escape deeper into Solarian territory, it was like a steel behemoth, studded with a myriad of what could only be described as communication towers, and four huge weapon-like emplacements.

The scientists were busily trying to secure their newly captured charge in the Faeriath's science suite.

"Contact that ship," Televis announced.

"Opening communications," another Solarian bridge officer replied from out of sight.

"Unidentified vessel this is the Solarian battlecruiser Faeriath, we mean you no harm. We are conducting a peaceful mission attempting to investigate what happened to the world below us. You have strayed into Solarian territory, do you require assistance?"

After almost a minute of tense silence the bridge officer cut through the quiet when he announced, "there is no response."

"Did they get the message?"

"They received the message, but there is no response of any kind."

The ship loomed before the crescent shaped Solarian vessel, as if regarding this insignificant little craft for a brief instant. It was far larger than the Faeriath, and like the Solarian ship was silvery in colour, though not as resplendent as its Solarian counterpart, its hull was dull like aged metal as opposed to the bright almost chrome looking hull of the Faeriath.

It was rectangular as well, like human ships, but where their ships were slight and tall, these were lower, wider, and sleeker.

"Sir, I am reading some form of energy wave, low powered." The Faeriath's sensory officer Kelthris warned.

"A scan perhaps?" Tallis, the ships second in command offered.

"Agreed; let them take a look, we have nothing to hide." Televis replied, his bright purple almond eyes narrowing slightly as he sat, pensive.

The energy wave completely engulfed the Solarian vessel in a bright green haze then just as abruptly, shut down.

After a brief pause, Kelthris announced, "Still no communication, or communication of any kind."

Televis turned toward his sub-ordinate, "what do you think?"

"There could be several reasons, their communication system could be inoperable. The scan could be out of sheer curiosity, or they could be determining if we pose a threat to them."

"Comraa!" Kelthris shouted in alarm, pointing to the viewscreen. Televis's attention immediately snapped back to the screen.

On the underside of the ship, several smaller craft began to detach and head toward the Faeriath.

"Thirty small craft have separated, cylindrical in shape, they measure fifteen metres long, about the size of a small fighter craft, they also appear to be unmanned."

"Full power to energy fields, standby all weapons," Televis said.

The Flotilla of tiny cylindrical craft raced toward the Solarian cruiser, while the far larger mother ship slowly began to advance in their wake. Its giant engines gave a baleful green glow as it advanced inexorably toward the comparatively tiny Solarian craft.

Televis watched as the immense vessel neared them, then finally his worst fears came true.

"Smaller craft are opening fire!" Tallis cried in alarm.

Tiny bursts of bright white light impacted on the Faeriath's shields, which flared brightly in response. The small nimble craft darted and weaved, above and below the outstretched crescent arms of the ship.

E.D.F Chronicles – The Cyberian menace

The Faeriath rocked gently although there was no serious damage, the crew were stunned, half expecting to be blown to space dust by now. Instead there was nothing but a gentle rocking, as if the ship was bobbing about on a calm sea.

Tallis announced in a mixture of confusion and relief, "there is no appreciable damage to the ship."

Televis was dumbfounded, "well, if this all they can muster, I believe we had better let them be; obviously we have upset them in some way," he said with more than a hint of sarcasm.

It was then he noticed the four huge weapon mounts on the fore section of the giant enemy ship, which had now moved into firing position.

The first two jutted out from the front of the ship like some kind of mandible, it was these that unleashed their ferocity first. A dull green beam of energy shot toward the Faeriath at an incredible speed, tore its way straight through the Solarian ships energy fields, and caused an entire section of its crescent shaped main hull to simply melt away and vanish. The ship lurched violently, Solarians were blasted out into space as the ship vented oxygen, to die of exposure. Weakened bulkheads and entire decks blew out in an instant, the carnage was extreme.

"Damage report!" Televis screamed over the roar of explosions and crescendo of multiple damage alert sirens all blaring at him on what remained of his tattered, flickering bridge. "How the hell did they get through our shields!"

"Unknown, we have severe damage on decks six through eight, all three decks are open to space; emergency bulkheads have deployed; casualties reported." Tallis replied scanning over the flickering status readout.

It must be those drone ships, Televis thought. *It was never their intention to attack us, simply to obtain our shield frequency with that pulse of theirs then transmit it straight back to the mothership.*

"They are firing again!" Tallis shouted in alarm as he stared wide eyed at the viewscreen.

Another shot slammed into the Faeriath, this time stripping away a sizeable portion of its beak-like command structure, the blast of decompression rocked the whole ship, again crewmen were flung into walls, shattered consoles, and blasted out into the cold blackness of space to die a frozen death.

"Direct hit! Structural integrity is weakening, decks three and four are open to space."

Televis gnashed his teeth in consternation. He had no doubt any longer, these were the people behind the destruction of Arcanthis, the rape of that beautiful world. But he could not fight them here, he was hopelessly outgunned and outmatched by that other ship.

"Ready all weapons! Fire at will, target their weapons arrays. Then initiate emergency jump into plasma drive, get us the heck out of here!"

The Faeriath's own fusion cannon roared its anger, the incandescent blue beam tore into the hull of the enemy craft sending out a spray of metallic hull fragments. The deadliest, most powerful weapon the Solarian fleet possessed, once it had finished its machinations, could only tear a long, dark, scorched gouge into that giant enemy ships hull; it did not even penetrate.

The flurry of high energy torpedoes fired from the ships twin launchers did moderately better, they managed to blast apart one of the enemy vessels weapon mounts in a great, bright gout of flame that momentarily lit up the entire ship.

The badly mauled Faeriath, then instantly leapt into plasma drive and was gone.

In a way, Televis was relieved. They had barely escaped with their lives, though the damage his ship had sustained, the casualties suffered and the loss of an entire world, shocked him deeply, right down to his core. Equally so, was that strange ships ability to withstand a direct hit from his fusion cannon with barely a scrape to show for it. *The armour on that ship must be metres thick*, he thought as his ship travelled through the swirling morass of plasma drive.

He spent long minutes in his chair, going over what happened in his mind, trying to make some sense of it all, who were they? Why would they want to attack the Solarian people?

Finally he realised it was no use trying to go over and over events in his mind, he just asked, quietly and soberly. "Status report?"

Tallis just as quietly replied, "structural integrity is at fifty three percent and dropping, we'll have to drop out of plasma drive soon to make emergency repairs. Fourty four of the crew are unaccounted for and we have large hull breaches on decks three and four, and six through eight."

Televis closed his eyes for a moment while he listened to the litany of damage his ship had sustained. How could he have been so stupid, so blind. At least they had the damaged, captured unit in his science suite. He was determined to know who the hell these enemy were, and where they came from, that wounded enemy down in his science lab was the key. He would have to travel to Solaria, to his homeworld to find the answer, they have the scientific knowledge and facilities to learn about this new threat, and learn they would.

He also had a world to re-name, somehow Arcanthis didn't seem quite so appropriate given the millions of his kin who had died on that world and those of his own crew who defended it.

He would call it Orialis, the world of tears.

Corvoth,
North western tip,
Krenaran space.

The giant armada dropped out of plasma drive slowly almost lazily in an enormous line that seemed to stretch right across the system.

The Krenaran fleet, still badly depleted from their disastrous war with the humans and Solarians was slow to respond, and by the time they did they were completely outmatched.

The ships sent out to intercept this mass of metallic rectangular behemoths, was made up of a single command carrier and a smattering of no more than half a dozen escorting stealth ships. They were all that stood between the tide of strange vessels before them and the destruction of Corvoth, including the top secret intelligence training academy where Lathiel was once trained.

The enemy fleet advanced, silently, inexorably toward them, never slowing, just a long silent march of ships, exactly as the single vessel did against the Faeriath.

The Krenaran battlegroup confused at the lack of communication, attempted to open communications themselves.

Aboard the large command deck of the Krenaran command carrier Vornoth, Kormroth looked out suspiciously at the alien fleet encroaching on their territory. He knew they were not Terran ships as being a veteran of the war, he could remember fighting against them. No, these were a completely different configuration to anything on their records, this was an unknown force. Perhaps the Krenaran empire had a new enemy? Or even better, a new ally.

"Open communications!" He growled in his native Krenaran dialect to an operator within a recessed pulpit to his left

"Communications are open, but we are receiving nothing."

Kormroth grinned as he looked upon the thirty foot high viewscreen ahead of him, positioned at the end of a central aisle that effectively cut the command deck in half.

To both his left and right, in two enormously long pulpits, dozens of other Krenarans worked at terminals ranging from sensory systems scanning those enemy ships, trying to determine what they were; their strengths and weaknesses. To flight and launch control systems for the fifty Krenaran fighters carried within its vast bays, as well as numerous weapons control systems.

E.D.F Chronicles – The Cyberian menace

All the time this immense armada was edging nearer, and nearer.

"Ha!" Kormroth spat. "They are playing coy, well if they will not speak, then perhaps they will fight! Deploy H.O.T rocket pods one and two, launch all fighters; prepare for battle!"

The lines of operators nodded as they heard his booming voice ring out across the command deck and began to work furiously at their stations. The alarm sounded and the bridge darkened noticeably, signifying they were now at battle readiness.

Outside the giant flat-topped Krenaran carrier, the equal in size of its opposing ships, the twin H.O.T rocket launch pods rose up from the flat deck, already proven so deadly to E.D.F ships in the past, ominously locking into place with a dull muted clunk. The twin launch bays also opened up on the deck and dozens of small single seat Krenaran fighters swarmed out like insects from it.

The smaller, more agile fighters flew ahead of the larger stealth ships and the Vornoth, as still the strange enemy armada advanced, seemingly heedless of this new threat.

"Energy wave approaching!" An operator shouted out in alarm.

"What!" Kormroth bellowed in anger. "All ships fire at will!"

The Stealth ships and fighters all raced forward as the giant carrier hung back, directing the battle from afar and giving itself plenty of time to unleash those devastating missiles, a typical Krenaran assault tactic that humans and Solarians had seen hundreds of times throughout the war.

They knew they were outnumbered, and most likely far outgunned yet they were prepared to sell their lives dearly to defend this world.

Hundreds of small cylindrical drones separated from the undersides of the giant enemy craft, quickly dispersing throughout the Krenaran fleet, peppering Stealth ships, fighters and the Vornoth alike with the same bright energy bursts as they did the Faeriath.

It was at this precise moment, when the first of those baleful green energy beams hit, that the Krenarans realised their reactive hull armour counted for absolutely nothing against this new enemy.

The beams lanced out in all directions catching three of the Stealth ships almost immediately, stripping their outer hull completely away and exposing the weakened support structure within. They span out of control as they dived to the attack, shots from nearby ships finished off what the first had started until there was simply nothing left but for a few small hull fragments drifting slowly through space, cast adrift.

Fighters that were caught in the criss-crossing energy beams were reduced to nothingness, as more drones passed by constantly peppering the remaining Krenaran flotilla.

The surviving three Stealth ships fired everything they had at these invaders, these steel behemoths who were systematically slaughtering them. Particle cannon beams slammed into the giant enemy ships hulls as they jinked and dived to avoid the deadly mass of fire directed at them. However, those particle beams which had wrought carnage amongst E.D.F ships a decade ago, barely glanced the immensely thick outer hull armour of these vessels.

"Fire all H.O.T rockets!" Kormroth roared from the centre seat of the Vornoth.

The huge torpedoes packed with immensely powerful high explosives, and supremely accurate guidance systems shot forth in a spray of bright contrails from the carriers' twin launchers, roaring toward their assailants. Some came into contact with the beams and were reduced to their constituent parts, utterly useless. Others though, by sheer blind luck, made it through the latticework of beams cross-crossing space all around them, slamming headlong into the enemy ships and detonating in massive explosions, blasting deep fiery craters into the hull armour of several of the craft.

Only a single enemy ship was penetrated, the breach bleeding out fire and debris fragments into space. Unperturbed the wounded ship continued to advance, silently and stoically, in-fact the damage had barely slowed it down.

Those surviving Stealth ships were finally caught as the weight of fire upon them was simply too great to avoid, although before the last one was reduced to a spinning ball of debris, it had managed to launch its final salvo of torpedoes. They smashed into the forward-most weapon mount of the closest vessel at point blank range, detonating and blasting it apart in an almighty fireball that lit up the entire ship.

The few Krenaran fighters still in the fight relentlessly pressed their attack against their gigantic opponents. Their weapons hitting home in bright explosions as they strafed, peppered, and harried these unknown attackers. Although when it came down to it, they were just a nuisance, their weapons simply not powerful enough to penetrate the awesomely thick armour of their opponents.

Kormroth looked out upon the final ebbs of battle playing out in-front of him bewildered, his fleet dashed, reduced to little more than scraps. They had thrown everything they had at them and barely succeeded in scratching them. Even a Solarian fleet would not have taken such a fierce pounding and emerge unscathed.

"How long until the launchers are re-armed?" He asked dejectedly.

"Another thirty seconds."

"We don't have thirty seconds!" He roared, just as the last remaining fighter collided with a drone, both dying in a small but bright ball of flame.

"Divert all power to the engines, set a collision course."

The four massive engines of the Vornoth glowed an intense emerald hue as they strained to propel the vast weight of the giant ship forward, accelerating all the time.

The deadly green energy beams fell upon the vessel, slowly stripping away its own considerable hull armour, exposing the decks beneath and its crew to the extreme coldness of space. The Vornoth's hull was slowly coming apart as it weathered the plethora of energy beams all shearing away at it, its launchers completely destroyed.

Kormroth closed his eyes and offered a small fearful prayer for the safety of the world he was about to die to protect, for its people, for its very existence against such a monstrous enemy.

A final energy beam swept over the raised command superstructure of the carrier, stripping away the outer hull of the command deck.

And for the briefest of instants Kormroth, commander of the Krenaran command carrier Vornoth, saw starlight before the energy from that strange weapon engulfed him and his entire staff in its green light, quickly and quietly erasing them out of existence.

The devastated, out of control command carrier smashed headlong into the enemy craft, the force of impact immense as their hulls collided, smashing and grinding into each other. Finally the Vornoth burst apart in a gigantic explosion, debris and hull fragments hurling out in all directions.

The enemy ship, while able to withstand the depredations of the Krenaran weapon fire levelled against it, could not withstand the awesome impact of a Krenaran command carrier crashing headlong into it, and slowly it too succumbed to the catastrophic damage it had sustained, exploding in an equally almighty blast that consumed several nearby drones in its ferocity.

The loss of one of their ships seemed to have an affect on the others around it, suddenly they were not so fluid as before, the drones slowed becoming ever so slightly erratic, a general look of sluggishness and disorder came over the entire fleet, as though in a daze. It lasted only for about a minute, then resumed their inexorable march toward the Krenaran world of Corvoth, as implacable as before.

The people of that hot, arid, dusty world looked up to the heavens in both fear and wonder to witness the faint white contrails of a myriad of small oval shaped landing pods streaking through the cloudless blue sky toward them.

The silvery egg shaped craft descended gracefully on a series of maneuvering jets, landing in utter silence. Not a single Krenaran dared to speak, not a bird cawed or fluttered its wings, nothing. In an extraordinary display of synchronicity every single craft landed at the exact same time.

Metallic panels around the edges of these pods opened like the petals of some hideous flower, and from within extending outward came rack upon rack full of metallic warriors. Once lowered to the ground, they began their silent march, the baleful red of their eyes unblinking, uncaring, no remorse or feeling of any kind toward the genocide they were about to commit. They had stepped forth onto the dusty windswept surface of Corvoth for the first time.

Birds, animals, everything took flight before their inexorable advance, startled by this new mass of metallic bodies now forming into a single silvery tide. They moved like mercury, a living mass of metal swarming over every single living thing in its path.

The silence was total, utter, it seemed to envelop this strange robotic host as though it was another weapon in its arsenal, and every living thing seemed to fear it.

The Krenarans themselves however, looked upon this vast tide of metal slowly advancing toward them as though they were perfection personified. The Krenaran military routinely took part in ritual graftings, cutting open parts of their bodies and attaching technological 'enhancements' was perceived as a sign of strength and status amongst the military, and every Krenaran loved the military, it granted them power and wealth in society.

The leader of this world, an aged, fat Krenaran well past fighting age, took it upon himself to make his way toward this ever approaching machine army, and in his native Krenaran tongue he called out to them.

"On behalf of the Krenaran people, welcome to Corvoth. Please make yourselves at home, we humbly offer you our hospitality."

He nervously reached out a green reptilian hand in friendship.

Without even breaking their stride, this tide of metal warriors silently levelled their weapons and nonchalantly opened fire. The green energy pulses struck the aged Krenaran dead in the chest and within a millisecond his body was utterly consumed, as though simply erased from existence, all that remained was a blackened patch of scorched ground.

The adoration of the Krenaran people quickly turned to fear and then terror, as slowly and unstoppably the swarm descended upon them, the pulses of their weapons flashing out in bright bursts of emerald light, systematically eradicating them from existence itself. Utterly silent, unyielding, the metal sea carved through them without missing a single step or slowing down. This was nothing but a wholesale slaughter, and within hours Corvoth was left a barren wasteland where not a single living being called that world its home. The deaths of those that once lived recorded as blackened shadows upon the dusty ground and on the scorched sides of the buildings themselves as they fled in desperate terror.

The badly damaged Solarian battlecruiser Faeriath plunged out of plasma drive unsteadily within the uninhabited Tartirius system, no longer able to sustain its flight through the plasma wake. It had managed barely thirty minutes travel away from the unknown but devastatingly powerful vessel it had encountered while investigating the destruction of the Solarian world now known as Orialis.

The once gleaming, proud ship listed, adrift, its hull blackened buckled and scarred. With two great breaches suffered at the hands of that enemy ships' deadly weapon systems.

"We are running on emergency reserve power only," Tallis announced from his station.

The main bridge lights had all gone out, bathing them in the ethereal glow given off by those workstations that were still functioning, an automated procedure designed to conserve what little power actually remained.

"How long?" Televis asked with a depressed sigh.

"Fifteen hours, then we begin to lose life support," Tallis looked back forlornly at his commander.

Well, at least we are alive, Televis thought, *something to be thankful for at least.*

"Comraa, should we send out a general distress signal?" Tallis ventured, the battered defeated look on his face matched his own.

Televis struggled within himself to answer his subordinate, if they did send out that signal there was still a danger that it could be intercepted by the alien ship. And if they didn't, they might all die here, frozen to death within his own ships hull, their precious cargo would never get to Solaria.

Finally with pursed lips he realised that the risk was great, but so was the outcome. "Send out the distress signal."

Tallis nodded in agreement, silently working at his flickering station, "transmitting signal on a Solarian coded channel."

Televis hoped he had not just put out a big neon sign highlighting their position, but he had no other option.

Standing up from his blackened and scorch marked chair he turned to Tallis once more, "have all hands except those that are not already engaged make emergency repairs. I am going to take a look at our little prize for myself."

Tallis acknowledged him with a curt nod as his commander left the darkened bridge. The elevator tubes on his ship were damaged, so the elevators themselves were rendered inoperable, there wasn't power to teleport him to where he needed to go. So Televis braved the emergency escape shafts to clamber his way down to the science suite ten decks below. Even then he had

15

to pick his way around debris strewn crawlspaces, flailing power conduits, and half smashed supports.

He was surprised the ship was still in one piece actually, after they had barely made it out by the skin of their teeth. He smiled quietly to himself; that was another human phrase, he really needed to stop doing that.

Soon he made it into the science suite itself, stepping through shattered glass doors that surprisingly still opened before him. He got his first glimpse of this robotic organism still writhing at the magnetic bonds that were keeping it pinned to the inspection table.

Four other scientists were stood around it, studying it and talking amongst themselves. Televis strode toward his captive; its legs blasted away just below what resembled its knee, the two limbs ending in a mass of flailing circuitry, wires, and twisted metal. It had what appeared to be a leering skull like face, pock marked with dirt, the occasional dent, and small nicks and scrapes no doubt received in the battles it had fought in since this unit was constructed. Its eyes, if they could be called eyes blazed red, and to Televis seemed to blaze with a hatred, a malice that made him shudder. Beneath its 'cheek line' its face tapered into a long deep set elongated metallic jaw, though it had no mouth to speak of.

So that's why they couldn't communicate, Televis thought, *they do not speak. Obviously this thing was built to inspire fear in those it fought against, the question is why attack us so openly, we were certainly not their enemy, not yet, we have no idea what these metallic creatures are?*

One of the scientists came over to him, "this is a remarkable display of technological advancement, possibly even beyond our own."

"What have you found out?" Televis asked, not taking his eyes off the thrashing captive for an instant.

"Not much so far, we have tried linking it up to the ships computer in order to try and get to its programming, although so far we are having a hard time even trying to find some sort of compatible connection port."

"Perhaps it was never meant to have one, maybe it is meant to be completely autonomous?" Another scientist mused.

"I doubt it," Televis said. "The landing party mentioned that they acted like a swarm, one giant mass sweeping everything before it. That takes communication, co-ordination to move such a large body of troops in such a way, they must be communicating somehow, even silently."

"Like some form of machine telepathy?" another scientist asked.

"Or a network?"

"Exactly, it is the only thing that could explain how they move and react as fluidly as they do," Televis replied.

"Their ships seem to react in much the same manner, you saw how those smaller craft manoeuvred, could they be on a separate network as well?"

"Or the same one," Televis cut in. "Think about it, what would be the fastest way of getting orders out to a vast number of machine soldiers?"

"A download?" One of the scientists asked in amazement.

"Precisely."

"So taking that theory to its logical conclusion, where are these warriors getting their orders from?" One of the scientists asked.

"The ships themselves; imagine our own computer system, we have a main computer core that disseminates information to all the various workstations throughout the ship. The workstations then disseminate that information to us. Could that not be what is happening with these machines, just on a far grander scale?" Televis stroked his blue tinged chin for a moment while he contemplated what all this meant.

"So the ships themselves are passing on information between each other, as well as downloading orders and information to the soldiers themselves such as this fellow here?"

"Correct." Televis nodded.

"So theoretically speaking, how far could such a network extend?" Another scientist asked.

"As far as there are ships to transfer the data to one another, hypothetically speaking it could stretch right across the galaxy."

"By Enoru!" One of the scientists gasped clasping his hand to his mouth as he realised the enormity of what they were thinking.

"So even if we managed to destroy one of their ships, as difficult as that may be. It still would not shut down the network, it might slow it down temporarily until other ships re-initialise data connections to take into account the lost vessel, and simply divert the flow of information." A third scientist said.

"The only way to shut down the entire network, and therefore this fellow here, is to find the central core and destroy it. There has to be some kind of command ship still out there somewhere."

"True," Televis said nodding. "Finding it would be easier said than done, theoretically it could hide anywhere in the galaxy, as long as it had a stable data link to another nearby vessel to maintain the network."

"We should learn more when we get to Solaria anyway," the group of scientists all agreed.

If we get to Solaria, Televis mused. His thoughts returning to the dilapidated state of his ship, *let's hope we do because time is against us. The more we delay, more worlds will suffer the same fate as Orialis, and this machine people will get even stronger.*

E.D.F Chronicles – The Cyberian menace

A nearby control panel signalled an alert, Televis keyed in the appropriate access code and Tallis's face appeared on the tiny monitor.

"Comraa, I'm afraid we have more bad news."

My ship is lying adrift in an uninhabited system, on minimal power and barely functioning, with two giant breaches in its hull. How could this possibly get any worse, he thought, but deigned to say nothing.

"Three more ships have dropped out of plasma drive, exactly the same configuration as the one that attacked us."

Televis wondered how they had managed to track them, could it be the coded distress beacon? But then as he looked back at the still writhing form of that robotic warrior held on the inspection table he realised the much more likely prospect that his captive could still be connected to this network they had all talked about, and that somehow even though he was damaged, his captive had in some way alerted those ships to his presence.

Quickly pulling up a star chart of the Tartirius system on an auxiliary display in the science suite, he studied it. Realising they were not far from a large inert gas giant Tartirius VII, he hoped against all hope that the interference from the magnetosphere of that world would help to mask his ship and his captive from the encroaching enemy vessels, and that the pressure would not all crush them to dust at the same time.

"Do we have enough power remaining for a short sub-light burst, just enough to take us into a low orbit of Tartirius VII?" Televis asked.

"Barely; although it will use up almost all of our reserves."

"Do it, take us into a low orbit but keep the distress beacon running."

"Yes sir," Tallis nodded before ending the communication.

The main sub-light Ion drives of the Faeriath, flickered, blinked and then painfully came to life in their customary blazing electric blue. The ship gradually re-oriented itself, and then in one final desperate lunge of speed, lurched forward toward the swirling sapphire blue gases of Tartirius VII. As the gases slowly enveloped the beleaguered Solarian cruiser, its engines winked, faded, and died for the last time.

The three huge metallic monstrosities that had only just arrived in the system were confused by the sudden disappearance of their quarry, they split up and began scouring each and every planet.

The Faeriath; no longer powered, was gradually being pulled toward the core of this immense gas giant. Drifting out of control it descended deeper and deeper as the hours ticked by. The pressure upon its already broken and fragile hull steadily increasing, the crew watching their consoles nervously plotting the rate the ship was sinking, helpless as its outer hull slowly began to buckle and crumple in the weakened areas due to the immense pressure exerted upon it.

Life support systems were failing all over the ship, the temperature plummeted, ice began to build up on the numerous control surfaces, the crew shivered. Breathable air was slowly becoming a premium; time was running out for a rescue.

Three of the giant metal behemoths were closing in on Tartirius VII, closing for the kill. As they were about to enter into a high orbit, a brilliant flash of light heralded the emergence of another fleet dropping out of plasma drive. Sixteen Solarian battlecruisers all raced toward the defenceless Faeriath. In a storm of fusion cannon fire they fell upon the enemy vessels arrayed ahead of them, blindingly bright electric blue beams of energy cut through space like a laser show. Torpedoes raced headlong toward their targets, exploding in immense blasts as they slammed into their unknown enemy.

Though the damage they were inflicting individually was but a nuisance to their massively armoured foes, the sheer furiosity and weight of fire directed at them had taken them by surprise.

Televis shivered in his now ice encrusted command deck, his hands and feet had become numb, his breathing raspy, barely clinging on to consciousness, desperately gasping at the last few precious wisps of oxygen still lingering in the room.

Many of his crew had already passed out, the crackling of a transmission heavily garbled by the magnetic interference given out by the gas giant's poles broke through the almost deathly silence.

"Faeriath are you receiving! This is Comraa Atanis of the battlecrusier T'elareth, we are attempting to get to you, do you require assistance?"

The sheer elation Televis felt upon hearing that voice was palpable, punching the air, he cried out in joy. The warhost had finally heard his call, though Tallis was unconscious at his station. Televis forced himself out of the command chair, weak, his breathing unsteady, footing uncertain. His legs refused to respond and he fell awkwardly to the ice cold deck plating; yet still he carried on, dragging himself through sheer will alone to Tallis's console. With a last burst of effort he hauled himself up, slamming his fist down on that acknowledge control.

"T'elareth, thi....this is the Faeriath, in dire need of ass…assistance. Life support....failed, no power remaining……in dire need." Then having expended his last vestiges of energy, Televis himself collapsed, slumping down at the feet of his second officer.

Atanis, sensing in Televis's voice that they couldn't delay ordered his ship to peel away from the battle raging all around them. The T'elareth plunged into the deep blue gaseous soup of Tartirius VII, getting a rough fix on the Faeriaths location after triangulating Televis's reply.

E.D.F Chronicles – The Cyberian menace

The thick gases swirled and parted about the ship, as like a dart, the T'elareth cut through them, gradually the misty indistinct form of the adrift Faeriath was revealed, broken, twisted, listing heavily and slowly being dragged to its ultimate demise.

Atanis hoped against all hope that the crew of the Faeriath were still alive as he ordered his crew to bring his ship alongside it, and to immediately teleport all surviving lifesigns aboard. The T'elareth then locked onto the Faeriath with a tractor beam and began to pull the beleaguered vessel free from the deadly embrace of that world.

The battle was still raging furiously above as the T'elareth re-emerged from the clutches of the gas giant, dragging its wounded charge behind it.

Six of the fifteen Solarian ships were now ablaze, their devastated, twisted hulls drifting forlornly, trailing fire and debris like the tail of some tiny comet as explosions continued to ravage them.

Atanis looked on through his viewscreen, this new enemy fought like nothing he had ever seen before. The smaller craft continuously peppered the Solarian ships with their bright energy bursts, doing no damage themselves except being a nuisance. The larger ships however, fired everything they had straight back at them. The bright blue fusion beams, and furious explosions of torpedo impacts, interspersed with the muted green energy beams of the enemy ships. While the Solarian weapons were having a hard time even damaging them, the enemy ships weapons tore right through the battlecruisers shield grids, stripping away whole sections at a time.

A bright explosion heralded the death throes of another battlecruiser, its power core went into a violent meltdown and blasted it apart in a bright shockwave that flung devastated parts of its hull out in all directions.

Although the remaining Solarian ships were pouring fire into them, many of them were by now badly damaged, the initial impetus of their attack halted by the immensely thick hull armour of these strange vessels. Although one of the metallic ships was beginning to buckle, its hull pock marked by dozens of torpedo impacts, black scorch marks raked across its hull by fusion cannon hits. It slowly began to come apart, finally exploding in a blindingly bright fireball that lit up the entire battle; Atanis had to shield his eyes at the intensity of the explosion.

Then something strange happened, something he didn't expect. At the death of one of their ships the others seemed to momentarily waver, as though suddenly unsure of themselves, the fluidity of their attacks gone, the co-ordination non-existent. He briefly thought about ordering the remainder of the Solarian fleet to press its attack, then just as quickly decided against it as the brief moment of uncertainty passed.

"Order the retreat, we have what we came for," he said as he looked down to his second officer.

The Solarian nodded as he transmitted the retreat order to the remainder of the flotilla. The badly mauled remains of the Solarian fleet, together with the T'elareth all whirled around, leapt into plasma drive, and was gone.

Who are these people, able to do this kind of damage to the Solarian fleet? Atanis thought, shocked.

Televis and the remainder of his crew were being treated for a combination of hypothermia and oxygen deprivation. The carbon dioxide within his bloodstream had risen to dangerous levels and it would be several hours before he and his crew returned to anything like normal again.

Luckily for him, the T'elareth and its eight surviving ships travelling alongside, were heading for the fleet yards at Ventaris, a journey of some seven hours at present speed.

With the Faeriath as badly damaged as it was, Televis knew full well how imperative it was that he get his wounded prisoner to Solaria.

E.D.F Chronicles – The Cyberian menace
4. Exodus

The highly advanced and spacious, by E.D.F standards at least bridge of the brand new only just commissioned Valley-forge bristled with people, even though they had barely taken off the protective shrink wrapping on the displays that surrounded it.

After all it should be crammed, the Valley-forge was a project envisaged five long years ago. A powerful symbol of the advancement of mankind, and of the perilous times they had oft found themselves in. The Valley-forge was a new kind of battleship for a new age, bigger and more powerful than even the mighty Danitza class that it was scheduled to replace, the first of its kind, and the new flagship for the entire E.D.F navy.

E.D.F naval officers proudly tended to the plethora of modern ultra-sophisticated duty stations, their smiles lit up the room as they basked in the media limelight, rubbing shoulders with civilians, honoured guests, as well as news crews from the outer colony news service all gathered together to witness the maiden voyage of one of the grandest and most auspicious projects ever undertaken by the E.D.F. Currently moored at number one berth at the Charlie base fleet yards orbiting Gamma IV, a planet of particular poignancy to the E.D.F.

Twin elevator doors opened out at the rear of the bridge revealing a lone man dressed in the immaculate royal blue of the navy, on the epaulettes of his thick deep blue velvet overcoat bore four black bands inlaid in white, identical markings were clearly visible on his cuffs. On his chest were medal tapes of numerous citations earned through years of fighting at the very forefront of naval battles ranging from the Krenaran war, anti-pirate operations while the E.D.F recovered from its devastating losses, the Dracos incident, and several others besides.

Silently he cast a glance around the room; surveying his bridge. His head topped with a mane of fiery red hair; his keen eyes an almost emerald green looking out over the chaos.

This was Captain Quinn Kinraid, the newly appointed commander of the most powerful ship ever built by mankind. He had been at these fleet yards before, a decade ago he had fought tooth and nail for them in the greatest battle the E.D.F had ever known. Then, as now he felt the weight of history, of expectation bearing down upon him. The difference was; then he was greener, less seasoned. Now he was older, wiser, and in command, now he accepted it as a force that made him strive to realise this expectation. Confidently he strode out of the elevator to the smiling expectant faces of his crew and the clamouring press.

He barely made it a foot before a microphone was shoved in his face. "Captain Kinraid, how do you feel about taking command of one of the largest, most advanced and powerful ships in the entire fleet?"

"Just grand!" was the typical thick Celtic reply.

Reporters and civilians threatened to overwhelm him, microphones and recording equipment thrust out toward him at every angle, clamouring for his next words.

With a wave of his arm he beckoned them back to give him some space as he took his place in the brand new ergonomic cream leather centre seat. He could smell its newness, savouring the scent of the leather, as though the wrappings had only just been taken off it.

An expectant hush fell over the room as he prepared to address his crew.

"Today marks the beginning of a new day, a new era, one where we let go of the shadow of the past and embrace a new future. With the launch of this new vessel let us send out a beacon of hope, of peace for all E.O.C.A citizens, secure in the knowledge that their worlds are protected by the E.D.F so that they may go about their daily lives unhindered by the machinations of other species; content that we, the crew of the Valley-forge watch over them."

The entire room burst into a warm, understanding applause at Quinn's speech.

"Today we begin our two day cruise to Sigma XI, and then back again; just a nice, easy trip out."

Kinraid looked toward the giant semi-circular wrap around ultra-high definition viewscreen dominating the wall of the bridge ahead of him, it depicted the numerous panels viewing gantries, and portholes of number one berth directly in front of the ship. The outer structure of the colossal Charlie base fleet yards where this ship was moored, tiny black silhouettes of people scurried past brightly lit windows that shone out back at him. He smiled wistfully, before turning toward his executive officer.

"Commander Anizeres, contact Charlie base command and control, request permission t' depart."

His number two nodded back at him, her long raven black locks almost seemed to clash with her pale complexion, giving her a kind of ethereal beauty that Quinn found striking as he watched her work at her station. If he wasn't already her commanding officer he might have been tempted to ask her out, but such things are unseemly between a captain and his crew.

"Charlie base confirms, permission granted, we are clear to get under way."

"Excellent Commander," Kinraid said with a nod. "Contact engineering, tell them to bring main power online," he turned in his seat slightly to face his new pilot. "Lieutenant Jansen, release all moorings and take us out slowly. One quarter sublight speed, thrusters at your discretion, let's see what this baby can do."

Jansen smiled nodding, "understood Captain."

Lieutenant Jansen had took part in dozens of simulations on piloting the new ship before even being offered the post, but it was nothing like actually sitting there at the helm of a near three and a half kilometre long battleship, the navy's new pride. The power of the thing, and the sheer size made him a little nervous.

Keying in a series of controls, he released the primary docking hatch with a blast of escaping air, the three thousand four hundred metre long, twenty eight deck behemoth of a ship began to drift clear of its berth.

Navigation lights began to blink across its vast structure as the fore docking arm smoothly retracted within the semi-circular forward hull, an odd feature for E.D.F ships as all those that had preceded it had gently sloped pyramidal fore sections, thus giving the Valley-forge a kind of hammerhead like appearance. The reason for such a departure was obvious, it provided the space necessary for its twin fighter bays and acted as a support platform for those huge twin high bore fusion cannons that were its main armament.

The rest of its shape was not too dissimilar to the Danitza class it was due to replace, except not as deep, the ship was longer but sleeker, and either side of this elongated mid-hull, two giant turrets rested, both equipped with twin long range high power laser cannons. Its massive sub-light engines began to power up, again these were not the typical jutting solid fuel boosters used in other E.D.F ships, instead they were replaced by a bank of six huge Ion engines and eight smaller engines almost identical to the ones the Liberty used, these glowed an intense electric blue, banks of small thruster jets fired from its forward section as the ship gingerly began to reverse.

More manoeuvring thrusters fired, as the vast bulk of the ship, larger than many orbital installations gingerly made its way clear of the fleetyards and began to turn. The Valley-forge, for all its power, all its majesty was not that much more manoeuvrable than the older Danitza's. Both were great lumbering beasts, impossibly slow to turn. But its graviton shielding system, triple layer ablative armour hull, and carrying two full fighter wings gave it the edge over the ageing battleships, not to mention those massive fusion cannons.

Once the ship was safely clear Kinraid gave the order, "Set course for Eidolon, bearing two-one-seven degrees, elevation minus six."

"Aye captain," Jansen replied with a smile, he'd been itching to see what the ships new plasma drive engine could do for real, as he keyed in the controls the ship responded. The immense plasma drive came to full power; barely contained energy crackled and arced about its semi-spherical orb like appendage on the underside of the ship, then unleashed its power in the form of two identical arcs of pure plasma energy from the twin plasma emitters jutting out like tiny needles at the front of the ship. The vast swirling plasma wake opened before the craft, bathing its hull in a myriad of swirling pinks, reds, burgundies and yellows.

"Full sublight speed," Kinraid said staring at the multi-hued spectacle on his viewscreen, "take us in."

Jansen simply nodded as he worked the controls.

The brilliant blue from the six huge engines momentarily increased in their intensity, as the massive ship began to build up speed then plunged headlong into the swirling morass before it. The wake collapsed in on itself with a giant burst of bright white light. The ship had now entered plasma drive, heading for what Kinraid hoped would be an uneventful maiden voyage.

With the fall of Orialis and now Corvoth, the immense fleet of this strange robotic race plunged ever deeper into both Krenaran and Solarian territories. The Krenarans in particular looked the most vulnerable. In the days following the loss of their world; Dalvosh, leader of the Krenaran military, and supreme overlord of the Krenaran empire tried in vain to organise some kind of effective defence against this new ever moving threat.

Although his closest advisors still advocated some kind of diplomatic contact, he argued there could be no diplomacy when they don't even speak. No, Dalvosh thought. They have come here for one purpose, and one purpose alone; to destroy them. He knew his homeworld Krenara prime had significant orbital defences, labelled as a fortress world on the galactic map, would they hold out against such a foe? He had no idea, it would put his world's label to the test. This was his last hope, especially as this alien armada seemed to be sweeping his ships away like twigs in the wind.

"The time is now!" Kelloth, his most senior aide said. "The battle calls you, and you must answer."

Dalvosh allowed his scaled eyelids to close over his deep red eyes for a second, he knew he was likely going to his death but he had to defend his people; Kelloth was right. He only hoped that these robotic monstrosities would dash themselves against the rocks of the defences of his world.

He opened his eyes again, "I will answer."

The two warriors stood side by side, clad in their traditional bulky metallic battle armour. "We will give them a fight they will never forget." Kelloth said before they both strode out of the deserted palace of Helioth; seat of power for the entire Krenaran race and out into the scorching hot surface of Krenara. Its red giant sun seemed especially bright today, coating the sky in a deep ruby red.

E.D.F Chronicles – The Cyberian menace

It almost seemed like the sky rained blood, *by the end of today it just might,* Dalvosh thought.

They walked toward a waiting Krenaran fighter and once they climbed inside, the cockpit glass closed over them. Kelloth being a capable pilot himself, flew them both through the dusty cloudless arid atmosphere of Krenara prime and into orbit, passing the numerous unmanned orbital defences that had kept this world safe for hundreds of years and continued on-course to dock with the flagship of his people, the Kralath-kar, meaning death bringer in the Krenaran tongue.

The deadliest ship his race possessed, a command carrier with one notable improvement that no other ship in the Krenaran fleet possessed. A Solarian shielding system, scavenged from the wreckage of a destroyed Solarian battlecruiser during the war. His predecessor Alax had it integrated into the systems of this immense craft. Dalvosh hoped they would protect him against the inevitable onslaught they were about to face.

One of the ship's giant launch bays opened, allowing the tiny fighter inside the huge flagship.

Slowly the small craft glided along a wide central aisle, passing dozens of similar fighters on either side, until Kelloth manoeuvred the craft onto an empty magnetic docking clamp and with a dull 'thunk' latched onto it.

The gigantic fighter bay doors closed over them, blotting out the starlight beyond with deep grey bulkheads.

Once Kelloth received the all clear and normal atmospheric conditions were established in the bay, he pressed a control and the cockpit slowly lifted allowing them both to climb out of the craft and onto a narrow metal gangway next to the fighter.

They walked together for what seemed like an eternity before they were able to exit this giant hangar concealed within the Kralath-kar, eventually they made it to an elevator which led them up to the command deck.

It was the same layout as every other command deck aboard a Krenaran carrier, except this one had a more enhanced weapons officers screen in order to monitor the stolen shielding system.

Eighty ships stood between this implacable enemy and his homeworld, barely a fraction of what the Krenaran fleet once was. That fleet suffered heavy losses as the Terrans and Solarians fought with a ferocity his people never thought existed in order to safeguard one of the Terrans key supply worlds, Gamma IV. Even though Krenaran ships outnumbered them two to one, their enemy had still prevailed. It was one of the heaviest losses his people had ever suffered, and because of that he had personally put an end to that war overnight, it was his first act upon taking the mantle of supreme overlord after

Alax's death. Alax and Axus's scheme was bold and grand, overthrowing the Terrans before they became the power that they now are, it would have brought unimaginable wealth, power, and glory to his people. But in the end they had misjudged the fighting spirit of those Terrans, and badly underestimated the Solarian involvement in that war. Once Alax was defeated and Dalvosh replaced him, he made the only decision he could; to end the war. After all sacrificing an empire to win a war was no victory; he never regretted that decision.

Now a decade later he faced that same choice, looking out at the star filled blackness of deep space at the head of a depleted fleet, knowing that a new enemy was coming for them. One that if the rumours were to be believed, were even stronger than the Solarians. And in that final hour as he waited silently, nervously for the first glimpses of the inevitable approach of the enemy armada, Dalvosh, supreme overlord of the Krenaran empire; feared for his people.

The Kralath-kar was in the centre of a phalanx of six command carriers, to either side of this centre over thirty stealth ships lay in wait. The plan was for the stealth ships to quickly outflank the enemy fleet and bottle them up in the centre, where the command carriers and planetary defences were waiting for them. It was a long shot, but it was all they had.

Dalvosh caught the first glints of the enemy ships hulls as they reflected the ruddy light from the Krenaran sun and he knew the time had come. Over the course of the next few hours, the fate of an empire would be decided. The comparatively tiny Krenaran fleet, already at battlestations simply maintained position, and waited.

"Deploy H.O.T rockets," Dalvosh's nervy voice broke the tense silence, "order the others to do the same, place all fighters onto hot standby."

Kelloth nodded, "done my lord."

Dalvosh watched as the immense enemy fleet closed, arrayed in a gigantic long line as far as the eye could see, there were no tactics to this, no strategy. It was an enormous tidal wave, come to engulf them all.

Still they came on, these metallic behemoths, never slowing, never stopping. Just as they had done at Corvoth; sweeping through Krenaran space and now they were going to sweep through their homeworld the same way, Dalvosh grew angry. He was not about to just cede his people to them without a fight.

"Ready all weapons, fire at will!"

In a flurry of activity, all six command carriers launched their entire salvoes at the mechanoid fleet. Dozens upon dozens of missiles roared toward them lighting up the very space itself in their wake, and for an instant it seemed that the enemy fleet wavered under the furious barrage. Some of the nimble agile little drones altered course and flew straight into the path of the onrushing fusillade, sacrificing themselves in immense fiery explosions and sparing the larger more important cruisers behind.

As the missiles rushed toward them, muted green energy beams flicked out criss-crossing space at every conceivable angle, picking off the deadly warheads before they could even impact.

Despite the sacrificial drones and the weight of firepower just levelled at them, some of the warheads managed to make it through and several ships were hit hard, two, three, four times; each warhead smashing home, burying itself deep into thick hull armour and then detonating in immense fiery explosions, blasting deep twisted craters into their shining hulls.

One of the enemy ships lurched, overcome by the damage it had taken, even through its armoured hull. It listed badly, nose down, as explosions ravaged the stricken vessel.

The Krenarans gave out a great cheer at witnessing the demise of one of their foes, all except Dalvosh. He knew from experience that it was far too early to celebrate yet.

It was then that the Krenarans realised their fatal mistake, how could they outflank something that could not be outflanked?

Executing their part of the plan perfectly, the stealth ships all raced forward in an attempt to get around the sides, above or beneath of this huge wall of ships. The beams flaring out towards them were so intense, so all-consuming, that the stealth ships themselves could not avoid their deadly touch; and as they flew headlong into them their hulls disintegrated, stripped away, entire sections broken down into their constituent parts and simply erased. Many simply did not get through this latticework of energy, reduced to nothing more than a few fragments of floating scrap. Others emerged as wrecks, cast adrift, in places their hulls remained intact, in others stripped to their very core, bereft of life, they looked like a collection of ghost ships.

Barely a handful of stealth ships sent against them had made it through, now they veered around, dodging and yawing for all they were worth to avoid those lethal beams.

Dalvosh looked on in horror at the plethora of twisted, broken forms of his ships laid out before him. "How long until the H.O.T rockets are re-armed," he whispered in desperation.

"Another minute at least."

"Damn you we won't have a minute!" He bellowed, slamming his fist down onto the arm of his chair. "Launch all fighters, and order the other command ships to do the same."

"Understood," Kelloth nodded.

At Dalvosh's order, a second wave made up of hundreds of small fighter craft swarmed out of the opening launch bays of all six command carriers. They looked like insects compared to the enormous enemy armada before them.

These smaller, nimbler craft were much more adept at dodging and weaving through the intense barrage of weapons fire hurled at them. Even still, some were caught by the deadly touch of those beams. Many made it through, and together began peppering the giant ships with their own wing mounted lasers. Small explosions constantly flickered and lit up the hulls of the lead ships in the enemy fleet as these bothersome little craft continued their attacks, strafing close to the giant cruiser's hulls.

Though the smaller, far less powerful weapons the fighters carried could barely scratch the surface of these gargantuan metallic titans, they still pressed their attacks, as though trying to kill the enemy with a thousand stings.

The first hint of a smile came across Dalvosh's reptilian lips, as he watched the constant harrying of the fighters from his viewscreen.

"Are they within range of the orbital defences?" he asked.

"Almost, another thirty seconds."

He hoped it would be enough, so far for all their efforts they had managed to down just one measly ship, it was a poor return. Also the fighters were now making a sufficient nuisance of themselves that the enemy had recalled a sizeable portion of its own drone flotilla to intercept them.

The few surviving stealth ships then began to press their own attack, particle cannons and torpedoes raking the enemy fleet as they flew in fast and close on attack runs similar to what the fighters were doing.

The damage was beginning to mount up on the incredibly thick outer armour of the enemy vessels, several now bore battle scars where particle cannons had gouged deep trenches, and torpedoes had left dark blackened craters in their hulls. Yet this mechanoid armada still advanced, unstoppable, unrelenting.

Krenaran fighters were now embroiled in an intense battle with the un-manned, weapon-less drones that far outnumbered them. Multiple explosions lit up space ahead of the advancing enemy fleet as fighters and drones buzzed about one another like a swarm of angry bees.

Although the drones themselves were unarmed, quickly their intentions became clear as they deliberately flew directly into the paths of the fighters themselves, immolating them both in bright explosions. Again the pesky drones were sacrificing themselves for the greater good of the fleet as a whole.

Dalvosh had to admire how the enemy fleet functioned, working together, the fluidity of their actions, and how one part of the fleet worked for the benefit of another, as well as their ruthless single mindedness to sweep all before them; he had never seen the likes of it before, neither in Terran or Solarian fleets.

Finally Kelloth broke him out of his musings, "torpedoes re-armed."

"Give them the full barrage, everything we have."

The command carriers together unleashed a second salvo at the vast embattled armada closing steadily in on them, the glow from the rockets of the warheads briefly visible as a bright plume of contrails before separating off and racing headlong toward their targets.

With the drones and fighters locked in a deadly cat and mouse battle with one another, the drones, being tied up already could not intercept this fresh wave of torpedoes streaking out towards their motherships.

This time the mechanoids paid a heavy price for their continual advance as they concentrated their fire on the incoming warheads, over twenty got through the curtain of weapon fire, slamming hard into the cruiser's hulls and instantly detonating in a swathe of immense explosions. Three of the giant cruisers began to list, stricken, before fires spreading within consumed them, a few seconds later they burst apart in almighty explosions that lit up half the armada. Debris blasting out in all directions slammed into ships nearby damaging them also.

Dalvosh breathed a sigh of relief, it was a ripple in an endless ocean, but at least they had made a ripple, he just hoped it would be enough to begin to turn back the tide before it was too late.

As those ships died a wave of unease spread through this massive machine armada, the stealth ships still harrying them continued to press their attack virtually ignored by the ships they were pounding with torpedoes and particle cannon fire.

The drones seemed to behave haphazardly, several crashed into one another instead of the fighters they were supposed to be chasing. It was as if suddenly the enemy had lost its focus, unsure of what it was doing.

Then it came into range of the orbital defences of Krenara prime itself, giant orbital particle cannons the size of entire ships began to gradually power up in a deep rumble as the enemy fleet neared.

This was the last roll of the dice for his world, his people, the enemy fleet constantly advancing were almost upon them now. Soon those ships will be turning their weapons upon the command carriers themselves.

Dalvosh winced and shielded his eyes as a blinding flash of emerald energy consumed the viewer, one of his command carriers listed, hit amidships, a massive hole blasted straight through the vessel. Stricken, it was pulled back toward the atmosphere of Krenara prime itself and began to burn up.

Disaster had struck for Dalvosh, the unmanned orbital weapons emplacements did not unleash their devastating firepower on the enemy fleet as he had planned. Instead they had released their fury on his own ships.

A second equally bright flash and another command carrier was blasted apart in a spectacular explosion, raining debris down through the atmosphere of his world.

"All ships, full retreat! Get us out of here!" Dalvosh screamed.

The Kralath-kar and its four remaining command carriers, together with the badly mauled remnants of the stealth ship flotilla fled with all speed away from their homeworld, the birthplace of their empire; abandoning their own people to their fate.

It indeed rained blood on Krenara that day.

Almost two days into their journey as the Valley-forge cruised comfortably through plasma drive, Commander Anizeres broke the relaxed silence.

"Captain; I've got something just coming into sensor range."

"What?" Kinraid replied a little startled, there goes his uneventful journey, and it was all going so well. "There shouldn't be anything out 'tis way."

"Well, there is now and it's heading toward us." Anizeres replied.

"Put it up on the viewer," Quinn sighed.

He could barely make out the forms of tiny dot like objects far in the distance, squinting at the viewer there was no chance he could identify them.

"Magnify."

In an instant it was revealed to them all, four Krenaran carriers and twelve stealth ships, some of which looked badly damaged were racing straight for them.

"For 'te love 'o mary! It's a new Krenaran incursion, go to general quarters, power up graviton shields, ready all weapons!"

Red alert sirens blared out across all decks, people startled at hearing those sirens on their maiden voyage, ran to their stations, graviton shields came to full power. There was not supposed to be an alert like this on a maiden voyage. The immense high bore fusion cannons, the ships main armament began to power up also.

The last thing Kinraid wanted was a repeat of the Krenaran war, not on his watch. The ships continued to close rapidly, getting ever larger on the viewscreen. Quinn's lips pressed together tightly, his eyes narrowed. He knew he was outgunned but he could not let this fleet cause havoc inside E.O.C.A space, just one of those carriers had killed thousands in the past. Mental flashes came up of the devastation wrought at the Aurelias colony during the war when a Krenaran command carrier decimated an orbital troop training facility, its wreckage plunged through the atmosphere to decimate the colony below.

"Wait!" Anizeres shouted just as Quinn was about to give the order to open fire. "Their weapons are not powered."

"They have invaded E.O.C.A space," Quinn shot back.

"But why? Take a look at those stealth ships, the damage on their hulls. I don't think they have come for a fight."

"Then why are they here?"

"Maybe they were fleeing one." Anizeres raised her eyebrows as if to emphasize the point.

"But who? What could cause an entire Krenaran fleet to just turn tail and run?"

The image of those approaching Krenaran ships was replaced with the visage of a Krenaran that Quinn knew well. After all a decade ago this Krenaran helped to foil an assassination plot against the then president of E.O.C.A himself, James Rushfeldt. Quinn had also been there at the time; it was Dalvosh. This time however he looked different, back then he was a proud strong Krenaran warrior, just taken over leadership of his people, now he looked a shadow of what he once was, a broken man.

"We are formally here to request asylum within E.O.C.A," he announced with a palpable hint of defeat to his voice.

Quinn reacted as though he had just been shot; *the Krenarans requesting asylum? What in God's name could have happened?*

"Dalvosh, where have you come from?"

"We are two days out from Krenara prime, we are badly damaged and sustained heavy losses."

Dalvosh gave Quinn one of those looks, a look which indicated that there was more going on here than he was letting on, but could not talk on an open channel.

"We'll escort you to the nearest E.D.F naval facility for repairs, then we'll discuss your request for asylum and its terms."

"I understand," Dalvosh replied abruptly.

The battered remnants of the Krenaran fleet fell into formation with the Valley-forge and gradually limped toward Delta gamma base, a small naval waystation that served as a temporary refuelling, repair facility, and stop over point on route to foxtrot base at Sigma XI in the Connaught sector.

Kinraid turned his attention toward Anizeres, "Contact D'mitry, have him place all our fighters on hot standby, ready to launch at a moment's notice."

Anizeres looked back at her Captain, "Don't you trust them?"

"Not for an instant."

5. Revelations

As knowledge quickly spread that the homeworld had fallen and the Krenaran leadership had collapsed, other remnants of the fleet stationed at other worlds began to break up, their morale shattered, many fleeing before the inevitable onslaught of this seemingly unstoppable robotic race.

Worlds throughout Krenaran space rapidly began to fall, bereft of the military chosen to protect them, some of which fled into E.O.C.A territory as Dalvosh had done, to be intercepted by patrolling E.D.F naval vessels, others hid within smaller fringe empires such as the Drullux and the Apathu. The collapse of the Krenaran civilization was underway and at each world the machines invaded they subjugated the population, with a speed unmatched they built giant factory complexes belching forth great plumes of smoke and noxious vapours, where those who hadn't been slaughtered were put to work building more robotic warriors, ships and drones. Any who resisted, the sick or the infirm were simply shot, reduced to nothing more than a charred patch of ground.

Thus these mechanoid terrors grew stronger with each passing world they conquered, in a never-ending wave of destruction spreading across the face of the galaxy.

Dalvosh trudged dejectedly into the cramped main operations centre of Delta gamma base with his closest aides, and Kelloth his advisor. The five of them flanked by a full squad of troops from the two hundred and fifty seventh 'ice maidens' reconnaissance platoon who had stopped over while their Stockholm class lander refuelled, they were so named for the freezing conditions of their world, Tarantis.

The entourage all came before the glass doors of Captain Marcus Drake's office, the commander of this rather backwater and forgotten outpost. As the doors gingerly opened they stepped through, Drake was sat at his desk, a balding man in his late forties, his office was a dimly lit rash of half opened storage crates containing all manner of junk. His desk a swamp of data navigators piled one on top of another haphazardly. The confines were so cramped that it was an effort to squeeze the fifteen strong party inside.

"I have come to request permanent asylum within E.O.C.A." Dalvosh repeated in his typical, deep gravelly Krenaran voice.

"Yes, yes I know that." Drake replied before sneezing loudly then wiping his snot laden nose with a tissue, much to the disdain of the Krenaran leader.

"Excuse me," he said as he tossed the tissue into a waste paper bin to the side of his desk. "Captain Kinraid apprised me of the situation, the question we all want to know is: What are you seeking asylum from? What could have caused such a catastrophe to befall the great and powerful Krenaran empire?" There was a heavily sardonic tone to Drake's voice as he asked the question, he had no love for Krenarans, the ship he served aboard during the Krenaran war was surprised and destroyed by a Krenaran stealth ship, resulting in the deaths of almost all of his shipmates, only he and a handful of others managed to escape floating in a lifepod for almost a week.

Dalvosh didn't rise to the man's jeers, he was used to being a hate figure amongst the Terrans, "we seek asylum because of something else, the Krenaran empire itself has been invaded and overthrown by a new race, a race of machines so powerful and so numerous that none can stand before it. The age of the Krenaran empire is over, our people are broken, reduced to a handful of wanderers and scavengers, now we come to you to ask for your help."

So this was what he couldn't talk to me about on an open channel, Kinraid thought but remained silent as he let Dalvosh tell his story.

Drake was tempted to say, help! Help the very species that just a decade ago caused the greatest loss of life since the second world war, you know what you can do with your help! But instead he refrained, this required the delicate diplomatic prowess of an E.O.C.A ambassador, not the strong arm of the E.D.F.

"If you and your men would prefer to wait here for a few days, we will send for an E.O.C.A diplomat to hear your case. We as a military force do not have the power to grant asylum to any outward alien people. We will prepare temporary quarters for your men."

Dalvosh nodded respectfully, "that will not be necessary, we have quarters enough aboard our own ships, we will continue to make emergency repairs while we await the arrival of your ambassador."

"Then we are in agreement," Drake nodded gently, secretly happy he didn't have a couple of thousand Krenarans disrupting his station. "Thank you." He said while he calmly showed them out of his ramshackle office.

Dalvosh and his entourage were escorted back to his ship, the rag-tag flotilla of eighteen ships gradually circled the small station, almost threatening to swamp it. With the impressive silhouette of the Valley-forge keeping a close watch from a slight distance away, the facility looked all the more insignificant.

***

Televis and his crew had been carefully nursed back to their full health by the ministrations of the skilled medical staff of the T'elareth. He had lost a lot of brave men during the attack at Orialis, and his ship was still badly damaged.

Although they had spent a day at the fleet yards at Ventaris undergoing emergency repairs, and taking on fresh supplies before the race to Solaria itself.

He had thanked Atanis personally for his help in the rescue of his ship. He, Atanis and the commander of the Ventaris fleetyards spoke with Primar Saltovos himself; the head of the entire Solarian military. In response to the attacks and the loss of Orialis, he had placed the warhost on high alert, patrols were being doubled for a twenty light year radius around Orialis itself. Although as of yet, they had found nothing. Televis had also made Saltovos aware that the Faeriath carried within it the only member of this robotic species, and he had agreed that it was imperative that it be brought to Solaria for further study, so that they might find a way to defeat this deadly new threat.

With that in mind, Televis bade both Atanis and the commander of the Ventaris fleetyards a fond farewell as the battered Faeriath gradually jettisoned from one of the numerous outer docking ports of the fleetyard itself. The silver crescent shaped craft gracefully came about, accelerated away from the station, and leapt into plasma drive to begin the final leg of its race.

It was over a weeks travel to Solaria even with the advanced plasma drive systems of the Faeriath. A journey that took them past the Sobris system, and through the swirling purple, greens and blues of the nebulae of the Oberon sound, then on to the Solaris system itself and the homeworld of the Solarian empire; Solaris IV, or just simply Solaria.

As they travelled, a communiqué had reached them notifying them of the fall of Bromis, together with a facility there that was used as a vital re-supply point for Solarian shipping across the entire Xinthis expanse, an area of space almost thirty light years wide and making up a large portion of the north eastern tip of Solarian space.

The Xinthis expanse was an area of 'dead space' were no stars or planets of any kind existed, a vast wilderness area with only the resupply point at Bromis providing essential food supplies and fuel for the Solarian fleet and civilian craft crossing this vast expanse. With the fall of Bromis, the entire north eastern quadrant looked very vulnerable indeed.

It was reported that these mechanoid ships attacked with such ferocity and in such numbers that the facility fell within minutes. The Solarian fleet posted there was smashed before it with extreme losses. Some fled to the expanse unsupplied, an almost certain death sentence, while others fell back and regrouped in outlying systems like Fulrix and Sobris.

Televis sighed in dismay at the news, at the inevitable losses of thousands more of his kinsmen, and at the very real possibility that unless the warhost is gathered to its full strength much faster, there won't be much of the Solarian empire left to save.

E.D.F Chronicles – The Cyberian menace

Just over a week later, after a long and tiresome journey the battered Faeriath emerged out of plasma drive on the fringes of the Solaris system, powered up its barely functioning Ionic sublight drive, and limped toward the homeworld, passing streams of all manner of craft busily hurrying to and fro like insects around this hectic world.

Televis's ship slowly manoeuvred into position and docked with one of several orbital stations, and contacted the station's overworked command and control staff as the ship gradually powered down.

"Your arrival was expected although you are slightly late," the female official manning this particular docking station said, she was hairless as all Solarians were, although her skin tone was a shade deeper blue than the males, it was one of the ways of identifying Solarian females.

"My ship was badly damaged," Televis retorted.

"Of course yes, yes." The woman replied with a stern nod, "you are due at the institute for advanced robotics. I would suggest you don't keep them waiting much longer," she said acidly before ending the communication.

Damn Solarian officials, Televis thought. *We must have some of the rudest, most abrasive figures in officialdom in the galaxy. It doesn't exactly set us in the best of light, being a supposed model of peace and culture and all that.*

He turned toward Tallis. "Have the captured robotic soldier magnetically clamped, secured, and brought aboard a shuttle to the surface." He said as he rose from his seat to join the entourage.

"Understood, sir." Tallis replied before turning back to his station.

Making his way through the battered confines of his ship, Televis passed half collapsed support struts, smashed consoles and trailing conduits as he made his way to the shuttlebay of the Faeriath, picking through a debris littered floor to the awaiting shuttle itself.

Once he was inside, the shuttle gradually began to lift off; collapsed hull plating fallen from the roof above during the battle fell from the bullet shaped shuttle like leaves falling from a tree as it levitated on its gravitic engines.

Televis watched the robotic warrior, still struggling against the magnetic clamps attached to its body in a never-ending, never tiring quest to break free. In a way he almost pitied it, a true sentient being would have given up its struggle and saved its strength for a better opportunity, or just accepted its fate long ago. But not this, it was running purely on its programming, all it knew was that it had to break free in order fulfill it again. And that was to systematically kill every single one of them.

The shuttle deftly flew out of the rear bay of the Faeriath and swung around in order to make its descent into the sapphire blue atmosphere of Solaria. As it passed the giant shape of the battlecruiser, Televis got his first glimpse with his own eyes just how badly damaged his ship was. The two giant rents torn into the command structure, again more damage on the secondary hull, the smooth flowing crescent shape of his beautiful ship now looked broken, torn, like a badly wounded beast. One thing he did notice though, and thought most peculiar, was that the breaches were not ragged as if hit by a solid shot or explosive; no these edges were smooth, as if the sections themselves had simply melted into nothingness.

He knew the weapons his people possessed; used only to defend themselves against a hostile galaxy were powerful and feared by all. They were nothing like this, this was a new kind of power, one that was, quite simply, beyond them. That, more than anything scared Televis.

The small shuttle carrying their robotic captive punched through the upper atmosphere of the Solarian homeworld, down through a patch of dense cloud cover, and past a flock of Logethi birds migrating northward at this time of year to their mating grounds high on the cliffs of Dorathamon. The shuttle gently slowed to a halt and touched down onto a small landing pad near to the grand crystalline spire of the institute for advanced robotics itself.

Televis led the way, with two others following close behind. Their captive magnetically clamped to a steel stretcher. Already dents and the occasional tear appeared as the robot prisoner unceasingly tried to rip and claw its way free.

The cortège walked up a small flight of marble steps, leading to giant double glass doors that swung effortlessly at their approach. Once inside the gleaming lobby of this vast structure, they were quickly mobbed by a gaggle of excited scientists staring wide eyed in wonder at the captive still trying desperately to free itself.

"Thank you for bringing this to us Comraa Televis, I am Felluthis, the principal of this institute. If you would like to follow me I will show you to our robotic sciences suite; where they plan to find out exactly how our new enemy works."

"Thank you," Televis replied simply, falling into step behind the much older Felluthis.

"It must have been difficult for you," Felluthis began as they walked, "so far you and only a handful of other ships are the only ones that have ever survived an encounter with these machines."

Hard was an understatement, Televis thought. Capturing this one damaged robot had very nearly cost him his life, the lives of his crew, and had resulted in the destruction of several other Solarian ships. He hoped that this struggling array of metal and circuits was worth the sacrifice they had all made, though all he could manage was a meek reply, "it was."

E.D.F Chronicles – The Cyberian menace

The small group proceeded down a marble floored corridor, the skeins of bright emerald green seemed to flash across the floor as though arcs of lightning. Finally the group came to a second set of doors which duly opened at their approach into a giant room.

Inside was all manner of sophisticated equipment, diagnostics, computer control terminals, and various other weird and wonderful machines.

The captured robot was carried to the centre of this room and a myriad of scientists crowded around it. The first task was to render their captive safe, otherwise the second they would try to connect any equipment to it, it would kill the person attempting to connect it.

This process alone took several hours and necessitated the robot be attached to a giant magnetic plate, from which it could not move.

Studying the robot carefully over the course of the next few days, they found several access ports along the rear cranium and the machines torso. Diagnostic, input and display devices were attached to the damaged unit. Bundles of cables lay splayed out from the body still attached to this magnetic plate, its arms outstretched, it looked for all the world as if it was being crucified.

Televis wondered if it even knew the meaning of torture, yet dismissed the thought just as quickly.

As the weeks passed he continued to make regular daily shuttle trips to and from the facility. Word had spread to him of several other attacks on Solarian shipping and the collapse of the Krenaran empire; by far the most alarming. He felt frustrated, helpless, as his ship was undergoing emergency repairs in an orbital repair facility at Kyo, the Solarian moon. He had to remain here while his kinfolk were fighting and dying against this implacable enemy, truly dark times had come to the galaxy.

Then like a lightning rod news of the breakthrough struck, Felluthis contacted him personally to inform him, summoning the Solarian Commander back to the institute urgently.

Once there he was hastily ushered through the doors, to the laboratory itself and confronted once more by the splayed out form of their captive, held in its torment by wires and constantly flickering displays showing complex datastreams.

He was shown to one of these displays by the band of excited to the point of feverish scientists. "It took us weeks to break through the incredibly difficult encryption algorithms built in to safeguard the machine core operating structure." The scientist went on, "once we did finally break through though, we found everything."

"Like what?" Televis asked growing impatient, time was of the essence and thousands of people were dying out there.

"We learned that these robotic warriors were built by an organic race, tens of thousands of years ago. These machines are called Cyberians, and were built to fight a war between what they know as 'the builders' and another race, the Xarathis. The Cyberians were programmed solely to kill the Xarathians."

"So if they were built to settle a war between two races we know nothing about, why are they here?" Televis asked.

"That's the other piece to this puzzle; you see the Cyberians were engineered as a completely autonomous force in their own right. Totally self sustaining and constantly on the move, they attack one system, completely destroy everything in that system and then move on to the next. But, to keep up this rate of advance, they have to have vast supplies of troops, ships, and equipment. So they were programmed to re-create themselves as well, on each conquered world, they rapidly build factories churning out hundreds of thousands of new Cyberian warriors, building new ships to replace ones lost in battle. In this way are not weakened as traditional forces are when they take new ground and their supply lines are stretched. Instead the Cyberians become stronger, more numerous."

"So what happened to make them attack us and the Krenarans?"

"The Cyberians do not come from our own galaxy, but a neighbouring one. When they fought the Xarathians, something also happened to them. Something corrupted their core programming, changed it irreversibly so that their primary function changed, instead of purging all Xarathians, they are now following their new function, which is to purge all organic beings. They perceive this literally as any machine would, in the tens of thousands of years since that war ended they had scoured their own galaxy, killing everything within it. Now they have come here to fulfil the same basic programming; a never ending quest of extermination."

"So if these Cyberians are tens of thousands of years old, how do we stop them?" Televis asked.

"Their one and only weakness lies in their communication channels with each other. You see, it's a double edged sword for them. Each Cyberian warrior is connected to the other by a data-link, in effect creating a vast network spanning the galaxy. Their ships are connected much the same way, which is how they are able to co-ordinate so fluidly and react so quickly. The ships themselves act as information hubs for the warriors, passing data and commands back and forth across this vast network. However every network must have a central core, a server, in order for it to function. The loss of a ship might slow the network down, albeit temporarily; the loss of the central core would collapse the network completely."

"So, where do we find the central core?" Televis frowned.

"I believe it would be within a ship, a command ship so to speak, something we have yet to encounter. Although everything we have learned thus far would lead me to conclude that this command ship would be a formidable adversary, they would take great pains to protect it. The problem is that this command ship could be anywhere, as long as it had a stable data-link to a nearby Cyberian ship it could theoretically transfer commands from one side of the galaxy, to the other."

"This would explain why Cyberians do not need to speak," Televis pointed out, looking toward their captive. "What do you need speech for, when all instructions are simply downloaded to you automatically."

The scientist nodded, "precisely."

Felluthis motioned to Televis, "the Solarian council are already convening an emergency session, they have asked for the report into our findings. I think they are going to gather the entire warhost."

"It's about time," Televis nodded in agreement.

"They are also sending the governor of Celtris III on an urgent diplomatic mission to Earth, in order to enlist the aid of the Terrans. The former ambassador has had close relations with Terrans in the past and with his help, they feel they would be amenable to our plight due to our mutual alliance through the Krenaran war."

"The humans have indeed grown powerful since that time, but does the council believe they are now strong enough to oppose this new enemy?" Televis whispered.

"The threat will be upon them soon whether they choose it or not. The more allies we have searching for this command ship, the greater our chance of success. This is an enemy that not only threatens ourselves, but every race in the known galaxy - We must prepare."

"Understood," Televis nodded in agreement, turned and left for his ship for the final time.

6. Pilgrim's journey

Kerulithar was now a week into his journey and harbouring an eager excitement to visit Earth, mainly due to the prospect of seeing his old friends Michael and Nikolai again, though he wished it was on happier terms. Another reason was that despite the close relationship he had helped to build with humanity, he had never actually visited Earth himself.

The tiny Solarian shuttle he was piloting was cramped and basic, yet he would not dare requisition a battlecruiser or even an escort for the journey. His people needed every spare ship they could muster just to stymie the implacable advance of the Cyberian assault, right now the warhost was buying time, nothing more, with their lives.

Truth be told, they needed humanities help. For the first time he had ever known his people actually needed *their* help. In fact, the whole galaxy may need the Terrans help in the end, which was why he was sent to speak with the E.O.C.A president, a Terran by the name of Franz Baumholt in order to negotiate their assistance, he just hoped humanity was able to….what was that human expression…….step up to the plate.

His shuttle, despite being small, cramped and slightly uncomfortable, did offer him the greatest asset of all right now - anonymity. The movement of a small shuttle wouldn't even be recognised, not so with a battlecruiser or an escort.

The navigation computer in his flight systems console alerted him that he had crossed the border into E.O.C.A space. The E.D.F waystation Charlie gamma base was nearby. He made up his mind to spend a night there refuelling and re-supplying, before continuing on his journey deeper into E.O.C.A territory.

Eidolon system.
Near the E.O.C.A / Krenaran border.

Squadron leader Daryl Mc'Kinsey banked his peregrine fighter to avoid a hunk of floating space junk, he was almost through with his routine sweep of the system. It had been largely uneventful so far, just the one hint of excitement to break through the tedium.

A freighter was trying to smuggle contraband narcotics out of the system. He and his wing had been ordered to intercept, they quickly surrounded it, and staring down the barrels of five fully armed peregrine fighters, the freighter wisely returned to port. There the freighter was searched and the crew quickly dealt with by local law enforcement officers. Once Mc'Kinsey had finished escorting the freighter, he and his wing returned to their patrol to finish off their sweep.

The monotony was not to last as in the blink of an eye several plasma wakes opened up instantly, suddenly all hell broke loose. Through the swirling wakes emerged the kinds of ships the like of which he had never seen before. Giants they were, silvery like Solarian ships, but dulled, faded. They had sleek rectangular forms and four large weapon mounts that were bigger than his entire craft, the huge leviathans powered up their engines and swept towards them.

"Holy shit!" was all that Mc'Kinsey could say, until it registered what it was he was seeing.

"All units break off, get back to Eidolon right now!"

The tiny group of five fighters banked sharply to avoid this marauding armada, one of the ships flashed out a strange dull green energy beam toward them. One of his wingmen flew straight into its path and Mc'Kinsey was forced to watch helpless as blue five, piloted by his closest friend Drew Collins was quietly and effortlessly reduced to its constituent parts, and then even they were gone. Drew didn't even have time to scream.

"Bastards!" Daryl spat in rage at the loss of Collins, then slammed his console as he rammed all the extra power he could muster into the turbines, overcharging and almost cooking them, his craft shot forward, he had to get away from these things and warn Eidolon otherwise they would all end up the same way as Collins just had.

Keying in the long range microwave radio transceiver, he contacted base command back on Eidolon. "Alert five alert five, we have just been attacked by a massive unknown enemy fleet just dropped out of plasma drive about a quarter the way into the system. One wingman down already, repeat we are under attack, alert five alert five!"

Mc'Kinsey risked a glance out of his cockpit window, alongside his port wingtip, something was flying alongside him. Not one of the other wingmen, this was cylindrical, barrel shaped. With a weapon mount at the front and a small engine at the rear, a complex array of sensory antennae adorned the top of it, it looked unmanned, he couldn't pick out a cockpit.

That was the last thing squadron leader Daryl Mc'Kinsey saw as the Cyberian drone deliberately swooped toward him, smashing headlong into his fighter and destroying them both in a spectacular explosion.

None of the five strong flight of blue squad returned to base that day.

Mc'Kinsey's distress call did eventually make it through to the forward operating base of the 58th tactical fighter wing, dubbed the 'flying 58th' where the scramble was immediately called. Over fifty peregrine fighters took to the skies from this and two other forward operating bases on Eidolon itself in a roar of twin afterburners.

The E.D.F naval flotilla stationed in orbit of Eidolon also intercepted the mayday call, although they had already detected the vast enemy fleet as soon as it emerged out of plasma drive and were now powering up their engines to intercept. As if waking from a deep slumber, the Washington class heavy cruiser New Jersey, together with the Jefferson class cruiser Warspite, a dozen Ghandhi class destroyers and Mandela class light cruisers all powered up simultaneously, heading out toward this new emerging threat, their engines glowing like miniature suns accelerating all the time.

On the bridge of the New Jersey, Captain Adel Rodriguez eyed his viewscreen intently, stroking his smooth clean shaven chin. *If the Krenarans have begun a new invasion, this time they would pay dearly,* he thought. A lot of things had changed since the last war, humanity was no longer the pushover the galaxy thought it was.

"Captain; fighters have broken orbit of Eidolon, requesting permission to join with the fleet." Lieutenant Curtis, his communications officer reported.

"Request granted," Rodriguez replied still fondling his chin, Eidolon was the closest system to the Krenaran border, who else could it be?

The fourteen ship flotilla advanced upon this unknown fleet now threatening the safety of their border world of Eidolon. The planet was behind them, the enemy ahead of them. Just where Rodriguez wanted them to be; he would defend Eidolon to the last, even if it meant the lives of every man in his fleet.

"Captain, information is beginning to come through from our scanners, from the looks of them, they're definitely not Krenaran. Ship's computer is struggling to find a match."

"A new enemy?" Rodriguez contemplated aloud rising from his chair, "are they hostile?"

"Well, judging by the size of that fleet coming toward us, and what they did to those five fighters, I don't think they have come for a picnic." Curtis replied, studying his readouts. "I'm picking up forty large contacts coming this way."

"All hands battlestations! Order the fleet to do the same." Rodriguez barked straightening his tunic, "We'll show them what it takes to invade an E.O.C.A colony world."

On every ship right across the hastily prepared E.D.F flotilla, red alert klaxons blared out, lights dimmed, people rushed to man consoles coated in a dull ruddy glow from the emergency lights above them, as the fleet was brought up to full battle readiness.

E.D.F Chronicles – The Cyberian menace

The forty huge Cyberian cruisers detected the activation of the E.D.F vessels weapon systems almost immediately, yet unfazed they continued closing in their unceasing, tireless advance.

The high definition sensor arrays, recording devices, and passive scanners onboard a tiny satellite orbiting high above Eidolon itself were all working intently, capturing every frame of the enemy ships advance, together with the E.D.F flotilla arrayed to stop them, then automatically transmitted this accumulated data to a small ground station on the surface.

Both the satellite and the ground station were operated by the E.D.F intelligence services, and this was but one of many listening posts dotted throughout E.O.C.A space. The experts manning the tiny listening post typically used to track Krenaran ship movements along the border, should they violate the terms of the peace treaty that ended the war a decade ago, worked furiously to decode and immediately forward the data via secure carrier signal, to the giant intelligence hub known as Foxtrot base at Sigma XI, a full sector away. Speed was of the essence and they hoped Foxtrot base would receive the data in time.

As the two fleets closed, the E.D.F flotilla was suddenly engulfed in a blazing green light, this wave of energy seemed to permeate through the outer hulls of the arrayed ships, covering all aboard in an unearthly light.

"They are scanning us; orders?" Dane Blackmer, Rodriguez's executive officer asked.

"Let them take a look, probably just trying to work out who we are." His focus fixed on the sight of those huge ships now filling his viewscreen.

The scan was finished within seconds, the blazing green light simply shut down, all around the fleet interiors returned to their darkened ruddy glow.

Suddenly it was as if their was a change in the behaviour pattern of those tiny drones, buzzing hither and thither like tiny parasites riding along with the larger craft. Now they broke off, heading straight for the E.D.F flotilla, the New Jersey, the Warspite and their attendant escorts, and began to pepper them with bright white energy pulses, flashes lit up the hulls of the craft as if caught in some kind of lightning storm.

Rodriguez was confused, they were peppering his ships with these bright energy flashes, yet doing no actual damage, was it even an attack? He had no idea.

"Should we return fire?" Blackmer replied, casting an ever-so-slightly questioning look at his commanding officer.

"Negative, they haven't actually caused us any harm yet. For all we know it could be their way of communicating with us."

"It could be some kind of passive scan, designed to find out our weapons and defences?" Curtis ventured.

"Order the fifty eighth to chase them away, but hold fire for now." Rodriguez replied, brushing back an errant strand of raven black hair from his immaculately smoothed style, while still fixated on the viewscreen trying to figure out that these things were actually doing.

Blackmer sighed a slightly disappointed sigh, "aye Captain."

The flock of Peregrine fighters from the fifty eighth banked hard to engage the drones. The drones themselves had other ideas, using their incredible agility they jinked, danced, swooped and climbed, then flew directly into the fighters themselves. Five of the craft were decimated almost immediately, their broken fuselages tearing themselves apart in small yet bright fireballs as the drones smashed into them.

"All ships, target the drones, weapons free!" Rodriguez ordered, *well this is it*.

The fighters of the fifty eighth dove to the attack, seeking revenge for their lost comrades, wingtip mounted lasers blasting apart drone after drone in their ferocity. However with every one they destroyed, more detached themselves from the underside of those giant cruisers and raced to the attack.

The massive Cyberian cruisers themselves now joined the fray, their weapon mounts spitting forth an intricate latticework of green energy, several ships were caught within the deadly touch of those beams. Entire sections simply stripped away, those aboard who had not been erased from existence entirely, were blown out into space through bulkheads that were no longer there.

A Ghandhi class destroyer, one of Warspites escorts listed lazily, before what was left of its weakened, shorn hull, blew itself apart in a dazzlingly bright explosion that lit up the entire starboard side of Warspite itself.

The E.D.F fleet retaliated, both the New Jersey and the Warspite poured fire into the oncoming Cyberian ships. Their high powered lasers scoring deep slashes into their immensely thick hulls, through all the maelstrom, the furious assault they were causing no real damage.

The fighters of the fifty eighth, caught in their dance of death with those deadly drones, were effectively kept out of the battle, much to Rodriguez's consternation.

One of the green energy weapons swept over another Ghandhi class destroyer, melting away a large portion of its sloped frontal section and command tower in one long arc, exposing the weakened decks and framework beneath. Rodriguez watched as tiny ant like dots were blown out through these devastated sections, the ship was bleeding its crew into space.

The stricken vessel began to pitch downward out of control, before a second beam burrowed itself right through the centre of the ship. The destroyer, now adrift burst apart in a bright plume of flame and shattered hull fragments, some of which peppered the side of the New Jersey itself. The ship shuddered under the impact of the shockwave, sending fragments clattering against its port hull armour. Rodriguez had to shield his eyes from the dazzling brilliance of the explosion.

"Damage report!" he ordered over the din of battle and wailing of alarms.

"Minor damage to the outer hull on our port side due to colliding with the hull fragments from that destroyer, but nothing too severe."

The E.D.F fleet threw everything it had against these monstrous behemoths, weapons fire lit up the surrounding space. Explosions rippled across the Cyberian ships hulls, though only causing minimal damage at best. *We might as well be throwing sticks at them,* Rodriguez mused. His brow creased, the sweat of desperation beginning to form.

Still they came on.

The surviving destroyers, through a quirk of fate, launched a co-ordinated salvo of torpedoes together. The giant flurry of warheads shot toward the cruisers, which had now slowed but still advancing, the brightness of their contrails visible over the myriad of laser fire criss-crossing the space around them.

Some of the torpedoes were intercepted by drones deliberately flying into them, sacrificing themselves to protect the larger craft, exploding in bright flashes as the remaining salvo rushed by. Finally slamming headlong into the thick armoured hulls of the Cyberian ships, then detonating, throwing out huge plumes of flame and broken hull armour into space. Deep, dark craters were torn into the Cyberian ships where the torpedoes impacted. Some had blasted their way right through the armour of the craft, causing immense damage within.

Rodriguez almost punched the air in delight, "they must be vulnerable to our torpedoes, order the destroyers to launch a second salvo!"

The badly mauled but surviving fighters of the fifty eighth were fighting a losing battle, despite now having destroyed hundreds of drones, for every one they destroyed more took their place. Eventually they withdrew back to the safety of Eidolon, only seven craft remained out of the fifty five sent against these metal brutes.

Now lacking any kind of fighter support, the E.D.F fleet was even more hard pressed, as the huge amount of drones buzzed to and fro unchecked seeking out the destroyers that launched that salvo, and intentionally ramming themselves against them. The fourteen metre long crafts smashed into the undefended ventral sections and booster turbines, blasting apart huge sections of the hull in their fiery demise and completely shredding the rear engines.

Several of the destroyers listed, fires raging throughout their broken hulls before exploding in intense fireballs throwing out debris in all directions.

The badly mauled E.D.F flotilla were being pressed further and further back toward Eidolon itself as the Cyberian armada resumed its relentless advance, the lattice of beams from the matter convertors, the Cyberians deadliest weapon, sweeping in wide arcs stripping whole decks away at a stroke. The broken hulls of destroyers floated aimlessly, adrift, and in some places still ablaze due to the devastating ramming attacks of the drones.

The long range laser batteries of the Warspite continued to flash out their anger, slamming into the heavily armoured Cyberian ships again and again, to no avail. The weapons themselves were just not strong enough, although several of the Cyberian leviathans bore scars on their hulls due to the ferocity of the E.D.F ships.

The badly damaged Ghandhi class destroyer, E.D.F.S Chesapeak with several of its decks shorn open to space and yet more ablaze, in one final, desperate act of defiance, unleashed a final salvo against these mechanical menaces. Completely emptying its torpedo bays, six warheads sped toward the Cyberian ships now closing for the final kill.

In the few seconds it took for the deadly payload to reach its target only two drones had managed to intercept the warheads, colliding with them in spectacular explosions, the other four smashing

headlong into the closest Cyberian cruiser already badly damaged by an earlier torpedo strike. Finally this was too much, and the giant craft began to list awkwardly as explosions wracked its outer hull. It crumpled and then exploded in an almighty blast throwing out debris far and wide, the shockwave and blasted hull fragments tore apart the Chesapeak along with it.

The shockwave slammed into other nearby Cyberian ships with such weight, such force that no amount of armour could shield them, the nearest vessel was struck several times, sharp heavy hull fragments hammering hard into its hull.

It too was now stricken and badly damaged, the New Jersey and the Warspite, being the only two ships still active in the engagement converged their fire upon the weakened, damaged areas of the ship, and in a blaze of high power laser cannon fire from the Warspite's four forward mounted short and medium range batteries, together with the New Jersey's twin forward firing laser array's and rotary cannons, all managed to combine to tear apart immense sections of this ailing cruiser. Within the space of a few seconds, it too tore itself apart in a storm of explosions, almost emulating that of its sister ship that had caused it so much damage in its own death throes.

Then something happened that Rodriguez did not expect, it was as if a wave of confusion and panic spread amongst this monstrous armada that now threatened to destroy them at any moment. It was as if they were suddenly unsure of themselves, unsure of what to do. Drones crashed headlong into other drones and their advance for a brief moment was halted. Just these two comparatively tiny ships stood before an armada that dwarfed them and threatened to engulf the entire planet.

Knowing they had done all they could, and victory was just not possible. Rodriguez swallowed hard and ordered his crew to shunt all available power to the engines. He fully intended to ram them, sacrificing his own ship in one last attempt to save their doomed world. The large twin turbines flared as they powered the ship forward, the Warspite followed suit, both ships guns blazing until their barrels glowed hot as they drove at the heart of the Cyberian armada, trying to cause as much damage as they could in this brief moment of confusion.

Rodriguez gently sat back in his chair as the immense hull of a Cyberian cruiser grew ever larger in his viewscreen, calmly accepting his fate, he had done all that he could. If he could not protect Eidolon from these mechanical 'things' then he would make them pay dearly for their prize. Time seemed to stop as he whispered one final prayer to his wife and children somewhere on that planet below, so that they may be spared the horror of what is to come. He barely got the words out of his mouth before the five hundred and seventy four metre long heavy cruiser New Jersey smashed headlong like a giant missile into the Cyberian cruiser, both vessels exploding violently in a devastating blast, lighting up the entire enemy fleet. The Warspite less than a second later followed suit. Two immense explosions that sent a message loud and clear throughout the Cyberian armada, humanity would be no easy target.

The E.D.F fleet had fought ferociously in the defence of their world, to protect their people. However their enemy was simply too strong and too numerous, and ultimately they had broken through. The trail of devastated broken ships a testament to the ferocity of the battle; the Cyberians had defeated them, but not without cost. Four of their own cruisers were destroyed, and their loss was keenly felt in the slowdown in the dataverse, the network came within a whisker of collapsing completely in this part of the fleet, and the numbers of operational drones were severely shortened, though new network connections had quickly re-routed the flow of data between the remaining cruisers and the far away, ancient command ship.

The vast Cyberian armada moved into orbit of the verdant green hued world of Eidolon itself, their weapons easily brushing aside the various orbital facilities and satellites of this outlying colony world. All except one however, that small inconspicuous little satellite operated by the E.D.F intelligence services. It had recorded the entire battle with its myriad of ultra high definition sensors, the small ground station on Eidolon itself manned by just four staff, sent the commands hurriedly to this satellite to transmit its telemetry via secure microwave data carrier to Foxtrot base. It had almost finished sending the encryption when it too went dark, the last image recorded was a close up of one of the immense cruisers, before it opened fire on it and erased it from existence.

The data that was sent would take several hours to reach a receiving station at Sigma XI, where the operatives of Foxtrot base could decode the information and analyse it. Then re-transmit it back to Alpha base, orbiting Mars, the headquarters of the entire E.D.F. It would take several days to traverse the thirty light year distance between Sigma XI and Mars, but at least the E.D.F would be made aware of what had transpired here.

Two large bays opened toward the rear underside of the Cyberian cruisers now encircling the planet, one after another a flurry of teardrop shaped craft began their descent into the atmosphere. Their Ion engines crackling as the charge interacted with water vapour within the cloud cover, the engines themselves glowed brightly as they strove hard to slow the rapid descent of these awkward looking craft.

People on the ground looked up to the night sky to catch a glimpse of these strange pods descending through the crackles of lightning and the driving rain to their world. The cacophonous boom! Boom! of anti-aircraft batteries flashed across the night air, as they attempted to thin the numbers of craft making it to the surface, the acrid stench of gunpowder filled the night sky, as streaks of tracer fire sought their targets.

Several of these pods were hit by anti-aircraft missiles, exploding in bright plumes of flame and trailing debris like some giant firework, others spiralled uncontrollably to the ground, yet more were pounded relentlessly by the anti-aircraft batteries from contingents of the eighth armoured battalion, the 'hell raisers' trailing smoke and torn metal fragments from ragged holes punched through their outer armour, yet through the storm of fire flashing across the sky, more came through, and the landing site was growing rapidly.

More craft began to descend through the hell of missiles, smoke, and bursts of flak, their engines lighting up the ground beneath them. There were screams of terror as people ran hither and thither, locking doors, hastily barricading windows. Anything they could do to escape the maelstrom. Within minutes the streets of Eidolon were utterly deserted, the only sound came from the occasional crack of a thunderclap, the patter of rain on windows and from the heavy tracks of armour and artillery being moved into position, the crack of asphalt breaking up under heavy metal tracks as huge war machines rumbled through the streets of the colony, the growling of their engines like the snarling of great beasts circling for combat, the stomp of soldiers boots following in their wake, and the deep resonating crump of a hydraulic footplate from a Dominator assault walker as they strode to the defence of their world, the continual ear-splitting pounding of the anti-aircraft guns, and roar of missiles providing a deafening accompaniment to the march of the defenders of Eidolon.

As the strange Cyberian craft came in for landing, the darkened, scorched heat shields housing the engines gradually separated, opening out like the petals of a flower, forming a base for the pod to land upon. Several large doors opened out in much the same manner, a telescopic rack from within extended outward from all four of these doors and began the release of dozens of Cyberian warriors. In regimented rows they advanced, their metallic skeletal forms reflecting the stars and the fiery explosions all around them.

The landing site continued to grow, already hundreds of Cyberians had been blasted apart, yet unheeding of their losses, more and more pods descended. The metallic warriors began their silent, eerie march, red unblinking sensors, eyes in the darkness fixed upon their foe; life itself, their dark weapons drawn.

Apollo main battle tanks, and Dominator assault walkers formed a defensive cordon around the outskirts of the colony site. Once the pods had finished descending and the anti-aircraft guns fell silent it became deathly still, not a single weapon fired as the Cyberians continually advanced without pause, without checking even a single stride.

Corporal Greystoke piloting the Dominator assault walker Big Bertha gave the order to fire as torrential rain ran in rivulets down his cockpit glass. The roar from the assault cannons of four Dominators deafening as they tore through the silence, the storm of heavy calibre armour piercing rounds scythed through the approaching Cyberians, in this vast sea of advancing metal it was impossible to miss, scores of the metallic warriors were literally ripped to shreds as rounds hammered into them, yet uncaring for their fallen brethren more still advanced scrabbling over the bodies of the fallen to take up the fight in their stead.

The terrifying boom from the cannons of the Apollo's took up the fight, the roar of their main guns reverberating loudly amongst the buildings around them, windows shattered from the force. The shells exploding amongst the Cyberian lines in great plumes of fire, blasted earth, and twisted metal from the bodies of smashed warriors. The E.D.F forces were exacting a horrendous toll on the Cyberian army, yet still heedless of their losses they advanced.

The troops around the tanks and those that had taken up position in the outlying buildings, began to open fire themselves, shots from their pulse rifles slamming into Cyberian after Cyberian, wreckage from hundreds of bodies littered the muddy rain-soaked battlefield, with every step they took more were blasted apart. So far these metallic monstrosities had yet to kill even a single man.

Once they got into range however, everything changed as they unleashed their own weapons, a smaller derivative of the cruisers own matter converters. With blasts like lightning they struck, with the stench of ozone and an intense sizzling and smell of charred meat, E.D.F troopers were simply atomised, their bodies converted into raw energy in the space of a nanosecond, the electricity immediately earthed itself. All that remained were blackened scorch marks upon the ground. Tanks were hit repeatedly, sections of their armour plating and tracks stripped away in a roar of steam and hissing metal. One of the Dominators was hit several times, its legs no longer able to support its weight, it toppled over backward with a loud thump. The pilot pressed the cockpit release and the cockpit glass slowly opened, and as he clambered out was blasted by a Cyberian weapon, the fat and flesh from his fingertips dribbled down one of the armour plates, the rest of his body consumed.

Casualties were rapidly mounting amongst the defenders, the stench of death was everywhere, the tanks, some of which where now disabled, their tracks in ruins continued to pour fire into the Cyberian ranks, huge explosions ripped through the sodden ground as artillery and tank shells landed amongst them.

Everywhere there was destruction, an Apollo blew itself apart as a lucky Cyberian shot stripped apart its fuel tank, the petroleum within igniting on the searing hot metal and the vehicle exploded in a shower of razor sharp fragments that scythed through Cyberian and E.D.F trooper alike.

The Apollo's having been hit again and again were looking extremely fragile, the order was eventually given to abandon them and fall back to secondary positions within the colony itself. Troopers ran in blind panic through the rain soaked streets, desperately trying to get back into cover.

The Dominators, swinging their assault cannons back and forth in huge arcs covered their retreat, shredding any Cyberians that came too close.

Though like an inexorable tidal wave of metallic bodies, the Cyberians swarmed over the ruined Apollo's and Dominators alike, surging into the colony.

More explosions continued to wrack them, artillery batteries positioned in the central shopping area of the colony, close to the hub, unleashed co-ordinated salvoes, blasting dozens apart at a stroke. E.D.F troopers who had took positions within the buildings themselves opened fire through broken windows and smashed doors, everywhere Cyberians were taking immense losses, but still, uncaring, they silently advanced, pouring into buildings like a tide of living metal to slaughter all those inside.

Corporal Greystoke and the remainder of the Dominators, were backed up all the way to the main square itself, he had never seen anything like it, such ferocity, such wanton destruction, even during the carnage at Gamma IV they had not experienced such an overwhelming foe.

The artillery illuminated by the streetlights were firing right behind them, their shells passing right over their heads to land with massive explosions amongst the oncoming Cyberians that seemed to fill every building, every street. It was just like one vast metal tidal wave sweeping through the colony.

Big Bertha itself was hit again and again, the armour on its right leg stripped away, the surrounding metal glowing hot from the effects of the Cyberian weapons, its frontal torso also hit, yet still Greystoke ordered his charge onward. *I will not lie down and die like a dog before this swarm of fucking locusts, I will die fighting.* His display was awash with damage readouts, yet his weapons were still intact, barely.

Slowly Bertha, and the other dominators staggered toward their foe, Greystoke willing his machine onward, beads of sweat trickled down his creased brow as he lined his sights on these metal demons now filling his cracked cockpit glass. They had fought together in engagements across a dozen worlds, bled together, Bertha was a friend to him as any machine could be. And if they were to die here, in this place, then by God they would make them pay. He gnashed his teeth and once more pressed the trigger on his assault cannon arm, emptying every last slug into these…these things. Bodies covered the street, ripped apart in a spray of metal fragments. The assault cannon now out of ammunition and steaming from the heat build-up, yet still Greystoke charged his twelve foot tall mechanical chariot into them screaming "Come on you little fucks!" all the while clicking the trigger for the pneumatic ram in his left arm hardpoint. The four thousand P.S.I titanium tipped ram smashed through Cyberian upon Cyberian, crushing them into walls, cars, smashing them down like a hammer fist. He swung it left and right, like a great club while the ram was still extended, smashing an entire line of Cyberian warriors to the ground. One was flung like a rag doll, crashing through the windscreen of a parked car ten feet behind.

Though wherever Cyberians were falling, more took their place, Bertha, in the open together with her accompanying Dominators, took one too many hits, the giant assault walker tottered unsteadily, and then collapsed heavily to the ground with a loud bang.

Greystoke, badly shaken but still alive, attempted to un-strap himself in order to grab his weapon and clamber out of his wrecked machine. He watched in horror as a Cyberian came into view through his smashed cockpit glass, it stooped down on-top of the fallen Bertha. Fixed him with those red unblinking sensors, and displaying no remorse nor emotion of any kind, smashed its fist straight through the broken glass and through the corporals head, coating the interior in a spray of blood and brain matter.

By the time the morning sun had arisen Eidolon had fallen, every living thing in the colony, eradicated. It became just another empty shell, a factory world for the Cyberians as they continued on their long bloody march through the galaxy.

Five hours later, the sensor data and video feed from that tiny satellite eventually reached one of a myriad of receiving stations on Sigma XI, and was then forwarded on to foxtrot base itself. Inside the vast enclave a team of imaging specialists, intelligence experts and scientific advisors pored through the data. Everyone was drawing a blank, they had never witnessed anything quite like this before. One thing they did agree on, was that it definitely was not Solarian, Krenaran or even Dracos in origin none of the major powers could have done this. So that led to the grim fact that a new enemy was out there, more powerful than anything that had come before, and humanity was now its target.

Kerulithar's tiny shuttle dropped out of plasma drive just outside of Venus, powered up its twin sub-light Ion engines, glowing in their customary bright electric blue, and then proceeded to make its way to Alpha base in orbit of Mars.

He keyed in a series of commands on a central communications console, contacting the base's command and control centre. A visage of an incredibly busy command centre showed up on a tiny overlay on his cockpit window, the face of a long dark haired female greeted him.

"I am governor Kerulithar of Celtris III, I am here on an urgent ambassadorial mission on behalf of my government, I formally request permission to dock and to speak with the commander of this facility at the earliest convenience."

"One moment please," the female replied as she seemed to talk to someone off screen for several seconds, confirming the ambassador's credentials.

Eventually she spoke again, "Solarian shuttle, you are cleared for docking at fighter bay six, manoeuvring instructions will be sent to your nav computer."

"Understood Alpha base; Kerulithar out," he cancelled the transmission.

E.D.F Chronicles – The Cyberian menace

The course corrections were quickly transmitted, decoded into Solarian script and flashed up on his nav console. The Solarian deftly flew the craft around the immense superstructure of the station, with its numerous communications and sensor towers, berthing bays for ships, and heavy weapons emplacements. Lights from thousands of rooms almost seemed to make the place twinkle, he thought. The sheer size and grandeur of this place impressed even him. He passed several transports and ships going to and fro from the station before eventually manoeuvring the tiny bullet shaped craft into a comparatively small fighter bay, though the hangar still dwarfed his miniscule shuttle.

Inside, numerous fighters, bombers and support craft were all neatly parked in rows, some had servicing crews in environment suits attending them. There was a bank of empty spaces, no doubt kept in reserve for smaller craft like his own. The shuttle gracefully glided into one of these bays, the interior of the hangar reflecting off the almost mirror like finish of the craft's exterior before slowly descending and coming to rest. His shuttle, a similar size to a Peregrine fighter, fitted easily enough within the confines of the bay.

A gigantic door folded down over the entrance of the fighter bay in one long movement, before sealing and locking itself with a loud, deep thud. The bay was re-pressurised and oxygen once again pumped in, allowing the governor to leave the shuttle.

A small party of three officers approached him as he made his way out of the powering down craft. "Ambassador, welcome to Alpha base, it is not every day we receive a Solarian dignitary with such a high prominence in government."

"This is no ordinary day," the Solarian replied, "but thank you," he said as he made his way down a small flight of access steps clutching a case containing several data discs. "This is a matter of utmost importance, affecting the future of all our races, I must be allowed to speak with your commanding officer and then to your president."

The officers nodded gravely, "I shall take you to see him, but first you must step through a bio scanner, and then another scanner for any concealed weapons or explosives you may be carrying. It's just a formality, but we have to perform these security checks to all visitors before they enter the station."

"I understand," the lanky, hairless blue skinned Solarian nodded, "please lead on."

He fell into step behind the officers he was head and shoulders above, a full foot taller, as they led him through a series of high definition scanning arrays, the first confirming that he was in-fact clear of any diseases he may be carrying that could affect them, as far as they could detect anyway. The second confirmed that he carried no concealed weapons. He followed the three officers through various corridors, passageways and gantries to the nearest elevator stop. Kerulithar quickly noticed how busy this place was, in some of the larger corridors the human military officers, troops, and lesser orderlies were in many cases having to push their way past civilians and other military personnel. To the Solarian it resembled nothing more than ordered chaos, though on a grand scale.

Eventually, after much pushing and shoving, where even the Solarian ambassador was jostled more than once, they came upon the elevator itself. Its doors opening out into a small oasis of zen and calm amongst the teeming masses.

The elevator quickly transported the four of them up to the command deck, where it deposited the occupants into a similar seething mass of activity.

The ambassador was shown to a large office, just to the left side of this vast floor, where Admiral Montrose was sat waiting patiently.

The Admiral nodded curtly toward the ambassador, "our two peoples have a long standing friendship, but never has a Solarian ambassador been sent to Earth. In any case, welcome to Alpha base, headquarters of the Earth Defence Force."

"Thank you Admiral, although I wish the manner of my coming was more pleasant. Unfortunately I bring news of dire events, never before has my government deemed events to be as catastrophic to the galaxy at large as these; hence why I have been sent."

"Please do go on," Montrose pyramided his fingers as the ambassador began, resting his elbows on his spacious ebony black desk.

"There is a new enemy at large, a mechanised race who call themselves the Cyberians, they have travelled long, from outside of our own galaxy with one purpose, and that is to eradicate all organic life everywhere in the galaxy. They have already destroyed one of our worlds, killing millions of Solarians, dozens of our ships have already been lost, and they have also overrun the Krenaran empire resulting in its collapse. The remaining few who have escaped have been reduced to wanderers, guns for hire, stragglers. Others have requested urgent asylum within your own borders."

Montrose frowned a little, *this Solarian was remarkably well informed about what went on inside our borders.* "Yes, I know about that, though what proof do you have of this new enemy and what threat they pose to our own people. The E.D.F cannot go to war based upon hearsay and conjecture."

Kerulithar handed him a small data disc containing what Televis and the science team had discovered on Solaria. "At great cost, one of our ships managed to capture one of the warriors, our study of it was rather enlightening.

This is a race that alone, no race in the galaxy can stand against. Although united, we might just stand a chance."

Just as Kerulithar finished talking, a lone young Lieutenant commander burst into the room, Montrose glared at him for his impetuosity and was about to severely reprimand him for breaking into a private meeting between him and the Solarian ambassador, before what the man said stunned him into silence.

"Admiral! Eidolon has fallen!"

"What!" Montrose immediately jumped up from his desk as though a thunderbolt had just gone through him, "the fleet?"

"Destroyed."

An urgent tone came to his voice, "get me the president, I want an emergency meeting with the admiralty and joint chiefs of the military within the hour. Initiate alert level two, repeat alert level two."

The Lieutenant was thunderstruck, *how could all this happen so fast.*

"Well don't just stand there, you can think about the implications later, go!"

"Err….yes, sir!" The Lieutenant saluted before stumbling out of the office.

Montrose turned back to Kerulithar, the tall blue skinned Solarian waited patiently for him to continue. "If you would not mind Ambassador, I would like you to be present at the meeting, your people's knowledge could prove invaluable."

Kerulithar nodded gently, "I shall be present."

"I will have someone prepare temporary quarters for your stay."

The Solarian smiled, "thank you that is most gracious of you."

The Admiral thumbed a control set into his polished black desk on his right, activating the stations internal comms. system. "Commander Birkenaar report to Admiral Montroses office please."

Commander Birkenaar was the head of hospitality management aboard alpha base, a lithe slim athletic woman, with a long mane of fair hair, and piercing brown eyes. She was a former attaché to Admiral Mason before he retired, and Admiral Kennelly until his death at the siege of Foxtrot base during the Krenaran war. As head of hospitality management, it was her duty to attend to the myriad of V.I.P's and guests, to ensure their safety while on the station, and to make sure that any guests do not stray into any sensitive or out of bounds areas as well as assigning quarters and to attend to any special requirements the guests may have. With anything up to a thousand V.I.P's and dignitaries passing through here from all over the galaxy every week, her job was a busy one.

She arrived a few moments later, panting ever so slightly, and straightening her hair as she cautiously entered the Admiral's office.

"Ah commander," the Admiral said with a respectful smile. "Ambassador Kerulithar here will require quarters for his stay; see that we have something suitable made ready for him."

"Absolutely Admiral," Birkenaar replied breathily, still trying to shake the effects of having to rush to the Admiral's office.

"Ambassador, if you would like to accompany me we'll find you a comfortable room for your stay."

Well, as comfortable a room as can be found on a purely military battlestation like this, she thought, though kept her musings to herself, not wanting to embarrass the ambassador after all.

Kerulithar nodded once more before falling into step behind the commander and leaving Montrose alone in his office again. The Admiral had an hour to gather all the information he could on what had happened ready for the briefing he had to give to the president. As he sifted through stacks of data navigators in a hurried attempt to compile and make sense of the data. An image flashed up on a viewer mounted on the left wall above a small row of seating, it grabbed his attention, forcing him to look up at it.

"Welcome to the outer colony news service, I am Annika Raumov, the top stories today. Disaster at Eidolon, E.O.C.A has lost all contact with the planet. In a shadowy reminder of the onset of the Krenaran war the planet has seemingly been devastated by an as yet unknown assailant. All troops and ships stationed on or near the planet have been overrun and utterly destroyed, the civilian population virtually wiped out. Hundreds of thousands of lives ended in what can only be described as the worst atrocity to hit mankind since the war a decade ago."

"How the hell has that managed to get on the news so fast?" Montrose thought out loud, "we barely even know ourselves yet." He continued to watch in interest.

"My freighter Dixie may, had just dropped out of plasma drive on our usual run when I saw these huge metallic ships encircling the planet, like nothing I had ever seen before. They looked real nasty so I turned the ship around and hightailed it out of there as fast as my drives could carry me. It was a good job I did too, as they seemed to not notice my ship at all."

"God-damnit!" Montrose shouted to himself, slamming his fist down hard onto his desk, "that's all we need, mass hysteria to break out amongst the colonies."

He gathered up several data navigators, piled them all into a black briefcase and headed toward the main briefing hall. He was not looking forward having to explain all this to the president.

E.D.F Chronicles – The Cyberian menace

When he arrived, the doors opened out into a large circular conference room, a giant oval table dominated the centre. Sat there were four other Admirals, and a series of vid-links to other Admirals and senior members of the military who could not be there in person. A vid-link was also open to the presidential office on Earth. Also sat at the table was the imposing form of General Joe Blake, commander in chief of the troop division and the most senior General currently serving.

Several of the vid-link screens suddenly blazed into life as those other commanders from across E.O.C.A territory joined in the meeting.

Last to appear was the president himself, Franz Baumholt. "It is three A.M here on Earth, there had better be a damned good reason for waking me so early in the morning."

Tetchy, Montrose thought. "I am sorry you had to be awakened so early Mr. President. A serious situation has occurred. Eidolon, a strategically important world close to the border of Krenaran space has been attacked. E.D.F assets stationed in the area have been completely destroyed and all contact with the planet was lost just over an hour ago."

"Sweet Jesus! loss of life?" Baumholt replied, his bleary eyes widening and suddenly alert at the news.

"Hard to tell this early Mr President; preliminary reports are still filtering in, with the destruction of military assets in the area, best guess puts it at around two to three thousand dead. With the fall of the colony itself, it could run into hundreds of thousands."

Baumholt rested back into his plush suede chair, tilted his head up as if to look at the sky, closed his eyes and let out a deep mournful sigh before slowly opening them again and fixing Montrose with an icy stare. "So what are we dealing with? another Krenaran incursion?"

The E.D.F's chief of intelligence and commander of Foxtrot base, Calvin O'donelly, spoke up. "I don't believe so sir; just before we lost contact we started to receive telemetry from one of our spy satellites above that world, it depicted a massive fleet of ships of a previously unknown configuration, far larger than anything the Krenarans have thrown against us, and attacking en-masse. Our forces stationed in the area were completely overwhelmed."

"So, if not the Krenarans, then who?"

"Mr. President. We have here a Solarian ambassador, just arrived who might be able to provide us with some answers." Montrose motioned for Kerulithar to take his place at the table, until now he had been waiting patiently in the darkened periphery of the room.

"Greetings and warm wishes from the Solarian empire on this saddest of days, Mr President." Kerulithar began. "The same enemy that attacked your world, has also attacked one of ours in much the same fashion. A world we now know as Orialis; the world of tears. For that world too was utterly destroyed, fifteen of our own battlecruisers were lost in the engagement."

"You have my deepest condolences for your loss," Baumholt interrupted. "How does this help us?"

"Thank you for your kind words," Kerulither replied with sincerity. "We believe that the same race that attacked our people, attacked your world, and also brought about the collapse of the Krenaran empire as we know it."

There was a stunned silence in the room as the seriousness of this information began to sink in. Montrose could scarcely believe it, the Krenaran empire – collapsed. Who was capable of such a thing?

"One of our ships managed to capture a specimen of their people, it was damaged, but still functioning. After several weeks of trying we finally managed to access its core programming, and in so doing learned a great deal about their race, and that is why I am here."

"Its?" Baumholt replied, his brow furrowing slightly as he tried hard to concentrate on what the ambassador was telling him, as an aide handed him a mug of strong coffee. He silently nodded a thank you to someone off camera.

"Yes, from what we have learned they are known as the Cyberians. A completely automated mechanoid race, there are no living organisms."

"Astonishing; a completely self operating robotic empire," one of the Admiralty said.

"Exactly, the Cyberians are thousands of years old, built as a race of soldiers, a military force to wage war in an ancient conflict between two worlds, completely autonomous and capable of building more of themselves to replace losses sustained in battle. Eventually, en-masse they utterly destroyed the Xarathian empire tens of thousands of years ago in another galaxy."

The president interrupted him again, "in 'another' galaxy, you mean they don't come from our own?"

"No," Kerulithar nodded. "When they finally overwhelmed and destroyed the Xarathian people, something also affected the Cyberians; their core data was corrupted. Possibly by the Xarathians themselves we do not know. What it did do however, was to irreversibly alter their programming, they were originally programmed to perform a single task, to eradicate the Xarathian race wherever they are found. This changed however, to eradicate all life wherever it is to be found. The Cyberians followed this literally, and in so doing they destroyed the race that created them, known only to them as 'the builders.' The Cyberians then went on carrying out their programming over the next ten thousand years. Slowly, systematically eradicating all life in their own galaxy, though their task was not complete, not while there is life left in the universe.

So they have travelled in their massive armada to our galaxy in order to fulfill the same basic programming."

Baumholt looked despondent, "this is a race that if your story is correct, utterly overwhelms and destroys everything in its path. How can we hope to defeat such an enemy?"

Kerulithar gave an understanding nod, his own people had asked that same question. "In our research, we found a single weakness; in the way that they communicate. All Cyberians communicate via an integrated network, known to them as 'the dataverse', rendering speech obsolete, and which also helps to keep their plans from falling into enemy hands. However, this 'dataverse' acts as one giant network, with the ships themselves passing on orders to other ships, drones, and even Cyberian warriors themselves much the same way data is transmitted between a network of computers. However just as in all networks, their has to be a single computer that acts as 'the brain' of the network, the server. We have reason to believe that this is a command ship of some description. Still lurking out there, which we have yet to discover, due to the strategic importance of this vessel it will likely be even heavier armed and armoured than typical Cyberian ships."

Baumholt stroked his chin for a second, mulling over the information Kerulithar had just given him. "So what you are saying is that 'somewhere' in the galaxy is a ship that is directing all the other ships attacks."

"Yes," replied Kerulithar. "That is why we need as many races as possible working together, not just to provide a more robust defence to this new enemy. But also the more ships we have out there looking for this ship, the higher our chances of finding it."

Baumholt stared at the softly spoken Solarian ambassador, as if trying to comprehend the enormity of the task that lay ahead of them. "So, right now all we have is a working theory, without any tangible evidence that there is a ship out there calling the shots, and that we need to search the entire galaxy, find it and destroy it." He shook his head incredulously, "that is a hell of a thing to base an alliance between four major powers upon."

"Do we even know if the Dracos will get on board with this?" Montrose asked.

"Although their methods are extreme, at their heart they are survivalists. Eventually the Cyberians will come for them too, and they, like us, cannot prevail alone. An alliance is in their best interests too," the Solarian pointed out.

"It would take virtually every ship we have to find this proverbial needle in a haystack, and with Cyberian advances tying up resources in other areas, we would be hard pushed to do both." Another of the Admiralty said.

"Which makes it all the more necessary to forge alliances," Kerulithar argued.

"We've already received an asylum request from Dalvosh, so I think it is fair to say we have what remains of the Krenaran fleet at our disposal. Although from what I have gathered so far, the Krenaran empire has totally collapsed, there are still fractured elements of the fleet out there. We could ask Dalvosh to try and unify these pockets into a cohesive force again, it would give us that bit more to throw against this thing." Montrose suggested.

"Great idea Admiral," Baumholt replied. "If the Krenarans want our protection, they are going to have to do something for it first. As of now, I am officially declaring an alert level one situation and passing all emergency powers to the military."

"Yes Mr. President, have all battlegroups report in and form up." Montrose replied, "as of right now we are officially at war with the Cyberian race."

"One last thing," Kerulithar interrupted.

It's a bit late now, Montrose thought.

"It appears that Cyberian cruisers are highly resistant to all but the most devastating of energy weapons, though they seem more vulnerable to direct fire. Torpedoes and fusion cannons should be our weapons of choice."

"Direct fire weapons?" Montrose put his head in his hands, "like railcannons – Goddamnit, we completed the changeover from railcannons to high power laser batteries nine years ago."

"We might still have some railcannon equipped ships in the surplus yards," another of the Admiralty suggested.

"Good; have them crewed and battle ready as fast as humanly possible. They will be our little ace in the hole." Montrose smiled, and if all else fails at least they can be used as fire ships.

"If that is all, then I declare this emergency session over." Baumholt replied, a gentle yawn escaping his lips. The light beginning to filter through to where he was sitting indicated to all that the sun was coming up on Earth. "Win this war for me gentlemen."

The screen went blank.

"Oh we intend to Mr. President," Montrose whispered. A promise to himself more than anything, "okay people we all have a great deal of work to do, prepare the battlegroups, ready the troop division, and bring those retired ships up to full battle-readiness."

"As we speak the Solarian warhost is being gathered, we stand by your side." Kerulithar added.

"Thank you," Montrose nodded. "The fate of the galaxy rests on our success."

E.D.F Chronicles – The Cyberian menace

7. The drawing of the lines.

Over the course of the next few days, the E.D.F navy began to form itself into its constituent battlegroups. Hundreds of ships from dozens of installations massing ready for the signal to commence operations, not since the beginning of the Krenaran war a decade ago had such a gigantic mobilisation taken place.

Human and Solarian ambassadors were dispatched into the veil to alert the Dracos to the impending threat, and to enlist their help in defeating it.

Once again sleek Solarian battlecruisers and their constituent escorts stood side-by-side with slower, bulkier more rustic E.D.F. ships.

Aboard Delta Gamma base negotiations were still ongoing with the Krenaran asylum application, ambassador Jacques Chaveaux was presiding over a sullen Dalvosh within the cramped briefing room of this backwater way-station operated by the navy. Captain Kinraid of the Valley-forge was also seated opposite, next to the ambassador. The visage of his immense ship dominated a row of floor-to-ceiling windows behind. Another Captain, Marcus Drake, commander of the facility was also present. Together it was they who had the un-enviable task of informing Dalvosh of the changes imposed by E.D.F command.

Chaveaux began, "we know from the blast patterns found on your ships that you were escaping something, something so powerful that the Krenaran empire, one of the most powerful of all the major powers in the known galaxy, could not defend themselves from it. Could you elaborate?"

"I have told you this four times already!" Dalvosh raged, his green reptilian features turning a slight shade of puce as his anger became more apparent. "They were mechanical, their ships did not register a single lifeform, and the smaller ships, the drones. They were automated too, controlled by the larger ships. World-by-world, system-by-system they swept through our territory, all attempts at stopping them or even trying to slow them down; failed."

Chaveaux whispered to Drake, "that ties in exactly with the attack on Eidolon."

Drake nodded, "if they attacked from the galactic north, through the centre of the galaxy, then the Krenaran empire would have found themselves caught between these new invaders, and the borders of our own territory."

"And if they were forced over the border we would have had no option but to treat it as another attack, and as is the E.D.F mandate, we would have no choice but to engage them in order to protect our own colonies."

"Talk about being caught between a rock and a hard place," Drake sighed. He was beginning to see the desperation of the Krenaran position.

Chaveaux turned toward the Krenaran leader once again, "it seems that your asylum application has proved fortuitous for mankind also Dalvosh."

The giant Krenaran raised a scaled green mass of bone that was the Krenaran equivalent of an eyebrow.

"We will grant your asylum request on the conditions that your ships and crew will work alongside our own and our Solarian allies in the defence of E.O.C.A and Solarian citizens against the Cyberian threat."

Dalvosh snorted, "fight alongside Solarians; why should we fight next to those cowards, hiding in their ships while we fight and die in blood soaked battlefields across the galaxy!"

Kinraid then interjected, "because if ye' don't, we'll feed ye' all t' the bigger enemy."

Dalvosh gulped hard, he had no desire to join the fate so many of his kind had already faced. With a dejected sigh he muttered under his breath, "it seems that I have no option but to accept."

Kinraid smiled and nodded, "no ye' don't."

Chaveaux sat back, betraying just a hint of smugness, smugness that a decade ago these Krenarans had almost brought humanity to its knees, and now in just ten short years it was they who now needed mankind's help - oh the irony.

"One more thing, and this too is conditional. The remains of your fleet are fractured, broken up into smaller forces as they fled to outlying empires in order to escape the Cyberian invasion of your worlds." The ambassador said.

"Yeah, what about them?" Dalvosh interrupted.

"We want you to re-form them, you are to take the Kralath-kar, travel to these systems, re-unify the Krenaran fleet, and then merge with our own and our Solarian allies. You have one month to complete this mission, we will try to hold out until then."

"One month, that's not much time." Dalvosh argued, his deep red eyes narrowing.

"That's all the time we can offer, if we wait much longer we risk being overrun ourselves."

With a hint of sadness Dalvosh lowered his head, "I understand."

"You had better leave immediately," Drake said.

Without another word, the burly Krenaran leader stomped out of the room with his two aides to rejoin the crew of the Kralath-kar.

"Tink they'll keep their end o' the bargain?" Kinraid asked Chaveaux.

"I think so, their survival depends upon it after all."

E.D.F Chronicles – The Cyberian menace

Volgograd, Russia.
Earth.

Nikolai Vargev turned toward his slightly aged T.V. "Viewer on."

The viewer blazed into life, coating the chilly spartan lounge in a dull glow, shadows clung to the bare rock walls, above the viewer the stuffed head of a Stag leered back at him, its antlers displayed proudly.

The outer colony news service was just about to start. Nikolai had retired from active service with the E.D.F commandoes just over six months ago at the ripe old age of fifty four. Although he still liked to keep an eye on what was happening 'out there'. These days the outer colony news was his only lifeline to the galaxy at large.

"This is the outer colony news service, the top stories today. After the destruction of Eidolon, widespread panic has spread throughout the border worlds, sporadic rioting has broken out, there have been violent protests and clashes with local law enforcement have resulted in arrests and dozens of injuries."

The image abruptly changed to a bedraggled man, bleeding from a small gash to the forehead and waving a placard, "we just want to get off this fu<beep> world god-damnit! What if what happened at Eidolon happens here at Agemman, we're next in the <beep>ing firing line! We've only just re-built from the last time this happen….."

The man was forcibly shoved to the ground as the Agemman planetary police advanced upon the baying, shouting mob."

The image returned to the blonde haired Raumov, "similar scenes have erupted at the Aurelias colony, at Gamma IV and Sigma XI, E.D.F facilities on those key worlds are being besieged as civilians seek protection from the advancing Cyberian armada. E.D.F forces are already on high alert following the loss of the colony world, and we are still unable to bring you updated pictures of Eidolon as news crews are unable to approach anywhere near the planet. The navy has already begun to form into battlegroups ready for an all-out offensive against this new enemy, Solarian allies have also pledged their support to the campaign."

Vargev relaxed back into his worn green leather chair, sighing mournfully and stroking his trimmed grey flecked moustache. He reached down and picked up a hip flask from a side table next to his chair, lifted it to his lips and took a deep swig of vodka. *So it is beginning again, the galaxy is going to shit all over again. Well, this time they'll have to pull their asses out of the fire without me.*

Ian J Smethurst

He rose from his chair to polish his statuette of the greek god Atlas holding up a small bronze world, a gift every commando received upon retirement. Together with a golden 'R' to affix above his colonel's rank slides for officers mess meetings. He had attended a couple since his retirement, though it just reminded him of his past. His time was over now, although he was struggling with the transition to civilian life, it was just like the old saying, 'you can take the soldier out of the army, but you can't take the army out of the soldier'. The days of him charging through a muddy, blood soaked, bullet ridden battlefield were long gone; proud memories, nothing more.

Solarian shuttle
On route to 'the veil'.

Kerulithar was a week into the long journey toward 'the veil', an area of intense magnetic distortion that rendered sensors virtually useless, he would be flying by visual aids only. This was the most unnerving part of his mission, simply because he had no idea what would happen. So far, whoever entered this area of space, never came out again. This was the Dracos's domain, a race that harboured a total hatred of his own people and the E.D.F in equal measure. They are one of the most feared and universally shunned of all races in the known galaxy, mainly for their propensity of torturing live captives for their own perverted 'amusement'.

However, Kerulithar knew that what was happening throughout the galaxy would soon affect them too, they were simply not strong enough to oppose it. They could no longer hide in the subterranean tunnels of Corvandris either. The Cyberians are unceasing, relentless, and would simply massacre them in their own caves, with no way out.

He dropped the shuttle out of plasma drive just before the swirling morass of blues, purples and sickly greens that was the veil. Slowly, almost hesitantly he manoeuvred the tiny Solarian shuttle into the depths of this vast cloud. His sensors began to lose their accuracy, then went totally blank. From here on in he had to navigate by vision alone.

Hoping the Dracos would see sense and not execute him over a three hundred year old transgression by his people, one they were not proud of. He was prepared to die if need be, as long as it brought the Dracos out of hiding and into the inevitable war that was now right on their doorstep.

For several hours he kept the shuttle on a perfectly straight trajectory, not deviating for one second. He would systematically scour this miasma of gas and dust looking for Corvandris, even if it took him weeks, even if it ultimately cost him his life.

E.D.F Chronicles – The Cyberian menace

The dark shape of a lone Dracos warcruiser slowly emerged through the clouds directly above him, seemingly unaware of the passage of the tiny craft. Its jet black shape completely dwarfing his own craft as it passed by overhead. Kerulithar, not realising he was holding his breath, exhaled loudly. He surmised that the craft must be heading for Corvandris itself, deciding to shadow it, he kept the shuttle about ten kilometres from its rear engines. Close enough to still make out its shape but far enough away for the shuttle to be rendered invisible to the larger crafts proximity sensors by the effects of the veil.

Gradually from out of the swirling morass of dust clouds of darkest violet, greens and blues there emerged a small planetoid, as if a tiny bead of jet was dropped into a swirling sea of ink, Kerulithar smiled. Corvandris, the world of perpetual night; he had found it.

Around this small, barren, rocky world he could see three orbital stations just coming into focus through the last vestiges of dust clearing. *So this is where the Dracos cling to existence, on this dark, cold, lonely planetoid bereft of life or atmosphere.*

Instead the Dracos dwelled within deep subterranean caverns, bored through this tiny world's largely solidified mantle, warmed largely by what little heat still remained in this dead planet's core.

He doubted if any of the Dracos still living had ever seen a sunrise, or gasped at the beauty of a bright cloudless sky, alas, he almost mourned for them, although as he closed and Kerulithar got his first real glimpse of Dracos orbital stations, the black charred landscape of the planet below, the remains of a violent volcanic past when this planet was young. The whole vista took on a dark foreboding sense, a sense of dread, and for the first time the Solarian ambassador felt his blood run cold in his veins.

He was almost thrown from his seat as a blast rocked the shuttle violently; snapping him out of his dark thoughts, they had found him. To his port side another warcruiser was coming around for another pass, intense violet beams filled his cockpit screen, almost blinding him and clashing hard with the flaring electric blue of his shields. He desperately tried to manoeuvre the tiny craft against the onslaught of weapons fire. Two more blasts from starboard rocked his shuttle hard, the Solarian was launched from his seat landing painfully, the blaring of alarms swirling around his throbbing head, warning of damaged systems and shield overload.

He threw himself back into his seat as the shuttle careered wildly, straight into the path of another warcruiser, jabbing hard on the starboard thruster control barely avoiding a collision. Then he cut all power to the engines, as he was quickly encircled by three Dracos warcruisers, several others, now alerted by the weapons fire were also approaching.

A badly garbled transmission came in, "Solarian! You will surrender immediately…..you have strayed upon our world and now you can never leave it….you are a prisoner of the Dracos, any attempt to leave will result in your destruction. I hope you enjoy pain as much as we do!"

The transmission ended, and Kerulithar's blood ran cold for the second time that day.

One of the orbital stations locked onto his craft with a tractor beam and gently pulled him toward the stations small, disused fighter bay. He guessed the Dracos no longer had a use for fighters anymore.

The craft was set down by a second beam that took over the duties of the first, then with a groan of aged metal the doors gradually closed over the bay sealing it behind him, and plunging both him and his craft into utter darkness.

A troop of Kallan warriors hurried across the small, dark bay, and surrounded the vessel. The lighting was then raised, though only to a pitifully dull twilight like glow.

Kerulithar keyed in a control and the side exit ramp slowly opened from just behind the front winglets jutting out from the fuselage of his craft, the gangway slowly lowered to the ground, and Kerulithar emerged from the craft straight into the muzzles of several Dracos eviscerators pointed straight at his face.

The leader of the troop addressed him, "a Solarian, and an ambassador no less, you have some guts coming here, but we have some special techniques lined up for you. The all-mother will be pleased," the Kallan leader sneered as one of his sub-ordinates bound his wrists.

"I need to speak with your leader, it is a matter of utmost urgency, the fate of the galaxy is at stake!" Kerulithar pleaded.

Without saying a word, the Kallan smashed the butt of his weapon hard into Kerulithar's face, sending him sprawling to the ground in a heap, a whimper of pain escaping from his lips, much to the delight of the other Kallan watching. A small trickle of purple blood began to run from the ambassador's fractured nose.

"You will speak when you are spoken to Solarian! Not before."

They half-escorted, half-dragged him to a row of dark, dank cells, reeking of blood, urine, and other filth that made his stomach churn. A heavy metal door was opened and he was kicked hard inside, before the door was slammed shut and locked.

Kerulithar began to wonder if all this was a good idea, his hands were still bound, his nose sore and bloody. Crouching low into a corner of this dark filthy cell, weakened, in pain and alone, the only sounds to accompany him was the drip drip of the damp walls as the condensation mixed with stale urine creating this awful stench. His thoughts turned toward his family, his wife and child, wondering if he would ever get the chance to see them again, he missed them dearly.

After three full days of agonizing electric shock treatment, being fed just enough to keep him alive, and several nicks and cuts from the Kallan's lethally sharp knives. A lone warrior stood outside of his cell door, the malicious, uncaring red eye slits of his battlehelm looked down through a grate upon his frail battered form with unashamed amusement. "The all-mother will see you now – it is time."

Pain ravaged his body with every movement, yet finally he had got what he wanted, a weak smile played across his cracked parched lips, "th….thank you."

"Don't thank me," the guard shook his head. "It has been three hundred years since one of our ancestor-kin sought us out, you have become 'interesting' to the all-mother, and she has sent for you."

And my pain ridden screams of the past few days, the writhing in agony as more 'treatments' were inflicted, the fact I provided everyone with a 'good show' had nothing to do with it? Kerulithar doubted it, he was being kept alive for a reason, he just didn't know what yet, perhaps it was merely morbid curiosity.

The heavy door was unlocked and opened with the screeching sound of rusted metal. Slowly, painfully he staggered to his feet, and was escorted down the dingy, dimly lit corridors by two guards.

Eventually they made it to a small shuttle bay, not stopping for rest or to catch his breath, he was to have no comfort. Catching a brief glimpse of his shuttle waiting in the bay just where he left it, it had not been tampered with, and for a brief instant he thought of making a break for it, to get far away from this accursed place, although he just as quickly dismissed it. He would be cut down before he even got half way to the shuttle. Even if he did somehow miraculously make it out of here, he had no idea where he was going, the Dracos knew this area of space far better than he did, they could pick him off at their leisure.

With a dejected sigh, he felt a shove in the small of his back as he was dragged into the black assault lander ahead of him, it quickly powered up, levitated on its gravitic engines and turned to face the hangar bay exit before speeding out into the vast swirling maelstrom beyond.

E.D.F.S Valley-forge
Captain Quinn Kinraid commanding.

"We're not battle ready," Lisa Anizeres argued. "We're still on our maiden voyage, we've never been in a battle situation before, we don't know how the crew will react."

"Don't matter," Kinraid replied. "I've gone over 'te orders with 'te Admiralty meself, our orders stand, we 'r to act as flagship for battlegroup Midway. Made up o' ourselves, the Krenaran carriers, the Danitza class battleship Demeter, four Washington class heavy cruisers, the Montgomery class carrier Victorious, an' an escort force of eight Ghandhi class destroyers. We 'ave orders to travel 't Sigma XI to pick up th' rest 'o the battlegroup." Kinraid stared out at the starlit backdrop of deep space through the panoramic windows of the forward observation lounge, while Anizeres paced like a wildcat.

"I know ye' 'ave misgivins' about this Lisa, hell so do I, we are bran' new, with a crew greener than th' lawn in me back garden in Dublin. I agree it is too early to be throwin' us into a combat environment just yet. But I also 'ave faith in this ship, an 'er crew, an' that means you too Lisa, we'll do 'er proud, so we will." He stroked Lisa's shoulder, before turning back to the thick U.V shielded plexiglass, that served as the windows throughout the ship.

"I understand, sir." Anizeres nodded, "thank you."

Kinraid nodded as they both left the lounge together, and strode out onto the haze of activity that was the Valley-forge's vast command centre.

"Krenaran ships report they are ready to get underway," Lieutenant Jarvis announced as he gave up the comms. position to Anizeres in traditional fashion.

"Understood," Kinraid said as he took the centre seat; immediately pressing a control on the left arm of his chair and opening up a shipwide communications channel.

"All 'ands, this is th' Captain. Soon we are t' take our ship into war, an' although she is a bran' new ship, with nay history t' tell, our actions from this point on make up that history. For although we r' inexperienced, we have th' most powerful ship in all o' the E.D.F at our disposal, and I know we will do 'er proud. For like th' dogs o' war o' old, we the crew o' the Valley-forge, will fight t' the bitter end, t' the last drop o' blood is spilt t' defend our people, an' our worlds. Although we're pitted against a powerful enemy, when they see th' Valley-forge it is they who will know fear! To war!"

An immense cheer went up throughout the ship, from flight deck operators at the fore of the ship, through to systems technicians, medical staff and engineering personnel at the rear. Kinraid had instilled in all of them a fire, a sense of purpose, this was really happening, they were going to war.

"Commander, contact engineering, tell 'em to bring main ion drives up to full power, begin with a one quarter burst until we r' clear o' the station, then increase power to full and activate plasma drive."

E.D.F Chronicles – The Cyberian menace

"Understood Captain," Anizeres smiled. Although she did have her misgivings, she was glad that all the pomp and circumstance was over, they could now get on and just do their jobs, and that job was to win wars. She routed Kinraid's orders down to engineering via her console.

The six gigantic main ion drives lit up an intense electric blue, each the size of a Ghandhi class destroyer. It needed such large sub-light engines in order to get this colossal ship moving, the Valley-forge was almost a mobile base in its own right. The elongated rectangular hull of the ship, with its inset mid-section lined with banks of long barrelled high power laser cannons, before tapering out to the semi-circular fore section began to gingerly, almost lazily move away from the station which it was more than half the size of. Together with its plethora of destroyer, cruiser, and heavy cruiser escorts as well as the four Krenaran carriers and dozen escorting stealth ships, this newly formed battlegroup edged its way from the station. The fleet of twenty one vessels all increased speed together, and in an immense blizzard of bright light, activated their plasma drives and was gone in a blinding flash that lit up the entire facility.

"Commander, I want those fighter crews t' remain on constant alert, we could be dropping out o' plasma drive into a warzone, and might need t' deploy them in a hurry." Kinraid said as he watched the streaks of starlight pass by behind the translucent swirling tunnel of shifting colours they were travelling through, the plasma wake.

"Understood sir," Anizeres replied working at her console as she sent the order down to the flight operations deck where the wing of twenty four Peregrine fighters were housed.

Anizeres then turned in her royal blue suede seat to face Kinraid. "Sir, do you think we can really trust the Krenarans? I mean with the whole Krenaran war, they hate us just as much as we hate them."

"Personally Commander, I don't, I've seen first hand what they r' capable of, I saw th' devastation at Charlie base, an' when th' war first started I served aboard the Exeter, we witnessed the destruction o' Malthus colony. Bodies piled in th' streets, people left t' rot. I will never forget what they did to us. But this is different, ye' see th' Krenarans know that they cannot possibly win alone, they need our help t' stay alive. We're th' only people keeping them from annihilation right now, so they need us as much as we need them, th' enemy of my enemy…."

"Is my friend," Anizeres finished for him.

Kinraid nodded with a smile.

Over the next few hours, Captain Quinn Kinraid retreated into his private quarters, leaving Anizeres in command while he caught up with battle readiness reports and grabbed what little shut-eye he could. He awoke in the midst of one of his power naps to the opening melody of the outer colony news.

"I am Annika Raumov and this is the outer colony news service, the top stories today. Unrest continues to mount across the border worlds, intelligence staff at Sigma XI are being evacuated to worlds deeper within E.O.C.A territory. The garrison at Echo base on Gamma IV, another world close to the Krenaran border has been strengthened with the arrival of a second naval battlegroup. The E.D.F are keen not to repeat the mistakes made during the Krenaran war.

We now go live to the presidential office of the Earth and Outer Colonies Alliance, Franz Baumholt as he prepares to address the people."

The image of the newsroom switched to the plush surroundings of the E.O.C.A presidents office, with its polished ornately carved wooden panelled walls and large desk depicting the E.O.C.A seal. Seated at his desk was the grey haired, slightly lined visage of Baumholt himself.

"Friends and fellow citizens of Earth and the outer colonies, we stand once again upon the dark precipice of war. The greatest enemy we have ever known seeks to crush us, overwhelm us, and eradicate every last man, woman and child from the face of the galaxy. We are fighting for our very right to exist, we are facing a powerful enemy and it will be a stern test. There is one factor the enemy have not considered in their all-consuming advance. The human spirit, our will to survive, and because of this we can defeat them. Already our Solarian allies are massing with our own forces and those of the former Krenaran empire, once our sworn enemy now standing by our side to defeat this greater foe. All the peoples of the galaxy stand united in the greatest mobilisation ever attempted, and we will prevail." His piercing blue eyes fixed on the camera as he gave a gentle nod. "I thank you all."

From worlds across E.O.C.A, to ships of the navy travelling through the darkest depths of deep space, everyone gave out a single great cheer. They all sensed the same ripple of energy, that they were living through something momentous, this was mankind's defining moment, it had come down to it at last, it was do or die time.

The remainder of that twenty four hour period passed somewhat uneventfully, although now at full battle readiness, the entire crew was on edge. Kinraid understood, what they were witnessing was on a scale none of them could comprehend, he doubted that many of them would make it through this war. And yet still, they carried out their duties with the professionalism and dedication expected of them, he could ask no more. This green crew would be forged and hardened in the flames of war, he had a good idea of what was coming because he had lived through similar times before in the war against the Krenarans. Quinn felt a tinge of sadness that his crew had to as well.

The buzz of his wrist-comm. snapped him out of his reverie, and he thumbed the acknowledge button, "Kinraid here."

The voice of Anizeres came over the tiny speaker, "Captain, we are approaching Sigma XI."

"Very good Commander, I'm on my way, signal th' fleet to drop out of plasma drive on my signal."

"Yes Captain."

Kinraid hurried to a basin and quickly splashed his face with cool water, watching the droplets run down his wizened and slightly careworn face onto the ginger whiskers of his beard, "so this is it," he whispered into the mirror before drying his face with a nearby towel and heading out of his quarters.

Once entering the bridge, Kinraid re-took his seat from Anizeres who vacated it readily. *Being a commander was one thing, being a Captain of a ship this size was quite another I guess she's just not ready for that yet.* He could hardly blame her after all.

"Signal the fleet, order them to drop out of plasma drive on my mark.......MARK!"

Instantly the twenty one ship flotilla dropped out of plasma drive in a blinding burst of bright light, the Valley-forge emerged through the plasma wake re-joining normal space-time once again.

In the distance, the emerald green verdant world of Sigma XI could be seen, classified as a garden world, with gigantic rainforests stretching thousands of miles across its major continents, home to uncounted billions of native species, it was also the site of a major E.O.C.A colony, as well as Foxtrot base.

When the Krenarans invaded the world, much damage was done to the nearby rainforests in the fighting. Fires spread, turning the sky into a choking smog where before the colonists of this world praised the purity of the air they breathed, often remarking they had the purest cleanest air to breathe in all of E.O.C.A.

Due to many conservation efforts on the world, the rainforests are slowly beginning to return to normal, although the damage inflicted will take centuries to repair fully. The pall of smoke that hung about this world in the days following the end of that war was now, thankfully, just a memory.

The Valley-forge and its escorting Krenaran carriers all made their way further into the system, nearing the remainder of the battlegroup in orbit.

"Captain, I'm picking up something." Anizeres pointed out with a noticeable hint of alarm. "Another fleet has just appeared on sensors, the configuration of the ships exactly matches the ones seen at Eidolon."

Kinraid stroked his beard thoughtfully, "so they 'ave come at last, how many ships?"

"I am reading over two hundred, all in one massive formation, it stretches out right across the system."

Kinraid's heart sank, he could not abandon this world. It was far too important to the E.D.F and E.O.C.A as a whole. The problem was he was vastly outnumbered and outgunned. It would seem the legacy of the Valley-forge would be a short lived one.

"Contact command, tell 'em we have sighted th' Cyberian fleet and are proceeding to engage."

Anizeres gulped, "understood." She knew as well as anyone they would need a miracle to hold out against such numbers.

"All hands, BATTLESTATIONS! Ready all weapons, initiate graviton shielding system, prepare to launch all fighters."

The defining moment had arrived, the battle-lines were drawn, the touch paper lay before them, all they had to do to light it was fire that first shot and all-out war would be upon them all.

E.D.F Chronicles – The Cyberian menace
7. The All-mother.

The assault lander touched down into a widened entrance of one of the many tunnel systems on Corvandris, dug out by the first Dracos to settle on this dark isolated little world over three centuries ago in their desperation to flee the Solarians they attempted to overthrow.

Now, a Solarian was descending into *their* midst, a feat none other of his race had even come close to achieving. From a viewing window Kerulithar witnessed several large pipelines, spewing out gases into the almost non-existent atmosphere, surmising that it must be from various manufacturing processes going on deep within the tunnels themselves.

"Put this on," one of the masked guards said as he handed him a breathing mask. Without a word Kerulithar dutifully took it and slid it over his face, accidentally rubbing it against his nose and wincing as the broken bones underneath grinded against one another.

The hatch opened, and instantly the biting cold hit him as hard as any fist, making him shiver to his very core. He forced himself to walk the few steps up the tunnel bay, trying, and failing to keep up with his Dracos 'guards'.

"What's wrong?" One of the Kallan sneered underneath his battlehelm, red eyes fixed upon him, "your pampered Solarian body can't tolerate a little cold?"

The hate in his voice all too apparent, Kerulithar pursed his cracked and bloodied lips into a grimace of resolute defiance, and walked the rest of the way to the main entrance bulkhead unhindered. It was just one of many that allowed access to the caverns below.

The guards giggled and laughed as the struggling Solarian did his best to soldier on. Next to the bulkhead was an I.D. card reader which one of the guards swiped a pass-key through. A panel slid open to reveal a glowing hand-print scanner. The Dracos gingerly placed his hand into the device, and after a few seconds the giant bulkhead doors, several times their size gradually began to open releasing a blast of pressurised oxygen at them that threatened to blow the Solarian ambassador off his feet.

Another snigger, and the guards shoved him inside before the giant doors closed once again with a resounding 'thunk', blocking off any hope of escape.

After a wait of a few moments while the oxygen recirculated into the room, the guards took off their masks, the red eye-slits and matt-black armour of their helmets replaced by a sickly mottled grey pallor, and large dark, almond shaped unforgiving eyes.

There was only the barest minimum of light in the room, but it was enough for Kerulithar to discern their real faces. And instead of being afraid of these murderous barbarians, he pitied them. Because plain to see in the dimly lit passageway was what three hundred years of hatred and isolationism had done to the Dracos. They should look exactly like himself, a healthy blue-tinged colour, not this deathly pallor. Hate and fear had twisted the Dracos into something barely recognisable anymore.

They showed him to a second bulkhead, opening it much like the first, and from there they descended deep into the dark passageways of Corvandris.

It was warmer down here, much to the Solarian's relief, yet it stank, the occasional rat scurried about, its chittering echoing down the long tunnels, filth lined the edges running into slimy open gulleys that carried it off to who knows where.

Beggars dressed in little more than rags foraged on the excrement lined floors for the next crumb to eat or oddity to sell.

This was what the Dracos did not want others to see, the dark bleeding heart of their people, a weakened people, a dying people. Yet still far too stubborn to ask for help from the race that put them there, and the race that can help them out of their self imposed mess - his people, the Solarians.

"Recognise your handiwork!" One of the guards spat.

Kerulithar simply said nothing, too ashamed for words, his people were supposed to be better than this.

They continued onward through these fetid, filth strewn passages for what must have seemed like hours until they came to a wide circular clearing.

The room was dark, all except for a single shaft of light that came down from the ceiling and illuminated a seemingly frail old woman sat upright on a large throne like chair carved from solid rock, which in turn rose up from a circular dais of dark granite.

The all-mother.

Around the shadowy periphery of the room, forms silently shifted and moved as other high ranking Dracos allowed space for the entourage to pass through.

A second shaft of light seemed to engulf the Solarian ambassador, in this gloom it shone so brightly that it almost blinded him.

"Kneel Solarian!" One of the guards shouted. "Kneel before the all-mother!"

When Kerulithar hesitated the guards lashed out, kicking the back of his knees hard, so that he fell with a resonant 'thud'. Gasping in pain once again, the chains from his bound hands clattered noisily against the hard unforgiving floor.

Un-heeding of Kerulithar's poor state, the all-mother studied him for almost a minute in utter silence, fixing him with her dark, icy stare.

E.D.F Chronicles – The Cyberian menace

When she finally spoke, her voice was raspy, hoarse. "For three hundred years, no Solarian has had any contact with the Dracos, now you are here....why?"

"Because we need your help," Kerulithar replied weakly, but with sincerity.

The all-mother cackled, a throaty, gurgling noise, foul to all who heard it, if she were on earth she would have been labelled a witch. "The Solarians have not needed *our* help for three centuries, why now?"

"Because we have a common enemy, one that will wipe out every living thing in the galaxy if we don't find a way to stop it."

The all-mother harrumphed, "and this matters us, why?"

Kerulithar began to grow frustrated, "because if we do not stop it now, together, in the coming days it will come for you too, and when that happens it will already be too late."

"And we shall simply take refuge in the veil as we have always done," she sneered, cocking her head slightly at him.

"It won't work," Kerulithar interjected, pleading. "The enemy are too numerous, sooner or later they will flood this area with ships, some will certainly chance upon Corvandris, even without sensors. Right now us and the Terrans are all that stand between you and them, if we fall the veil will be swamped with Cyberian ships. They will find Corvandris and they will utterly destroy it. Those that do survive, and there won't be many trapped as you are down here, will be scattered, fleeing like cornered rats, they will be easy pickings for the Cyberian armada."

"And these....Cyberians?" the all-mother cut in, "they are this new grand enemy, who are they?"

"A completely autonomous, self-replicating machine race, hell bent on destroying all life in the galaxy. They go from world-to-world, completely annihilating every living thing found upon it, then move onto the next. They have been doing this for thousands of years, and have gotten very good at it." *Even though the little turns of phrase I picked up while spending time with the humans can be irritating, they can also be a boon when trying to get a point across, those little humans do have a flair for the dramatic,* he smiled inwardly.

The all-mother sat back on her hard throne, suddenly much more contemplative, three hundred years of mistrust and hatred was a long time. What if this wretched Solarian was telling the truth, what if there was a new enemy out there? Could she take the risk of her people falling prey to it? "What possible bonus could they get from destroying these worlds?"

"Nothing, they are simply following a programme, a programme we are unable to change. They were designed to do this, they do not need to sleep, or eat, they do not stop for any reason. When a Cyberian is destroyed as far as we are aware, another one is built to replace it, with the same basic programme already installed, repeating the process over and over in an endless circle of destruction."

"To what end?" The all-mother asked.

"The destruction of all life – everywhere."

That answer hit her like a stone.

A voice arose from the darkness, "why should we believe this Solarian, they were the ones who almost drove us to extinction themselves!"

"Silence!" The all-mother cried, although she was very old even for a Dracos, and still old by Solarian standards, her voice thundered around the room utterly convincingly, her power instantly silencing the dissenters.

Another voice gingerly spoke up and the all-mother made to swat it aside, yet refrained.

"The creepers have brought tidings of unusual events happening outside the veil, small scale battles, outlying skirmishes, fleet movements as if amassing for a major war; both Solarian and human."

It was Kerulithars turn to be surprised, how could the Dracos know so much about the events unfolding all-around them when they are so isolationist? And just who were 'the creepers'? He made a mental note to try and find out later.

"The most alarming news that has been widely reported is the collapse of the Krenaran empire, both Human and Solarian worlds have been attacked, which can only lead us to believe that there *is* a new threat out there that is behind this."

The all-mother rested her grey wrinkled and lined face in her hands, "if we do decide to join your alliance against these *Cyberians*, we will require certain guarantees." Her dark eyes narrowed in her shrivelled sunken eye sockets.

"I understand, and I shall forward your requests to my government."

Just when Kerulithar thought he might have garnered the support of the Dracos, the all-mothers aged, cracked lips broke into a wicked hate filled smile. "Our condition is that a new, clean, habitable world be set aside for our people to settle. To be left completely to ourselves as we are here."

Another voice made itself heard, this one however was familiar and carried more weight. "All-mother! How can you be considering listening to the lies sprouting from this *things* lips, he is our sworn enemy!" It was Calvaris Senergid, commander of the Dracos fleet.

"Be quiet, Senergid!" her voice boomed around the room like a thunderclap, even Kerulithar trembled. "This is about more than just who-trusts-who, this is about our future as a people."

"I do not see that it should be too much of a problem, as I said, I shall forward your request to my government." Kerulithar bowed his head low as a mark of respect.

"Release this man!" her voice boomed. "Escort him to his ship. Senergid, prepare the Dracos warfleet to leave the veil once adequate conditions are met."

Kerulithar was finally released from those heavy manacles that had been biting into his wrists all this time, he rubbed at them gingerly. "Thank you all-mother, your counsel has been most wise."

"Do not thank me yet, for if those conditions are not met, I plan to send a creeper infiltration squad, with a seeker drone to personally vaporise you where you stand."

There was a maliciousness about that last statement that made Kerulithar shudder, he knew she was not joking.

He had finally achieved what he had come for, and although both physically and mentally he had been beaten almost to breaking point, he emerged from that room triumphant. The Dracos were onside, albeit with a pretty large condition; still, he had secured a valuable ally.

The guards jostled and buffeted him again as they escorted him back through the filth lined, beggar strewn caverns. This time they did not need to push him onward, the Solarian's own pace was perfectly adequate, he just wanted to get the heck out of this wretched hell-hole. Occasionally however he felt the sting of a Dracos boot kicking him in his already bruised and tender legs.

Soon enough, they exited the giant bulkhead tunnel, donned their breathing masks, and headed back out into the biting cold where the lander was parked. One of the Kallan pressed a control and a side boarding hatch opened, the three of them clambered back inside the dark craft and in a roar of gravitic engines and ion turbines, shot forward into the smog filled atmosphere of Corvandris once more.

Kerulithar slumped down onto a hard bench, soon he will be with his people again, his mission had been a gruelling one, had tested him to his very limit, and he had genuinely feared for his life down there. Yet he was free at last.

Once the lander arrived back at the docking station and they disembarked, Kerulithar did not say another word, just made straight for his shuttle, climbed aboard, powered it up and left. He had had quite enough of this godforsaken place.

The tiny shuttle shot forth, quickly leaving Corvandris behind, the swirling clouds of the veil enveloping it once more as he left, hiding it away from prying eyes. He would likely have to return to inform them of the allies decision regarding their 'conditions'.

He did not look forward to the return visit.

Just as he was mulling all this over, from out of the thick swirling gaseous soup, the dark portside hull of a Dracos warcruiser loomed, its bladelike fins cutting through the gases and causing them to swirl and dance in odd patterns.

"Sweet Acara!" Kerulithar yelled as the immense ship loomed in front of him, blotting out his view. Panic raced through him, he was going to plough straight into it.

Mashing his finger into the downward pitch control so hard that it hurt, the shuttle dived sharply, almost throwing the ambassador aside. The tiny ship was threatening to go into a spin as he wrestled with all the strength his pulverised limbs could muster. By a matter of mere inches the craft barely managed to miss colliding with the giant cruiser.

His heart was still pounding in his chest as he levelled out the craft, flying beneath the giant vessel as it passed by overhead. *Just one of the dangers of navigating in the veil*, he surmised.

The shuttle managed to glide on a straight trajectory through the rest of the veil without further incident, several hours later and starlight began to emerge through the last fronds and trails of gas emanating from this giant strange nebulae.

His navigational instruments all came back to life, and the blackness of space was once more revealed to him again, filling his cockpit window just as it should be.

He immediately punched in the co-ordinates for home, keying the plasma drive controls, he could tend to his injuries on the way, right now he was desperately tired and just wanted to sleep. At last Kerulithar was going home.

8. Against the tide

Kinraid watched the silent advance of the Cyberian fleet on the bridge display of the Valley-forge. The Demeter had positioned itself port-side on to the enemy in order to bring its massive long range laser cannons into play. While the Valley-forge itself had her prow to the enemy armada, ready to unleash those twin high-bore fusion cannons for the first time. The Krenaran carriers had all deployed their H.O.T rockets and had launched their own fighters, acting as cover for the larger carriers.

It was a prudent strategy by the Krenarans, which was why Kinraid had already launched the Valley-forge's full complement of twenty four Peregrine fighters, now standing by just ahead of the giant battleship.

The Victorious had also launched its own fighter wing, but kept its bombers loaded with deadly cobra missiles in reserve, a little surprise for the Cyberians.

The Cyberian fleet continued to close, now entering extreme weapons range, although Kinraid knew full well that if he ordered the destroyers and cruisers to launch their torpedoes now they would be intercepted long before they ever hit their intended targets, and he could ill-afford to waste his shots. So he waited, as the Cyberian fleet filling his viewscreen continued on its silent, eerie advance.

"Today th' great question will be asked, which is better? Man or machine? Organics or synthetics, here at Sigma XI, with these two titanic fleets arrayed against each other this question will be asked. Will there be anyone left alive come the morrow t' answer it?" He whispered as he stoically watched the tide of bright steel ships advancing through the blackness of space, glinting from the light of the Sigma sun.

Seconds seemed to pass like hours as the immense invaders bore down on the vastly outnumbered and outgunned defenders lined up in the defence of this one world. The tiny drones began to separate from the undersides of a score of the giant Cyberian cruisers when Kinraid gave the order.

"FIRE!"

As one, six destroyers all launched their torpedoes in one devastating volley, a torrent of warheads racing towards these all-but invincible giants, their contrails blazing brightly as they hurtled toward their targets.

Still in the midst of being deployed the drones were unable to react, and only a couple managed to intercept the incoming barrage, ramming themselves into the warhead itself, two bright explosions briefly lit up the still advancing cruisers as the drones sacrificed themselves to defend it. The latticework of ubiquitous green energy beams that were the deadly matter convertors blazed out in all directions in a desperate attempt to shoot down the incoming salvo.

However, even a machine intelligence has limits to its reactions, and the warheads smashed home with devastating force, blasting huge deep holes into several of the cruiser's thick armour plating. In some places it had punched straight through.

The destroyers switched to their close range laser batteries while their torpedoes reloaded, behind them the gigantic Krenaran carriers launched their own immense spread of even bigger H.O.T rockets in a second wave, the destroyers themselves were lit up as the bright contrails of the huge missiles passed them, racing toward their foe.

By now, more and more drones were separating, beginning to act as a skirmish screen for the larger ships behind. The Krenaran fighters surged forward in a wall of tiny craft, ready to draw away the immense flock of drones so that the big guns of the larger ships could engage. Some of the drones broke the screen and went after the dummy run of the Krenaran fighters, others jinked and danced to intercept the bigger threat of the oncoming H.O.T rockets.

Three, four, five drones died in tumultuous explosions lighting up vividly the ships behind, yet a goodly number of the deadly rockets managed to make it past the drone screen. Again the lattice of matter convertors lit up in bright emerald green streaks, and several more warheads were caught, stripped to their constituent parts, and then reduced merely to atoms. Those that got through however enacted a bloody vengeance, their powerful explosives blasting apart huge chunks of plating, smashing through armour and causing catastrophic damage within. Three of the cruisers slowed, consumed by fire, damaged beyond all hope of repair they eventually blasted themselves apart in monolithic explosions that showered the nearby ships in debris, some merely bounced off the thick plating, others like jagged house-sized knives sunk deep into the sides of those that fought alongside.

A great cheer went up on the bridge of the Valley-forge as they watched the fiery demise of those ships, though Kinraid knew that was but the opening shot of what was to come.

The Demeter then opened up with her guns, her immense turrets firing out great pulses of vivid blue laser energy. Abruptly though the cheering stopped, as the great guns of that giant battleship failed to cause any appreciable damage, all that remained after the punishment meted out by those powerful laser batteries was a few blackened scorch marks.

"Ready main fusion cannons, target the closest ship, FIRE!" Kinraid curled his hand into a fist as though physically assaulting the ships out there himself.

Throughout the ship lights dimmed, plunging the crew into a brief twilight. A thunderous groan so deep in pitch that it vibrated throughout the entire ship as massive amounts of power was syphoned through one of its three Solarian power cores and into its twin fixed, forward firing high bore fusion cannons, which unleashed the built up energy into a vivid sapphire blue beam of such incredible power, such magnitude, that it forced the three thousand metre long battleship backwards several metres.

The awesome power of the two onrushing beams simply immolated drones that crossed their path or even came into contact with them, like moths touching a giant flame before smashing headlong into the closest Cyberian cruiser with such ferocity that it pitched the giant craft upward before blasting it to pieces in one almighty explosion.

Another great cheer went up as a fourth Cyberian ship died, the Valley-forge had let loose its fury for the very first time.

The Cyberians appeared staggered, as if dazed, drones flew haphazardly, colliding with other drones, the Demeter pressed its attack, blasts from its powerful main guns hammering home time after time, although its ministrations were largely ineffectual, it was an impressive display.

Kinraid almost gave the order to advance himself, then stopped as he saw the bout of strange, almost groggy like behaviour begin to dissipate, drones were once again regaining their co-ordination, and the silent advance picked up its pace once again. *It's nothing more than a ruse,* Kinraid thought, and he was not fooled for a second.

After diverting all that energy to the fusion cannons, his ship had to wait until sufficient power was restored so that it could fire again.

The Cyberian fleet was now well within weapons range, the green lances of their guns darted back and forth, trying to disrupt the mass of E.D.F and Krenaran fighters performing attack runs along their hulls like swarms of angry insects. The drones largely ignored them, they had bigger fish to fry and soon began peppering the outlying destroyers and stealth ships with their energy disruptors, instantly scanning any shield impacts as they hit; there were none.

The drones continued to swarm amongst the fleet, peppering them with pulses of low powered white energy. The Demeter responded by firing its multiple point defence lasers, flashes of energy lashed out at the tiny craft destroying several of them in tiny blazing fireballs making the giant battleship almost twinkle to those watching on the Valley-forge.

Several times the flagship itself was hit, causing its graviton shields to flare at the impact points, yet not powerful enough to cause any damage.

"Point defence turrets, open fire; get those damned things off us," Kinraid ordered.

The six twin turreted batteries nestled in sites across the battleship opened fire in a searing cavalcade of rapid firing laser energy. Dozens of drones were caught and destroyed in the withering fusillade, although the drones already had what they came for. The operating frequency of those graviton shields, and instantly the information was fed through to the larger Cyberian cruisers. It no longer mattered that the drones died, their task was done.

The stealth ships pressed their attack, dodging and jinking around the intense latticework of matter convertor beams, their deadly emerald touch cleaving through another two of them as they passed, reducing their black and silver hulls into little more than a smattering of drifting hull fragments. Krenaran torpedoes blasted deep craters into the thick hull armour of the cruisers, their particle beams scoring deep furrows in several places, gouging out fiery gulleys into their hulls, before veering off for another run.

Despite the pounding it was taking, the damage inflicted upon it, still the Cyberian fleet advanced, unheeding, uncaring.

This time though, the E.D.F/Krenaran fleet was within weapons range of those lethal cruisers, and they used their numerical advantage and weight of fire to deadly effect. First the destroyers were hit, although fast moving and agile, even they could not evade that lethal criss-cross of beams and three of them – almost half the formation was systematically reduced to floating scrap. The remaining destroyers aborted their attack run, and peeled off to form up with the stealth ships.

The drones locked in bitter combat with Krenaran and E.D.F fighters, began to break off the destruction derby of their ramming spree, instead heading for the Victorious, Demeter, and Valley-forge themselves.

The Victorious knew its time had come, and her Captain Abel Rankin did not order the badly mauled fighters to pursue, but to form up a second defensive wing ahead of the lumbering Montgomery class carrier while it launched its nasty little surprise. A full god-hammer bomber wing equipped with those deadly cobra anti-ship missiles, if *they* couldn't penetrate the Cyberian's ships hides, then nothing would.

From out of the carrier's two upper launch bays, the bombers swarmed out into the explosions and flashes of battle just as the remainder of the fighter escort had re-formed. Barely eight craft remained out of the Victorious's twelve and the Valley-forge's twenty four.

It would be tight, Rankin just hoped the bombers would be able to unleash their payload before they were pecked to death by those drones, once the Cyberians found out what was happening.

The twenty strong bomber and fighter formation set forth at full speed, dodging and weaving around floating half-destroyed bulkheads and hull plating, and through the dangerous minefield of energy beams that were the matter convertors of those deadly cruisers.

E.D.F Chronicles – The Cyberian menace

Suddenly in one fluid motion the drones immediately turned about, making a bee-line straight for this fighter contingent. Rankin knew the Cyberians were now well aware of the plan, it was a race against time now. Several fighters were consumed by the constantly shifting matter convertors, erased into non-existence as the remainder of the unit flew by grimly resolved to their task.

The remaining Krenaran fighters, realising the onrush of the drones and the peril of their E.D.F counterparts, re-formed amidst the carnage around them and quickly launched themselves in an intercept vector at full speed. Several of them rushing through, and being wiped out by the deadly touch of the Cyberians energy beams in the process.

An intense burst of rapid firing Krenaran pulse cannons tore through the chasing drones. Dozens of which collided with them in a sea of flaming destruction, the Krenaran fighters themselves were all but wiped out in the process, yet they had helped pave the way for what was about to happen.

The E.D.F fighters skirted close to the metallic hull of one of those strange cruisers, which to their surprise had no anti-fighter defences at all. Rankin, co-ordinating the attack from his bridge, surmised that the Cyberians, being so heavily armoured, figured they didn't need fighter defences. They were about to find out just how wrong they were.

The remaining fighters climbed hard, veering out from the hull like a giant fan, allowing the bombers behind a perfect shot. In one single flurry the ten strong bomber squadron fired their under-wing cobra missiles, shooting out in a blur of intense white contrails and hammering home, smashing deep into the armoured hull of this metal leviathan as the tiny bombers also jinked hard, accelerating away from the force of the blasts.

In a ripple of massive explosions the warheads detonated, blasting apart immense chunks of armour, entire decks were decimated, secondary explosions ripped through the giant ship, then slowly almost fatefully, the cruiser itself began to list, before finally tearing itself apart in one dazzlingly bright almighty explosion.

A great cheer went up on both the bridges of the Victorious and the Valley-forge, watching as the fiery remains of the ship drifted outward, colliding into anything unfortunate enough to be in its path. *The fighter and bomber crews had acquitted themselves well,* Kinraid thought with an appreciating nod. *Their heroics will be remembered here.*

"Fusion cannons are now recharged and ready for firing." Lieutenant Iuliov, the Valley-forge's tactical officer said from his station behind Kinraid.

"Fire!" He shouted without hesitation, he wanted to press what little advantage he had.

The ship's most powerful weapon system duly unleashed its ferocity once again, the twin sapphire blue beams of raw energy raced out once more from the battleships gigantic main guns, pitching it backward momentarily again, the raw fury, the incredible hitting power smashed into a second cruiser near to where the other had disintegrated, instantly blasting it to pieces in an equally bright explosion.

With the destruction of these two ships a hole had formed in the immense tidal wave of Cyberian shipping bearing down upon them. It was as though a rock had been placed in a stream, separating its flow, though it was still but a drop in a vast ocean to the Cyberians. To the E.D.F/Krenaran defenders however, it was enough, and they grasped it with both hands. Before Kinraid could even issue an order, the entire battlegroup broke formation and raced headlong toward that tiny gap; all except for one ship, the Valley-forge itself.

"Captain?" Anizeres questioned. "We have a chance to break through and attack them from the rear where they are most vulnerable."

Kinraid didn't reply, he continued staring through pyramided fingers at the mass of ships all fighting and dying in front of him, his eyes narrowed, thoughtful.

"Captain!" Anizeres shouted.

"That is exactly what they want you to think….." Kinraid fondled his ginger beard, deep in thought.

Anizeres shook her head, "think what? I don't understand."

"Why would such a large and overpowering fleet leave such an obvious hole in their lines?"

Anizeres considered this, and then began to come around to her Captain's thinking a little, "because they *want* us to take it."

"Exactly," Kinraid replied with a knowing smile. "It's a trap, bait to draw us in, once we head for the door, they slam it shut; crushing our fleet in the process."

"They have already headed toward it!" Anizeres shouted in desperation.

"Contact the fleet, order them to return to their original positions immediately." Kinraid ordered.

After a short pause, Anizeres replied. "The fleet are responding, although some are finding it extremely hard to turn in the press of ships."

Caught like ants on flypaper, Kinraid thought. "Who?"

"The Demeter and the Victorious."

Kinraid cursed, slamming his fist down hard on his chair; with that one impetuous charge they may have just gifted Sigma XI and Foxtrot base to the Cyberians.

E.D.F Chronicles – The Cyberian menace

The Valley-forge was now alone and vulnerable, even a battleship of her size and power could not hope to defend a world from a two hundred strong enemy fleet alone.

The jaws were closing fast, two of the Krenaran carriers had realised their fate turned about and managed to escape in time, though they were carrying wounds. Decks missing, bleeding oxygen, gases, and in some areas fire out into space from ruptured conduits.

The heavy cruisers however did an admirable job in forming a stop gap for the other ships to get the heck out of there, still armed with their rotary rail-cannons designed to pound a ship repeatedly from short to medium range, the three rotating barrels constantly firing, like a house sized Gatling gun unleashing a torrent of high explosive shells into the nearby Cyberian craft. Although the rail-cannon was an archaic weapon by modern E.D.F standards, rendered obsolete by the longer ranged and more powerful high power laser batteries, it was also a direct-fire weapon, and thus, a weapon in which the Cyberians were vulnerable.

Both port and starboard gun emplacements on all four heavy cruisers fired simultaneously in a blaze of explosive ordnance, their shells repeatedly hammering home on the encroaching cruisers, blasting apart great chunks of armour plating, and eventually like a particularly nasty hammer drill, tore into the ships hulls themselves. Three more Cyberian ships died, their hulls torn to pieces, shredded and ablaze from multiple high explosive shell impacts.

The heavy cruisers eventually buckled under the sheer weight of enemy ships around them, together with their own guns running desperately low on ammunition, their hulls were quickly shorn to pieces by several dozen matter convertor beams gouging great furrows into their port and starboard sides, dissolving outer hull armour and exposing decks to the deep freeze of open space, and eradicating all those within. The ships rocked and lurched violently as their pressurised hulls exploded, oxygen within rushed out through bulkheads that were no longer there in a desperate attempt to fill the void of space.

Finally the hulls of these four vessels were so weakened that they simply floated apart, lifeless. There was no final death scream, no gigantic explosion seen from tens of thousands of kilometres away to herald their passing to the galaxy. There was just a silent descent into nothingness.

Kinraid smiled through his frustration, although they had died, they died well. Those four little ships had single-handedly allowed the majority of the fleet to escape from the jaws of certain destruction.

The Demeter, unable to manoeuvre its vast bulk in the tight press of ships, elected to simply ram the cruisers attempting to slowly take it to pieces. All throughout the giant battleship, the deadly green energy beams of the matter convertors washed over it, removing entire decks at a stroke, weakening the ship to such an extent that it was struggling to hold itself together.

Kinraid knew the Demeter was doomed, and the Victorious too, there was just nothing they could do to spring them from the jaws of that deadly trap.

Explosions burst out brightly as gas tanks detonated, while matter convertors swallowed up walls, bulkheads and supply lines nearby.

Although, by now Kinraid figured with profound sadness that most of its one thousand six hundred and forty crew were dead, he watched in disbelief as those engines that still worked in the ramshackle rear cluster of inter-system boosters fired for all they were worth, scorching the nearby cruisers, propelling the devastated bulk of the ship forward. Then rather lazily, the immense battleship smashed itself into the Cyberian cruiser ahead.

Support struts shattered instantly, entire sections of already weakened hull gave way, ripped apart like tin-foil as the titanic impact tore into both ships, finally both of them exploded in one gigantic devastating explosion lighting up the ships around it, like a flame in a darkened room.

The shockwave threw out debris in all directions, heavy torn pieces of hull plating and armour smashed into other ships nearby. The blast front was even felt aboard the Valley-forge, where the ship was rocked violently, Kinraid had to hold on to his seat.

"Damage report," he said as he straightened himself. The ship was practically brand new and command would have his ass if it came back damaged.

"Graviton shields absorbed the worst of it, some minor buckling on deck fourteen though." Anizeres replied.

Well, it would seem command is going to have my ass after all, he mused, then the ship was slammed much harder, this time sending the captain sprawling from his seat to land with a crumpled thud on the deck plating. Everywhere alarms blared out, loudly signalling damage to his ship.

Anizeres clung on desperately to her console as lights momentarily dimmed and then returned to their normal brightness again. "Direct hit to deck twenty six, forward section. The whole area is open to space – casualties reported."

Kinraid picked himself up, gingerly rubbing his arm he landed upon when he hit the floor before re-seating himself. "How the hell did they get through our shields?"

"Unkown at this time, Captain."

The ship shuddered violently again as it was hit by another matter convertor beam, a power coupling ruptured across the roof of the bridge in a flash of miniature explosions, sending out a sheet of sparks and thick acrid smoke, a console linked to it blew itself apart in a shower of glass and yet more smoke. Its operator flung halfway across the command centre to land in a bloodied heap, shards of razor sharp glass jutting out from his throat and face.

Anizeres shouted over the din of explosions and violent shuddering, "another direct hit, deck sixteen, middle section - no casualties reported this time, but structural integrity is down to eighty percent. We cannot keep taking these kinds of hits Captain!" Her face lined with soot and sweat.

Kinraid agreed completely with his commander, if the Valley-forge took many more hits like that they were done for. If they stayed here much longer, they were done for. Yet they could not just abandon the planet either; he gnashed his teeth in frustration, what else could he do? The fleet was in tatters, he had four destroyers remaining, two Krenaran carriers and a smattering of stealth ships. The Victorious was ablaze and about to be finished off, he had no fighter cover remaining. Kinraid closed his eyes, a sigh of despair escaping his mouth, he was absolutely overmatched in every area; silently he prayed for a miracle.

Just as he opened his eyes again and was about to signal the retreat, the miracle came. In the form of a flurry of plasma wakes opening directly behind the Cyberian lines, so bright in their intensity that the giant enemy ships were silhouetted against them. Their heavy armour no match for the raw power of a Solarian fusion cannon. Several were cut to pieces before they could even manoeuvre to meet this new threat. Great plumes of torpedoes arced, and detonated on the already damaged ships, explosions tore through their hulls.

A giant fleet of some three hundred Solarian vessels had come to their aid. Kinraid watched in barely concealed jubilation, "Now we 'ave a fighting chance, how long until our fusion cannons are ready?"

"Another five seconds, although the targeting matrix for number one cannon has been damaged, it will have to be aimed manually," Iuliov said wiping the grime from his brow.

"Understood, fire when ready!"

Kinraid smiled as the battle unfolded ahead of him, the remaining Krenaran carriers and their own destroyers launched a fresh salvo of torpedoes and H.O.T rockets at the Cyberian invaders, all slamming home with horrific force, another Cyberian vessel succumbed to the catastrophic levels of damage it had taken, slowly it too tore itself apart in a blazing fireball.

A new wave of confusion spread through the Cyberian line, as the Solarians pressed their attack from the rear, and the remaining E.D.F/Krenaran flotilla renewed their assault from the front. Solarian battlecruisers darted in and out, like agile barracudas, their torpedoes and fusion cannon blazing away, causing immense damage. Suddenly it was Cyberian craft that were being scythed down, as though fresh wheat in a harvest.

The immense fusion cannons of the Valley-forge let loose their anger again, the intense blue beams blasting another cruiser apart in a spray of fire and debris. Kinraid could not believe it, they were actually winning, it seemed that panic and confusion was rife in the Cyberian armada, as if the machine intelligence of the Cyberian fleet could not comprehend being attacked in two places at once, ships darted between one threat and another, suddenly unsure of themselves.

With the Cyberian lines crumbling before their very eyes the remains of the fleet broke off their attack, and for the first time either human or Krenaran had known it, actually retreated.

The viewscreen blinked and the image of floating, battle-scarred hulls and half destroyed ships was replaced by the face of what appeared to be a middle aged Solarian. Although Kinraid guessed that for a Solarian to be middle aged he must easily be over a hundred years old.

"Greetings Terrans, I am Alvokar Tolaris of the Solarian battlecruiser Aedris, our warhost is but one of many come to help defend your worlds against evil, as we once did over a decade ago."

"Thank you….er Alvokar," he hoped he had got the pronunciation right, the word sounded important. "Our world is now safe thanks to the efforts 'o you and your men." Kinraid replied with genuine relief, the thought had crossed his mind for an instant that the world had been about to fall.

"Do not thank me yet, for this is far from over. Every major power in the galaxy is now involved in this great war. A battle to preserve the sanctity of life itself, elsewhere worlds are being fought and lost, we have victory here though I fear it is but a temporary reprieve."

"I understand Alvokar, nevertheless you have my eternal gratitude."

"Thank you, our scans show you have a fine ship, though badly damaged."

Kinraid nodded, "we took a few bad hits in the assault, we'll remain here a while affecting temporary repairs while another E.D.F battlegroup relieves us."

"As you wish," Tolaris nodded almost regally. "We shall stand guard with you until your new fleet arrives."

And with that, the communication ended. The silvery crescent shaped battlecruisers joined and interspersed with the battered, battleworn E.D.F and Krenaran defenders. It was a show of unity that almost made Kinraid shed a tear. Despite everything, the animosity, the bloodshed between races, the bitterness between entire empires, everyone now knew that this was bigger than themselves, it affected them all and only together could they hope to defeat it; today was a perfect example of that.

E.D.F Chronicles – The Cyberian menace

"I'll be in my quarters," Kinraid said as he slowly, painfully rose from his seat and turned toward Anizeres. "You have the bridge."

Anizeres nodded, "understood Captain."

Kinraid made his way across the blackened debris strewn bridge to his private quarters, and with a tired sigh slumped into a chair. That was some battle, now he knew how Michael Alexander, his former commanding officer must have felt after a battle like that.

Keying in a data display, he opened a comms. channel to the nearest major naval facility, which was ironically Delta Bravo base, a large resupply station on-route to the Solarian border and situated in orbit of the Perseus colony world.

"Valley-forge, what can I do for you?" Came the rather pointed reply from Captain Al-Tahar, a man of deep Indian descent, noted as being the only Captain in the navy to still wear a turban on duty due to his deep muslim beliefs. E.D.F command could not refuse him to wear it on religious grounds, although when fighting on the ground he usually wore an apex combat helmet like everyone else. He rather quickly found out, that a bright scarlet turban made quite an attractive target to an enemy marksman, and several times he was hospitalised while fighting in the Krenaran war until he learned his lesson.

"Please relay to command that we have successfully defended Sigma XI from Cyberian attack. We are badly depleted however, and require immediate extraction in order to properly effect repairs. Our own ship is badly damaged also, and we have lost all fighter cover."

Al-Tahar looked shocked, "how many did you lose?"

"Enough Captain, the fleet is badly mauled and well under half strength, some of my best men are dead." Kinraid replied with a solemn sigh.

"We've been hearing similar stories across the colonies, there is fighting on Tarantis, Agemman again, Aurelias. The entire Krenaran frontier is under threat of collapse, we simply can't get enough ships out there fast enough."

Kinraid nodded, he could well believe it. "It will be a while before we are operational again too, we took quite a beating out here. The fighting was intense, brutal at times. I haven't seen anything like this since the darkest days 'o the Krenaran war."

Al-Tahar nodded in agreement, "many other Captains are saying the same, others are saying even that war pales against the size and sheer scale of the enemy we are up against, we truly are witnessing some dark days. I'll transfer on the message."

"Thank you Captain," Kinraid replied with a smile before cancelling the channel and slumping back down onto his leather two-seater. *Dark days indeed,* he thought, his look grave, concerned, *dark days indeed.*

9. Re-emergence

"Can you believe what is going on out there?" Michael Alexander shouted from the front room of their bungalow as he watched the latest report come in from the outer colony news. It depicted a live report from a news crew that had landed on the devastated world of Tarantis, E.D.F troops were putting up a valiant fight, though they were almost constantly overrun, swamped, and then simply steam-rolled as swarms of Cyberian warriors stormed on right past them. Many were falling back in total disarray. The report was also describing the escalating humanitarian plight suffered by the colonists as they fled in their thousands from the embattled worlds with whatever they could carry, crowding into ramshackle aged transports bound for worlds deeper within E.O.C.A space where they hoped to gain some modicum of protection.

A heavily pregnant Kathryn Alexander hobbled into the room still clutching a handful of half chopped spring onions from the salad she was preparing.

"I know," she said between taking bites, "it's horrendous out there, I don't like to watch it, it brings back too many bad memories for me."

Michael turned in his seat to face her, seeing the pained expression on her face. "Of the Krenarans?"

"Yep," she nodded.

Michael Alexander, the former war hero of the navy, Captain of the most prestigious ship that ever flew, was now retired and finally happy. He had everything he had ever wanted, and he was finally able to let the ghosts to rest of the deaths of his previous wife Jana, and his only son Theo. He used a portion of his sizeable retirement payoff to purchase this large bungalow on the outskirts of Aspen, Colorado. And after striking up a romance while still aboard the Liberty, he finally married Kathryn Jacobs, the ships former medical officer three years ago. Once he officially retired, Kathryn took up a position as head nurse of a local hospital so she could be with him. Right now, however, she was on medical leave due to her pregnancy.

Together they stepped out onto the rear balcony, Kathryn bringing mugs of coffee for them both. They sniffed the cool, crisp air coming from the pine forests at the rear of a large meadow of freshly cut grass. The sun was about breaking the horizon, bathing the clouds and sky in vivid orange.

This was his favourite part of the house and every morning he came out here, his senses brought alive with the scents of jasmine, honeysuckle, and a dozen different rose varieties mixed with the heady scents of dew and pine.

Michael sighed a happy, contented sigh looking lovingly into Kathryn's eyes as he took the mug. The two of them sat back in their reclining patio chairs and silently took in the beauty of the mountains around them. He placed a gentle hand on Kathryn's arm as they sat together, "this is freedom, this is living my love."

They barely spoke as they took in the magnificent sunrise, yet hand in hand their hearts spoke volumes. After a few moments witnessing natures spectacle unfold in their own back garden, there was a knock at the door and Kathryn moved to get up.

"It's okay, I'll get it." Michael smiled back at her as he leaned in and kissed her tenderly on the forehead.

Opening the front door he was confronted with two naval officers, one with short cropped hair betraying several grey flecks across the temples and bearing an Admiral's insignia on his uniform. He instantly recognised the figure as Admiral Montrose, the other was a deep brown haired younger Commodore, one which Michael did not recognise.

"May we come in?" Montrose asked.

Michael was instantly suspicious of the two men's motives, then again Admiral George Montrose was a man he had come to respect over the years. He would not have come here unless it was a matter of utmost importance.

Silently opening the door, he gestured for them to come inside, closing the door behind them and following them through to the lounge.

"Is everything okay?" Kathryn asked from the balcony.

"Yes my love, everything's fine." He lied as convincingly as he could muster.

Michael stood rigidly upright as the two men seated themselves, in his mind he was already retired, he had done more than his bit for humanity, and had no desire to go back to the navy.

He watched as the two men seated themselves.

"Nice place you have here," Montrose broke the icy silence.

"Thank you, now why are you here?" Michael asked, a little flatly.

"Straight to business, that's one of the things I like about you," Montrose replied.

"Well, you know me."

Montrose smiled unconvincingly, "Look, I am just going to give it to you straight. Have you seen the news reports lately?"

Michael nodded a silent yes.

"Well you see the desperate situation we are in, don't you?"

"Well, yes." Michael replied, "You guys are getting nailed to the wall out there, the question is what does any of this have to do with me? I am retired now, my war is over."

"We really need you back one last time for one last mission, a mission of such importance that the fate of the entire galaxy may well rest upon it. Those news programmes don't tell the whole truth, the reality is that it is even worse out there. Do you know that the frontier worlds close to Krenaran territory, battlegrounds that you fought to defend, have all but collapsed already. The Cyberians are pushing further in, and right now we don't have the strength or the numbers to stop them. Hundreds of thousands of lives have already been lost."

"So you want me back, why?" Michael asked.

"So you can do what you do best, command a ship. While the navy tries to stem the tide of advancing Cyberian ships, we need you and your crew to search for a special kind of Cyberian vessel we believe is out there. We need you to locate it so that the fleet can destroy it. All our resources are tied up just trying to keep the Cyberians at bay, we have no spare ships."

Michael eyed the two men suspiciously, a hint of anger flashed across his face, his voice cold and full of menace. "Fifteen years ago you pulled this crap on me, it damn near tore my family apart. My first wife and child were killed because I wasn't there to protect them. Now that I finally have my life back you want to pull the same thing again?"

"I understand how you must feel Michael, if there was any other way....."

"You have no idea how I feel! And now I think it is time you should both leave." Michael retorted, threatening to burst into a rage, how dare they presume to know how he felt, they weren't there, they were directing the war from behind a desk sixty light years away. When the war ended he could go back home to his wife and family, Michael couldn't.

"If that is your decision," the two officers stood and made to leave, Michael opened the door and had to restrain himself from shoving the two men through it.

"We'll be waiting if you should choose to change your mind, but don't wait too long, time is running out and lives depend upon it." With that Montrose and the Commodore left the house, Michael slammed the door after them. Collapsing back down onto the settee he breathed a deep sigh of relief and closed his eyes, remembering the faces of Jana and Theo before he lost them to a Krenaran torpedo. When he opened them he saw Kathryn standing in front of him.

"You're going to go aren't you?" Tears began to gently trickle down those soft cheeks of hers.

"I don't know." Michael replied honestly.

For days afterward he was forced into this sullen, contemplative mood. As if the sheer gravity of his decision weighed him down, Kathryn did her best to comfort him but it was no use. Only he could make this choice, she understood either way of course. It was like a battle playing out within him, he did not want to leave her even for a short while, and especially now since she was pregnant with his child. Yet he also knew that millions out there could die if he did not. He wrestled with his emotions, and not for the first time in his life.

After days of soul searching, he realised that the stakes were far too high, and so he went to his terminal in the study of his bungalow and keyed in a secure channel to Admiral George Montrose now back at Alpha base, the Admiral's surprised face greeted him.

"Michael! I didn't think you would ever speak to me again after the incident at your house."

Michael cut him off tersely, "I will go on your mission, but there is a condition."

"What's that?"

"Give me the Liberty."

"Michael, the Liberty is sat in a surplus depot, mothballed just outside of the Orion system, are you sure?"

"Do you want me on this mission or not, that is the condition." Michael replied sharply, he was in no mood to be toyed with and was also letting the Admiral know he was not at all happy at having to leave Kathryn.

"Okay, it is done, I'll have you re-activated immediately, a shuttle will be sent for you in one hour. I'll also put in a request with the Epsilon zeta-one surplus depot, and have the Liberty taken out of mothballs and returned to active duty, I just hope they haven't cannibalised her parts too much, she has been in there a while."

Volgograd, Russia.

It was snowing outside and bitterly cold when two men in full military uniform and fur lined overcoats approached an old, seemingly ramshackle house near the great statue of the Mamyev Kurgan, the mother Russia herself.

Gently they tapped on the heavy painted steel door, with a rusted metallic creak a man opened it. He was considerably bulkier than the two facing him, with a deep brown moustache tinged with flecks of grey, and cold, dark, serious eyes.

"Colonel Nikolai Vargev?"

"Yes."

"May we come in?" The Soldiers asked, shivering slightly.

Nikolai chuckled a little within himself, obviously these two did not understand how harsh a Russian winter can get in these parts.

"Of course," Nikolai replied after studying them for some time, gesturing for the two men to enter.

The men were shown into a warm lounge, with a large open hearth dominating one wall, a viewer on another wall, and several shelves filled with war memorabilia, medals and trophies that he had collected over the years. Other than that it was rather spartan, not too dissimilar to the man himself, one of singular purpose, without distractions, one who got the job done no matter what.

They seated themselves on a rather harsh settee as Nikolai threw another thick log on the open fire, the whole room seemed unbecoming of one of the E.D.F's greatest ever soldiers, the two men looked at him questioningly.

"Oh I am Nikolai Vargev, you have the right address. I do not need many of the creature comforts that others do. Just a warm fire, some clothes to keep the elements away, some food, and my weapon at my side, comrade."

Nikolai studied the two men closely, "although this is not a social call is it?"

"Not exactly, I am Major Jack Allen of the twenty eighth airborne, and this is Lieutenant John Stewart of the fourteenth infantry."

Nikolai cut him off, "the hillrunners? My unit fought alongside them at Barnards star, during the Krenaran war."

"I remember, a lot of our guys died that day, you were the ones who managed to push the Krenarans back and allow our extraction."

"Look," Allen spoke up. "There is no easy way to say this, but we need you back for one last special mission."

"Yeah, so why me?" Nikolai quickly retorted, lighting up one of his customary cigars.

"You and your team are going to be our insurance policy, you have no doubt seen on the news how bad things are getting with the Cyberian situation."

Nikolai nodded, "yeah it's getting pretty brutal out there." He puffed, blowing smoke across the room and causing the two men to splutter and choke. His moustache parted as a slight grin played across his thick set features.

"Well, in reality it is much worse, the entire frontier worlds are on the verge of collapse. Everywhere we look we are in danger of being overwhelmed, soon they'll penetrate deeper into E.O.C.A territory, soon Earth could even be hit."

"So what do you want me to do?" Nikolai rested his still considerable bulk on a door frame, sliding one hand into his trouser pocket, and taking another long drag of his cigar with the other.

"You and your unit of commandoes are going to be our backup. The Liberty is being pressed back into service and tasked with locating a Cyberian mothership, a command cruiser that we believe is out there running the whole show. Once we find it, the fleet is ordered to engage and destroy immediately.

However, if for any reason the fleet cannot destroy it, we plan to insert your unit into the cruiser and destroy it manually with demo. charges."

Nikolai was suddenly much more interested, "that sounds like a hell of a mission, what are the chances of success?"

"Not great I'm afraid, if that command cruiser is out there we can expect it to be heavily armed and crawling with Cyberians. You'll have to form a battle plan very quickly based upon scans the fleet acquires while engaging it. You're going to have to think on your feet with this one Nikolai."

"So; overwhelming bad guys, a slim chance of success, well I guess it beats sitting on my ass on a Sunday morning." He said after taking one last puff of his cigar then stubbing it out in an ashtray by the side of him.

"Good, a transport will be along shortly to collect you." Allen smiled, offering his hand.

Nikolai took it in his typical vice-like grip, and Major Allen almost winced, "to the mission."

"To the mission," Vargev repeated with a nod.

***

The Shuttle arrived just an hour later, touching down in an area of parkland near to the great statue of the mother Russia towering above it. Nikolai not needing a great deal of equipment had already packed for the journey, dusting off his old standard issue combat fatigues and military boots one final time. It felt good to be back out there again, fighting wars, being on the battlefield in the thick of the action. He was Nikolai Vargev, he didn't do retirement very well.

Pulling open the gull-wing side hatch of the elongated bullet shaped fuselage he clambered aboard to be greeted with the sight of his old friend Michael Alexander also sat in one of the passenger seats.

"So, they brought you out of retirement too eh?" Nikolai grinned.

"Yep, the Liberty as well, although by the sounds of it I'll have a completely different crew to what I am used to."

The Russian took a seat and strapped himself in, in a spray of dust, loose grass and weeds the shuttle took off once again, it's atmospheric delta wings splayed out as it climbed through the sunlit atmosphere, wisps of cirrus clouds, and out into the starlit majesty of space itself.

"Your unit is already being transported to the Liberty," Allen said as he turned to face the colonel. "As of right now both of you are returned to active duty."

"So what kind of crew can I expect to be working with?" Michael spoke up.

"I don't have the details Captain, the only name I have heard mention in connection to the Liberty is a Commander Maxwell Thorne."

Thorne, Michael thought. Former first officer of the Eurinades if he remembered rightly, that ship was lost during the great battle for Gamma IV with many of its crew. The Eurinades was a great ship with a good crew, he must have made it to one of the escape pods and was picked up later.

From what he remembered of Maxwell Thorne, he was a good officer, if a little rigid and inflexible, he would have to watch him carefully.

After just over an hour of travelling, the tiny shuttle arrived at the gigantic headquarters of the E.D.F, Alpha base. Shuttles and other craft buzzed to and fro, like bees constantly tending to a giant nest. Its vast docking arms outstretched, on the ends of many E.D.F naval cruisers were berthed.

Michael leaned toward the viewport next to his seat for a closer look. There was the faint silhouette of the Apollo, one of the last Danitza class battleships ever constructed, to the left and right of her on separate moorings were the Alliance, an Alexander class medium cruiser named to commemorate the alliance the E.D.F maintained with the Solarian empire in order to win the Krenaran war. And the Euripedes, a Mandela class light cruiser named after the ancient Greek poet.

The shuttle gently glided past the giant form of the Apollo, past its enormous dorsal long range high power laser arrays, the barrels of which alone were several times the length of the little craft. Its command superstructure came into view, antennae jutting out from it as though delicate black strands of cotton reaching out into space. The occasional blink of a navigation light giving any hint to their presence against the dark backdrop of space. Its gently tapered main hull with its patchwork of armoured panels and tiny point defence lasers, and then past the almost pyramidal armoured frontal section of the ship, its docking arm outstretched and clamped securely to the berthing port of the station.

Several times Michael had seen the Danitza class battleships in his career, named for ancient Roman or Greek Gods, and that was exactly what they were, Gods of steel, marching proudly onto the field to do battle with their enemies in the name of humanity. Though even now, seeing one so close as this still took his breath away, the raw power and majesty they seemed to exude was unlike any other ship in the fleet. They were a slowly dying class now, about to be superseded by the more modern Valley-forge and her sister ships, although to Michael there was something about the old Danitza's, a sense of greatness, one of the reasons why their crews loved working on them so much, Michael couldn't help but feel that with their passing, an era was passing along with them.

The shuttle gradually came to rest in one of the station's myriad fighter bays, the armoured bulkheads closed down behind them protecting the occupants from exposure. Oxygen was automatically pumped into the bay as it was re-pressurised, creating a breathable atmosphere.

The occupants stepped out of the gradually powering down shuttle into the familiar flat expanse of a fighter bay lined with rows of Peregrine fighters poised to defend this place in a heartbeat, with their lives if necessary.

Michael, Nikolai and Major Allen headed together toward the nearest elevator terminal, the sounds of their footsteps echoing across the silent bay.

Once they had all entered the elevator itself Allen spoke into the speaker, "Command deck."

"Destination confirmed," the elevator speaker replied.

Michael watched as the doors gently closed, blotting out the fighter bay as if blotting out his life, he wondered if naval officers of any rank really had a 'life' or were they just a resource to be used when the time called for it. He suspected the latter, although he would never mention it in conversation.

The elevator gradually deposited them on the vast command deck filled with the bustle of officers going to and fro, to Michael it was like organised chaos, the hustle and bustle of men busily going about their duties was more akin to a city centre than a military command centre.

Along the walls, communications experts monitored hundreds if not thousands of communications and requests from bases large and small throughout E.O.C.A space. Live feeds were displayed on monitors showing how the war was progressing across the two main sectors currently under attack. The Connaught, and Molrav sectors.

Admiral Montrose himself strode across this immense hall to greet them, "depressing isn't it?" He said as he shook Michael's hand, "I am glad you've come."

He saluted Nikolai in turn, and the ex-commando snapped rigidly to attention and returned the salute, as did Major Allen.

The Admiral motioned for them to follow, and both Nikolai and Michael fell into step behind him, "The truth is gentlemen, we are completely outmatched, we are outgunned and heavily outnumbered at every single turn. The navy is in full retreat across both sectors being chased like a scolded dog. Even the Solarians are struggling, the latest report came in only an hour ago, they have lost six different worlds already."

"Jesus," Michael gasped. "If the Solarians are struggling having the most powerful fleet in the known galaxy with the Solarian warhost, then what chance do we stand?"

"To be honest, little or none," Montrose sighed depressingly. "Agemman colony fell this morning, although the loss of life was minimal, the colony had largely been evacuated. It's looking like Tarantis in the Molrav sector will be next."

Michael could scarcely believe it, the last time he had witnessed war on this scale, the Krenaran war had broken out.

"We are fighting an almost numberless army, capable of crossing galaxies, and they have a way of co-ordinating their forces that frankly leave us in the shade. We are looking at total defeat in four months at least. That's what our best analysts are saying."

Both Michael and Nikolai were stunned at the severity of the news, everything they had fought for, every sacrifice, every hard fought victory was unravelling right before their eyes. Nikolai stiffened visibly, his jaw set, he was not about to let everything just fall apart without a fight.

"That is why this mission has to succeed, and why it is so important." The Admiral went on, "the Solarians believe there is a command ship out there, as I've said. They also believe that this command ship can send orders over vast distances by 'daisy-chaining' commands through its cruisers, who pass those orders on instantaneously to whatever cruiser, drone or warrior is the intended recipient. That's how they can co-ordinate so damned fast."

Michael nodded his understanding, "the command ship does not even have to be present at a battle for the orders to get through. I can see the advantages, all they need is a stable link to another of their cruisers."

"Exactly," Montrose replied. "If we destroy their cruisers, we may disrupt a link, but only until a new link is formed between another ship, re-establishing the network so the effect is only temporary."

Vargev smiled, "like we give them brain fade."

"errr, yes." Montrose stammered casting a look at Nikolai as they walked. "What we need to do is cut off all their orders at once."

"That's pretty hard to do with a system like this," Michael countered.

"Not if we can locate and destroy the command ship itself," Montrose replied. "If we destroy that, no orders can get passed on to any ship, drone, warrior; anywhere."

"Like a computer network without a central server, it cannot operate so it collapses." Michael said nodding in approval.

"It's the only chance we have," Montrose replied.

"But I'm guessing something that valuable is going to be pretty well protected," Vargev pointed out.

"And hard to find," Montrose replied. "Oh yes, she'll be a tough nut to crack alright, but we have to find her first, and that is where you come in."

Michael then asked the question he had been itching to ask, "what crew will I have?"

"The Liberty will be staffed with a temporary, but experienced crew. This is not a mission for greenhorns. Your senior staff will be made up of Commander Maxwell Thorne, Lieutenant's Lars Brogan your Pilot, Anders Allstrom your weapons officer, and Lieutenant Commander Logameier."

At least I get my old chief engineer back, Michael thought. *A Lieutenant Commander now, when did he get a promotion?* He made a mental note to ask once he got back on board.

"Lieutenant Commander Logameier was chosen due to his familiarity with the Liberties rather unique systems," Montrose said as if reading Michael's thoughts.

He nodded approvingly, with the amount of alien tech on that ship, it could hardly have been anyone else.

"Also the Liberty will be carrying a one hundred strong battalion of E.D.F Commandoes, led by Colonel Vargev here. They will form the backup force, in case the fleet should fail to destroy whatever it is."

"Admiral that is a lot of men for such a small ship, the Liberty is all about speed and hitting power, it's not a troop carrier."

Montrose nodded, "I know it's a calculated risk, but it's one we have to take in this case. We simply cannot afford to fail. Your crew will already be there when you arrive, the Commando unit are on their way and should be there also. The Euripedes is due to leave to reinforce the defenders at Charlie base, and should be passing the surplus depot near Orion where the Liberty is currently lying. I wish you both the very best of luck and Godspeed, we are all counting on you."

"Thank you Admiral," Michael replied nodding solemnly, he felt the importance of the mission weighing down upon him, if he couldn't find that ship, the whole of E.O.C.A was dead.

10. Return of a legend.

Both Michael and Nikolai saluted the Admiral before leaving the chaos of the command deck, heading for the elevator that would lead them to the docking array and the Euripedes.

The doors slowly closed behind them, "docking area." Michael spoke.

"Destination confirmed," came the familiar reply as the elevator began its headlong descent through the bowels of this immense structure.

"Hell of a time to come back now," Vargev grunted while leaning on one of the walls.

"I agree, it just makes me wonder just what the heck have we been fighting for over the past fifteen years, just to see it all fall apart now?"

"For once, I agree with you comrade. I guess it's up to us," the big Russian replied with a shrug.

"Yeah, but we're not as young as we used to be, can we really pull this off?"

Nikolai shook his head slightly, "being older just means being smarter, we have to pick and choose our battles. We can't just charge in all guns blazing anymore, we just have to be a bit cleverer in our approach."

Michael contemplated this for a moment, realising that Nikolai was right. "Hey, since when did you get to be the wise one?"

The Russian simply smiled back at him, saying nothing.

The doors opened and the elevator gave a little beep to indicate they had arrived.

The docking section was far larger than the command section they had just emerged from, a long straight hall as far as the eye could see, along one side it was filled with windows looking out upon gigantic ships clamped to the berthing pods and the blackness of space beyond. The Apollo itself looked every bit the titanic ship that it is, with Michael and Nikolai stood before it.

Occasionally crewmen and engineers shuffled past, attending to the vessels this place housed. Michael was almost sad that he was not travelling on such a prestigious vessel although it was standard practice to keep at least one Danitza class at Alpha base at all times.

Together they walked on past the various berths, some taken and some empty, until they came to the Euripedes on berth eleven.

The two men took a sharp right turn, and walked up a smaller berthing corridor up to the ship itself, eventually ending in a guarded entrance manned by a rather fat Lieutenant who looked like he had spent too many years in space, and too many feasts as well.

Both Michael and Nikolai pushed their I.D. cards into a reader which the Lieutenant studied, "Yes, your all clear Captain you may enter."

"Thank you," Michael replied walking past nonchalantly.

"You may also enter Colonel," The Lieutenant said to Nikolai.

The big Russian did not respond, just gave him a look of distain followed by a low pitched menacing growl.

The Lieutenant blanched and turned away, while the Russian followed Michael aboard.

The Mandela class light cruiser Euripedes was spartan, bare looking, with only the occasional aged monitor or continuously displaying status readout to give any hint that the ship was even functioning. Being such a small ship, basically an escort vessel, it was a far cry from the comforts aboard the larger vessels of the fleet that they were used to. Both Michael and Nikolai were shown to a bunk with just a single storage locker to stow their equipment, there were no plush separate quarters here, just a male dormitory and a female one.

It reminded Michael of a prison ship rather than a frontline naval fighting vessel, Nikolai on the other hand was quite at home, much of the layout reminded him of the many military installations he had visited in the past.

"Not what you were expecting?" He asked.

"Hardly, I knew the Mandela class and Ghandhi class were small, spartan little ships, but this is ridiculous."

With a dejected sigh Michael finished up stowing his gear and trudged off to the nearest elevator, to get a look at what passed for a bridge on this ship. If the bridge was anything like the crew quarters, his expectations were not particularly high.

"Main bridge," he spoke aloud to the elevator.

"Deeestinaaation confiiiirmed," was the stunted reply.

Even the elevator doesn't work properly on this ship, is there anything that does? Michael thought, shaking his head.

Eventually stepping out of the somewhat dubious elevator, and onto an equally aged, broken down bridge, Michael sighed. His expectations had turned out to be correct after all, the chequer plate floor and occasional exposed metal grille echoed as he stepped on them.

The men surrounding the periphery of this cramped forlorn looking place were largely unaware of him, he counted six of them, a lone pilot-cum-navigation officer, the ships commanding officer sat in a badly decrepit centre chair, a tactical officer manning a station just to the left of him, and a sensory officer to the right. Two other men were manning stations behind, one of which Michael suspected was an engineering monitoring station.

He approached the Captain in the centre seat who heard his approach and immediately spun around in his chair to face him.

Michael recognised the man, it was Lieutenant Commander Johnathan Walters, an old acquaintance from his flight school days, Walters was in the class below his one, and occasionally took trials flying Michael's fighter after he had used it. His jet black buzz cut now had the occasional grey streak making its appearance on his crown, and he was thinning rather badly.

"Michael Alexander…." Walter replied, an ominous tone to his voice.

Michael immediately wondered what he had done to earn the apparent enmity of the Lieutenant commander, yet refrained from saying anything except, "hello Lieutenant."

"Hello Lieutenant, that's all you have to say?" Walters eyed him suspiciously.

Michael shrugged, "nice ship you have here." Trying to change the subject, lighten the mood a little, then almost immediately regretted doing so.

"Nice ship!" Walters spat, "the ship is nothing more than a bucket of rusting nails, thanks to you!"

Then Michael remembered, Walters was originally on the shortlist to be chosen as executive officer of the Liberty. When Michael gave that position to Quinn Kinraid, Walters must have felt very put out. Even more so now that command had picked Maxwell Thorne over him as well.

"Johnathan when I chose Kinraid as my first officer, it was nothing personal against you. The Liberty is a damned hard ship to command at the best of times, with systems and resources completely different to any other ship in the navy. I felt Kinraid was the more experienced, and better able to handle her, and it turned out I was right."

"And condemned me to a life of bit-part commands running the junk of the navy," Walters shot back.

"I'm sorry you feel that way, but I had to make the right decision," Michael began to wonder if Walters would ever get over the seething resentment he felt toward him. "Your career is your own responsibility, every man in the navy knows that."

Walters simply turned in his chair, returning his gaze to the viewscreen. "I have orders to drop you off when we arrive at surplus depot Epsilon-zeta one, so that you may re-take command of your precious Liberty; other than that get off my bridge."

Michael simply shook his head, left the bridge and headed below decks, eventually he made it back to Nikolai who was sound asleep and snoring so loudly Michael thought the support braces were going to collapse.

This is going to be a long trip, he thought with a depressed sigh.

It was a three week journey to Epsilon-zeta one, and by and large the first two weeks passed by rather uneventfully. Michael used the time visiting the various dilapidated parts of the ship, engineering, weapons control, helping out where he could. Compared to what he was used to many of the systems looked like something that had come from the ark. He often visited the observation deck looking out upon the swirling backdrop of plasma drive superimposed over the multitude of stars that streaked past, it was the one peaceful, serene area of the ship, it gave him time to think.

Lieutenant Fairlight, the ships young chief engineer he found to be surprisingly well versed in the way her ship operated, which when he cast a glance over the place he would never have guessed. She was also one of the few female engineers in the navy, and one of the busiest women aboard ship, her repair teams were always rushing to and fro fixing some equipment failure or breakdown. Fairlight once said to Michael that the Euripedes, "was one of the oldest Mandela class vessels in the fleet, and like an old lady she needed to be cared for constantly." Michael could very well believe it.

On the third day of the third week into the voyage, everything changed.

Suddenly the ship lurched violently, Walters was almost thrown from his seat, "What the hell was that?"

Alarms blared out, loudly cutting through the serene calmness of the journey like a knife.

"A highly charged burst of magnetic energy," one of his officers replied manning a sensory console.

"A magnetic charge, why?"

"Magnetic disturbances disrupt the plasma wake, basically diffusing the ionised plasma we are travelling through, and therefore forcing us back into real space."

The ship rocked violently for a second time, Michael was hurled from his bunk, landing hard on the unforgiving deck plating below. Rubbing his arm gingerly, he rushed to change into his naval uniform and bolted out of the crew quarters, leaving Nikolai in his wake.

"Another burst incoming!" The pilot shouted over the wail of alarm sirens.

A third blast rocked the ship, sending crewmen across various decks hurtling to the floor, though causing no damage to the ship itself. The plasma wake the small craft was travelling through had now completely collapsed, flinging the ship violently into normal space and directly into the path of a fully armed Cyberian battlecruiser nearly eight times its size.

"Hard to starboard! Take us under it!" Walters screamed.

Thrusters on the tiny vessel flared for all they worth, bright jets of ionised gas attempted to manoeuvre the ship beneath this colossus facing them.

The Cyberian ship immediately opened fire with its matter convertors, bright green lances of energy raked the facing port side of the ship. Crewmen were launched from their stations and thrown through the air as the pressurised outer skin of entire sections melted and then vanished completely under the strength of those beams.

"Damage report!" Walters screamed over the blare of warning klaxons.

"Decks six and seven hit sir; casualties reported, large sections are open to space. Structural integrity is down to sixty four percent!"

Another explosion sent the bridge crew scrabbling to stay at their posts.

"Sir! Main power is weakening, with power diverted to maintain forcefields around those damaged decks, our reserves won't hold for long."

Michael managed to stumble his way onto the bridge, "What the hell is going on!"

"We're under attack! What does it look like!" Walters shouted back.

"Cyberian vessel is manoeuvring for another attack," the tactical officer announced.

"Ready main guns, give them everything we've got!" Walters shouted.

The forward and port medium range laser turrets swung into position, and began to unleash a torrent of direct hits on the giant that was now closing for the kill, though for all the hail of fire the Euripedes was pouring into it, all it had accomplished was to anger the great beast even more.

"We've scored seven direct hits and there's not a hint of damage!" The tactical officer shouted incredulously.

"That's impossible, their must have been something?" Walters replied back in exasperation.

"They have energy dispersing hull armour!" Michael shouted, "your laser weapons are useless against that thing."

"Then what can we use?" Walters replied, "We have no rail-cannon or torpedoes."

"You are outmatched and outgunned, the only thing you can do is run," Michael replied. "Get away from that thing!"

Walters nodded in agreement swinging in his chair to his navigator, "Shunt all available power to the main inter-system booster, give it everything you've got pilot."

"Aye sir," the pilot pushed the throttle level to maximum on the booster, the ships main sub-light drive. The badly damaged Euripedes began to lurch forward. Although it was all too little too late as the Cyberian craft fired those deadly beams again, melting away an entire swathe of the Euripede's aft section and blasting apart the main booster in a shower of metallic fragments. The ship lurched violently forward due to the force of the explosion then began to list, limp as if hanging in space.

E.D.F Chronicles – The Cyberian menace

Damage alarms blared out all over the ship, across the vessel the extreme damage the small craft had taken was plainly evident, flailing conduits lay sparking and crackling from collapsed trunking, glass and various debris strewn across the floor from blasted consoles, the walls were scarred black from fires and explosions, lights flickered constantly. Dead or dying crewmen lay everywhere, some bleeding profusely.

Walters slowly, groggily got back to his feet, his own face blackened and scorched, bearing several nicks from flying shrapnel bleeding down his right cheek.

"All hands abandon ship!"

Nikolai sprinted onto the bridge also trying to figure out just what in the blue hell was going on.

"Get out of here now!" Walters shouted to the two of them, "ultimately we are expendable; you have to live!"

Without a second thought, Nikolai shoved a motionless, dumbstruck Michael into an empty escape hatch lying between two flickering terminals on the bridge, and jabbed the control to begin the launch sequence.

As the door closed Michael could only watch as the deadly green energy beam crashed through the bridge floor, melting half of Johnathan Walters's body away to nothingness, his severed upper torso slumping wetly onto the devastated bridge floor, all he could manage was "Goodbye......old......friend" before the rush of escaping air swept his body out into space and a thousand tiny metal fragments along with it.

The escape pod jettisoned from the half collapsed bridge, its tiny thrusters firing it clear of the devastated Euripedes, all Michael could do was watch from a tiny porthole barely bigger than a saucer, as the E.D.F ship finally, violently succumbed to its wounds in one giant blazingly bright fireball. The huge Cyberian vessel jumped back into plasma drive, its gruesome task complete.

They drifted like that for days, hungry and thirsty, though by some miracle still alive, over and over Michael had the same thought circulating in his mind, how could a man like Walters, a man who hated him so vehemently, ultimately give his life to save theirs. He did not deserve to die like that, yes in the end his bitter jealousy over what Michael had managed to accomplish in his career, in his life had gotten the better of him. Though Michael would always remember him for the kind, funny little man he was at the academy, the class prankster of his year.

How that battlecruiser had missed them he had no idea, just blind luck he guessed.

Suddenly there was a sharp jolt, and the two of them were jostled in their tiny capsule. Nikolai managed to struggle toward the only viewing port on the escape pod, the tiny porthole Michael had looked through, and saw a green shape pass over them, getting closer.

"I think something has got us," the Colonel pointed out flatly.

"Like what," Michael replied struggling to get a better view for himself.

"I don't know, but it's pulling us in," Nikolai replied a little more concerned, all he had was a pulse pistol sidearm, fat lot of good that would do against those mechanical beasties, he hadn't had time to get fully kitted out yet.

Nikolai drew it and charged the weapon anyway, well if this was going to be the end, he would go down fighting weapon in-hand, not like some cowering whelp.

Another sharp jolt knocked him off-balance and he tumbled heavily against the side of the pod, quickly getting back to his feet and rubbing his sore arm painfully.

The side hatch was opened from outside the pod, Nikolai levelled the weapon, his finger poised over the trigger ready to fire the instant one of those things reared its mechanical head around the hatch.

He was faced instead with humans, his own people, and in full military attire. The relief surged like a wave through them both as they stepped out of the pod, and into the main cabin of a Stockholm class lander.

Nikolai immediately recognised them as E.D.F commandoes, no doubt these were the backup force destined for the Liberty he had orders to command.

"We were lucky to find you Colonel, we picked up a very weak transponder signal as we passed by. Realising that it had come from an E.D.F escape pod, we changed course to pick it up."

"Well I'm glad you did," Nikolai smiled. "The Euripedes was destroyed on-route to the depot by Cyberians."

"I know, we are part of a formation of five landers, right now we are all running on silent mode, all our emissions are cut and we are operating on total communication blackout. We are hoping to just drift past them without them noticing."

Nikolai nodded, "Good idea...err..."

"Stormont sir, Lieutenant Stormont, codename Rapier."

Nikolai nodded his understanding, "okay Rapier, now that you've picked up that pod and let us out, I suggest you cast it adrift again."

"May I ask why, sir?"

"Because if you can pick up that transponder signal from the pod, you can bet your ass they can too."

Stormont nodded, "yes sir, at once."

E.D.F Chronicles – The Cyberian menace

In order to maintain the air supply and atmospheric pressure within the tiny lander, Lieutenant Stormont accessed a nearby panel and erected a dome shaped forcefield around the pod, before opening the main cargo hatch doors again. The cargo winch slowly lowered the pod back out into space, before releasing the magnetic coupler and allowing it to drift away helplessly once more.

Stormont then retracted the winch and closed the hatch doors before shutting off the forcefield.

"Good work Lieutenant," Vargev said. "If we had of carried that thing all the way to Epsilon-zeta one, we'd be lit up like a christmas tree to them."

Although the Stockholms were ugly, Vargev thought. *They did have their uses.* These were the newer updated craft. During the latter stages of the Krenaran war it had become all too apparent that the troop division lacked the capability to transport materiel and equipment quickly from one battlefield to another, so a select few of the Stockholm class landers were refitted with cargo hatches and heavy duty winches which allowed them to lift anything from a Raider A.T.V, to a Rapier light tank. Heavier pieces, such as the Apollo main battle tanks and groundhog artillery platforms required two landers working in consort to lift. These refitted Stockholms became highly prized to commanders on the ground, the E.D.F commandoes had switched over to the type II lander completely by the end of the war as it allowed them greater flexibility in their operations.

Michael had taken a seat in a row of bench like chairs lining the cabin, full of twenty other commandoes belching, farting, playing cards, cleaning their weapons, and a myriad of other mundane distractions to pass the time. He longed to just have quiet, to give him time to reflect, to grieve. In a strange kind of way he almost wished he had never met Walters, so he wouldn't have had to watch him die like that. Was that selfish? He guessed it was - Walters, his ship and his crew had gave their lives to protect them. Jealousy, hatred, was beside the point. With an effort he pushed his dark musings to the back of his mind, now was not the time, all that mattered was the mission.

Nikolai sat down next to him, although rather cramped in the little space on the bench that they had, putting a hand on Michael's heavily slumped shoulder as if reading his thoughts.

"He died with honour, saving us."

All that Michael could say was a rather hollow, "yeah."

Aspen, Colorado.
Earth.

108

Ian J Smethurst

Kathryn Alexander had just awakened from another restless night, partly from the baby kicking inside her, and partly because her husband was not with her. She had seen the news reports on the viewer as they steadily got worse, the Cyberians were pushing deeper into E.O.C.A space, thousands were dying everyday. She wondered about the horror colonists on those far flung worlds must be going through. It seemed just a matter of time before they would land on Earth itself.

She had no clue whether her husband, the man who should be here with her was alive or dead, Kathryn was out of her mind with worry.

As she pushed the bedclothes back to get out of bed, about to pull on her nightgown in order to head into the kitchen, it happened – she could not control it, a warm wetness flooded down her thighs and pooled onto the floor beneath her, she almost thought for a moment that she had inadvertently wet herself. Incontinence was common in women in the latter stages of pregnancy, then a sharp pain lanced across her belly. No, her waters had definitely broken, and the contractions were starting.

Panic gripped her, clutching at her belly she thumbed the communications terminal in desperation.

"Which emergency service do you require?" An emotionless computer voice spoke back to her.

She mashed the ambulance key repeatedly as another contraction felt like it was tearing her insides out, she screamed in agony and began to pant in ragged breaths.

"An ambulance will be dispatched to you now."

"It had better damn well get here quick!" She shouted back to the computer as she stumbled into the bedroom and grabbed the things she had prepared for her inevitable trip to the hospital.

Although she had understood why Michael had had to go, a part of her mind screamed for him to return, to be with her in this most precious of moments.

A third contraction brought another scream of pain, beads of sweat began to line her forehead. This ambulance had better come quick she thought, because this baby is not going to wait.

Within minutes the ambulance arrived, the emergency response team rushed through the door she had opened for them. Now barely able to move due to the pain, another medic brought in a motorised wheelchair and gently pushed her out toward the waiting ambulance.

Kathryn was now blowing hard, and had an uncontrollable urge to push already. Two of the medics gently lifted her onto a stretcher, and took a look at her inside the ambulance, shaking their heads.

Kathryn saw their response, panic gripped her, *why were they nodding? Was their a problem? God-forbid.*

"She's not fully dilated yet," one of the medics shouted to another.

Relief flooded through her, at least the baby was okay so far. The doors of the ambulance slammed shut behind her, startling her a little. Seconds later the vehicle sped on its way to Briar ridge medical centre.

Jesus, I'm being wheeled into my own hospital, Kathryn thought.

The medics noticed her breathing increase, perspiration lined her brow and her hair was become increasingly matted. "How close are the contractions?" One of them asked her.

"About every four minutes," Kathryn replied between pants. "Oh god!" She screamed as another surge racked her body.

"Try to resist the urge to push for now, you're not ready yet," another of the medics said.

"Try telling him that!" she screamed at them.

"We had better radio ahead, have the delivery suite prepared for our arrival, we'll need to rush her straight through."

The other medic nodded and patched in a direct feed to the delivery suite comms. terminal so as to alert them to their coming.

"Try to relax, we'll be there soon," one of the medics tried to soothe her.

"Don't tell me to relax! If you had something the size of a bowling ball trying to rip its way out of you, you'd be pretty damn freaked out too!"

The medic stifled a chuckle, smiling warmly. It was a fake smile of course, all a part of those patient care courses and a thousand other call-outs, but at least it was warm, and it did help to calm her a little.

They pulled up outside of the centre and immediately flung the ambulance doors open, rushing her inside still on the stretcher, straight past those in the accident and emergency section, much to the chagrin of those who had been waiting.

They rushed her into a small elevator just as Kathryn began to pant in deep ragged breaths as she could feel another contraction coming on, she screamed aloud in agony, almost giving in to the all-consuming urge to push, this was the strongest one yet and they were getting closer.

Once the elevator arrived at its destination, the three medics immediately rushed her through into the waiting delivery suite. Here the room was cool and fully air-conditioned, the cool air helped Kathryn to relax a great deal.

A middle aged woman in full surgical scrubs approached her, and repeated the question the medics had asked in the ambulance.

"How far apart are the contractions?"

"About one every three minutes now," replied a bedraggled Kathryn.

She took a data navigator from a tabletop nearby and peered at her notes, "you have requested an epidural as your pain relief, do you wish to change that?"

"Ummm….no." Kathryn replied between pants.

"Good," the woman replied. "I am nurse Alexandra Cox, I am the duty midwife. I'm just going to take a little look at you and take a measurement. It might feel a little cold."

"Okay," Kathryn nodded, she was a little scared, it was her first child after all, though she felt something else also, a strange sense of complete trust in this woman whom she had never met before. It was the oddest feeling, like a sense of calm and competence and trust the woman just seemed to exude. All Kathryn could think of was; *damn she was good.*

The woman kneeled down to work between her legs, then came the pang of cold.

"Okay you are eight centimetres dilated. You're almost there, at ten centimetres you are ready to give birth."

Kathryn nodded as another contraction began to ravage her, she screamed again, panting loudly.

"I know that your body is telling you to push. But I don't want you to just yet, it's too early, can you do that for me sweetie."

"I'll try," was all that Kathryn could muster.

"Okay, I need you to roll onto your side for me, okay?"

Kathryn nodded and tried to shuffle onto her side, although pain racked her body, with the midwife's help, she managed it.

Nurse Cox was now out of her field of vision, *what was she doing?* Kathryn began to panic slightly, then the midwife moved to a position where she could see clutching the biggest transdermal injector she had ever seen in her life, the sight of it scared her half to death.

She can't be serious, Kathryn thought over the haze of agony clouding her mind.

"This will hurt just a little bit, then the pain will go away," the midwife said in her customary soft soothing voice.

She is serious, Kathryn panicked. "Err…..I want to……recon."

Too late, she felt a sharp lancing pain in her lower back like she was being skewered, then the strangest feeling began to overwhelm her. The agony, the pain she had just felt seemed to simply melt away, it felt as though she was as light as a feather, as if she could walk on the clouds.

Gently, the midwife helped her onto her back again, another contraction was coming and she groaned loudly gripping the sides of her bed, teeth gnashing in consternation.

E.D.F Chronicles – The Cyberian menace

Sweat trickled down her brow, the pain lanced across her belly once more, though with the help of the epidural she managed to resist that all encompassing urge to push for now at least. This contraction lasted longer than the others, finally she screamed out in agony before collapsing back down onto the bed again, panting loudly.

"You're doing great sweetie, almost nine centimetres now," the voice of the midwife came from between her thighs.

Kathryn puffed hard, trying to get her breath back. That last contraction had almost taken every ounce of energy she had.

"It shouldn't be too long now, the baby is engaged and is in the right position."

A sense of light relief came over her, she'd heard the horror stories of breech births and ectopic pregnancies, at least there weren't any complications so far."

A wave of depression borne of fatigue swept over her, "why me!" Kathryn wailed, as tears began falling down sweat dampened cheeks.

"Why did he have to do this to me?" Then she gave out a scream of tortured anger, "Why isn't he here!!"

The other woman understood all to well these strange mood swings, in her thirty years as a trained midwife she had seen it all before. Every woman had them, mood swings, curses, shouts and moans, she had seen women go from wailing despair to the heights of ecstasy upon that child being born. However all she could ever do in these times was to offer a gentle voice, a compassionate hand, it would all be over soon.

Kathryn gripped both sides of the bed again, threatening to break it in her throes, another contraction was coming, this one felt big already. She began panting loudly, using every last ounce of will left to resist that huge urge to push even though it was all she could think about. Her body was screaming at her but she had to hold on, had to resist one last time. The pain subsided once more into just a dull ache, though she knew it wouldn't be gone for long.

"Okay, that's it!" The midwife cried with just a hint of elation. "You're doing marvellously, you're fully dilated now, on the next contraction I want you to push really, really hard."

Kathryn could only nod, exhausted. The midwife wiped her brow with a cool damp cloth, it helped and she calmed a little; the calm before the storm.

"Thank you so much for helping me," Kathryn smiled through tear flecked eyes, she breathed "I really do appreciate everything you are doing you know."

The midwife smiled back, "we're not out of the woods yet my love, but we'll get there."

"Thank you," Kathryn repeated.

A fresh surge of pain lanced through her like a hot knife, "Oh god!" the contraction seared through her with all the force of a lance.

"Ready! Now push!!" The midwife screamed encouragement at her.

Kathryn pushed with everything she had, screaming out loud, hands wrenching against the sides of the bed, fingers going white with the strain as she bore down as hard as she possibly could.

"Push!" The midwife repeated.

She pushed with every last ounce of strength left within her, screaming and weeping with the sheer physical exertion.

"Okay, the head is clear," the midwife announced, "one last big push, and it should all be over."

She braced herself, trying to sum up any last remaining vestiges of energy she still possessed. Barely a minute later this final contraction was violently upon her, she screamed again as her stomach tightened hard, bearing down and pushing with every last ounce of strength left, gnashing her teeth so hard her gums began to bleed.

Please, please let this be the last one, she thought as she mentally cursed Michael for doing this to her in the first place.

Then with one final burst the body was clear, and Kathryn utterly exhausted simply slumped back down onto the bed, a panting mass of sweat, blood and matted hair.

The midwife gently picked up the bloodstained baby with practiced ease, before gently clamping the umbilical cord at either end, and with one neat cut, severed the cord in place of Michael.

After a couple of gentle pats on the back to awaken it, baby cries echoed out into the room as the midwife carefully washed the newborn, before wrapping it into a thick soft cotton blanket and placed it down into an incubator to keep it warm for the time being.

"Congratulations, you have a lovely baby boy," The midwife smiled as she turned to her data navigator and input the weight of the baby while it showed on a readout within the status panel on the side of the incubator, six pounds eleven ounces.

"Do you have a name for the little man?" The midwife asked.

"Oh…..err, Richard," Kathryn stammered, "Richard James Alexander," she smiled at hearing those first little cries, a new rush of excitement, joy and energy washed over her, this was her boy, her first born child and all she wanted to do was cradle the little thing in her arms for the first time.

"We're not quite there yet Kathryn, it's important you pass the afterbirth," the midwife nodded. "Imagine you are going to the toilet, and I want you to push one last time for me sweetie, can you do that?"

E.D.F Chronicles – The Cyberian menace

Party pooper, Kathryn thought with a mischievous smile. With this new wave of energy, she felt she could do anything. "Okay."

She bore down and pushed one last time, gnashing her teeth again, the sweat forming once more on her face. Straining every sinew in her neck, she felt something loosen then slide out of her, something slippery, then a wet squelch as something plopped on the floor beneath her.

The midwife bent down, inspected whatever she had deposited on the floor for a good few seconds before rising back into view again with a smile, "That's my girl, the afterbirth is complete. We'll have to take it away for testing anyway, but I don't think there should be anything to worry about."

The midwife turned toward the incubator again, at the little newborn gently sleeping within, and very carefully lifted it out of the machine.

The sudden drop in temperature startled the newborn and it began to wail, its cries once again filling the delivery room as the midwife gently lowered this tiny, fragile, delicate little miracle onto Kathryn's right breast.

"You've earned this, congratulations….you have a son."

Tears of joy flooded out of her, "thank you so much." She sniffed as she held her little man in her arms for the very first time. His crying almost immediately settled down into a contented sleep.

"Hello, you." Kathryn smiled as she looked down upon the tiny bundle of joy resting on her breast. "I'm your mother."

After watching and cradling her gorgeous new baby in her arms for a few seconds more, she turned back to the midwife who was silently watching. "I don't know how to thank you, I could never have done it without you."

The midwife simply smiled in return, "you did all the hard work, all I did was give a little helping hand. All part of the service."

Kathryn chuckled a little in delight, before cuddling little Richard close.

Nurse Cox retrieved her data navigator, turned and said, "If everything is okay, I have a little paperwork I have to attend to about the birth. I'll only be a few minutes."

"Of course," Kathryn nodded. Right now she was clutching the most important thing in the world to her. At that moment the only thing in the world to her, he really was her little bundle of joy.

Stockholm class lander flotilla.
On-route to rendezvous point.
Epsilon Zeta-one.

The landers drifted slowly for two days, although to Michael it might as well have been two years. All power except for minimal life support was cut, the communications blackout was still in effect, engine emissions were down to minimal. They crept on by, alert to any hint of Cyberian movement. If the ship which destroyed the Euripedes was still out there and they detected the landers, they were as good as dead. Michael knew a Stockholm class lander wouldn't even last beyond a single shot from a Cyberian cruiser.

A couple of shivering commandoes were playing a game of poker to pass the time. Running on minimal life support meant that the temperature inside the craft dropped significantly, the system was keeping breathable air circulating and that was about it. He watched as their hands shook from the cold as they held their cards.

"Nav point has come onto long range scanners, E.T.A at present speed is fourteen hours." One of the pilots announced over chattering teeth.

Michael knew that the sensor systems of the landers were severely limited compared to those of a full fledged naval vessel, and were only reliable up to around half an astronomical unit. So the surplus station was close, but the fourteen hour E.T.A reminded him just how slowly they were going, soon he would be reunited with his old ship again, this alone gave him some comfort at least. It would be like being re-acquainted with an old friend, he just hoped those at the surplus yard hadn't treated her too badly.

He buried his arms inside his naval officer's jacket for warmth and decided to keep on waiting out the next fourteen hours, if only he could get his damned teeth to stop chattering.

Nikolai chuckled inwardly as he watched his friend, although it did get cold up in the high mountains of Aspen where he came from, it was as nothing compared to the biting Russian winters of Volgograd that Nikolai was used to. The Russian had a greater natural resilience to the cold than Michael. And here in this frozen lander it was showing, although it was beginning to grow cold even by his usual standards.

Over the course of the next four hours, the temperature dropped again, and the occupants began to show signs of hypothermia. Nikolai searched through the emergency supply kit of the lander and picked out a small portable laser heater. A simple device that often proved invaluable in times like this, it fired a continuous stream of low powered laser energy into a sac of fire resistant gel, the gel retained the heat well and its fire retardance meant it could be used almost anywhere. The small laser pod that came with it was only good for about eight hours of use though, but at least it would keep them warm for now and didn't rely on the landers own power reserves, making them an easier target for detection.

E.D.F Chronicles – The Cyberian menace

Nikolai set the small, compact device down on the cold, hard metal plating of the landers floor, attached the laser pod and flicked on the small operate button on the top of the laser emitter itself.

Sure enough a tiny red beam of laser energy began to warm up the gel, the sac began to glow as the contents inside were heated, and began to gently bubble.

Quickly the other soldiers all huddled around it for warmth, some had already broken out emergency blankets, Nikolai and Michael also gathered around the tiny device. As the hours passed however and nothing was heard from the cockpit, Nikolai grew uneasy, eventually he could stand it no more, got up and went to check.

He could see what looked like a vast parking lot of ships through the partly frozen cockpit window approaching them. Vessels of all shapes and sizes, many broken down, half collapsed, some showed layers of decks, their internal structure open to space. Others bore the scars of weapon impacts and damage no doubt inflicted upon them during whatever engagement these once proud ships fought in. Now all dead, not a single light, navigation blinker, or any other form of illumination came from them. Nikolai felt a keen sense of loss, sadness. *This is where once great ships go to die,* he thought.

He noticed the other landers slowing as they began their final approach to the depot, his one kept on going, still drifting at the same rate as before, the others had fired their retro-thrusters to kill the excess speed, his hadn't.

Jesus we're going to crash, he thought as panic began to grip him.

He looked down, began to shake the pilots, they were unresponsive. Looking at them more closely he noticed their lips had turned a deep shade of blue, their eyes frozen open. Fingers frozen to the consoles, they resembled frozen wax mannequins.

Poor souls, Nikolai thought. In their desperation to get them all to safety, they had frozen to death at their posts.

Being as careful as he could manage, he wrenched the frozen hands off the flight console surface, breaking several of the corpses fingers in the process and laid them down next to the two pilot's chairs. Then he took over one of the seats and quickly jabbed at the reverse thruster controls as the hulk of an old Trojan class frigate loomed before them.

The lander came to a dead stop barely a metre away from the derelict ship's hull, they were so close he could actually make out the old weld lines on its panels as it filled the view in front of them, dwarfing the tiny lander utterly.

Nikolai sighed with relief, then activated the anti-grav impellers on each of its wingtips to give the small craft lift, allowing it to climb over the huge hulk.

As the craft climbed over the edge of its badly cannibalised hull, a collection of small porthole lights were just about visible in the far distance. The other landers were all heading toward it.

That must be the depot facility itself, he thought as he manoeuvred the craft to follow suit. Once they arrived the other landers all aligned themselves in a ring around the rather ramshackle central facility structure, though the others left the docking bay free for Nikolai's craft. Carefully the lander touched down in the open bay, the bay doors closing around it.

The access ramp slowly lowered and the occupants quickly fanned out eager to escape the cold confines within, accompanied by the deep thrum of the craft as it continued to power down.

A side door opened and two men approached them, one was a sharp eyed, dark haired man in a wheelchair. His eyes had a questioning, suspicious glint to them, hook nosed and hollow cheeked, undoubtedly the thinner of the two, and a little gaunt in appearance.

His associate was stockier, his features more rounded, although his gait was sluggish, plodding.

The man in the wheelchair addressed them first, "I am Mr. Cosgreene, and this is my partner Smythe, together we run this surplus depot, any questions you may have can be directed at us."

Michael stepped forward, shaking off the last of the cold, "this is a civilian depot?"

"Well done, how very observant of you." Cosgreene sneered, "all the trash the E.D.F no longer needs or uses is dumped in places like this."

"We're after a ship called the Liberty, we were told it would be here." Michael said, choosing to get straight to the point with these two.

"Oh you were, were you? Got a service number?" Cosgreene asked pointedly.

"As a matter of fact I do, FAD-193751," Michael replied, a number he knew instantly over the years of commanding her.

"Smythe go and check the records," Cosgreene asked before snapping his attention right back to Michael, "so you must be the famous Liberty captain are you?" He asked with barely concealed sarcasm.

Michael simply nodded an affirmative.

"You'll forgive me then if I don't bow and scrape to your holiness."

Nikolai wasn't sure if he liked this little guy, or was just getting on his nerves, "as soon as she is up and running again, we'll be on our way."

Cosgreene stopped eyeing Michael for a second, and instead turned his attention to Vargev, "Oh I forgot, you must be his commando bumchum as well, Colonel Vargev if I recall."

E.D.F Chronicles – The Cyberian menace

Vargev recoiled from the insult, "why you little bastard! If you weren't in that chair, I'd tear your puny little head from your shoulders!"

Cosgreene smiled, "awww does ickle me in my ickle chair bother you?" Cosgreene sneered once more. "This is a civilian station, manned by a civilian crew, your threats and your orders mean absolutely dick here."

Smythe returned through the same side door, puffing a little, "S'definitely here boss, row nine, plot fourteen."

Cosgreene turned back to face the arrayed men, eyeing Michael in particular, "well, there you go, there's your precious little ship. Now, if you'd all kindly piss off, I'd be much obliged."

The little man wheeled his way back toward the side door again, silently turning his back on them.

"I hope there is still some of her left, and not been cannibalised too much." Michael shouted after him, "if you've taken any of her major systems!"

"You'll do what exactly? If you wanted her in one piece, she shouldn't be here."

At that Cosgreene disappeared out of sight, leaving the men alone.

"Napoleon syndrome?" Vargev asked as he stared after the two men just left.

Michael shrugged, "beats me, somebody put a bee in his breakfast this morning."

The men all clambered aboard the lander, Nikolai once again made his way into the cockpit taking up the pilots position, Michael climbed into the co-pilot's seat gingerly stepping over the still frozen corpses of the former pilots.

"Well, at least we got a little warmer anyway." Michael quipped.

"Even if the reception was colder than a bare arsed baboon in Siberia," Vargev laughed.

Nikolai powered up the craft, rotating the anti-grav impellers downward, the lander gently rose, then rotating them forward, the craft began to back out of the bay. The Russian manoeuvred the small craft around and began the search for the Liberty.

"You know when Cosgreene said it was in row nine, plot fourteen?" Michael asked, looking out at the seemingly endless array of broken down ships and various junk ahead.

"Yeah," Nikolai replied, frowning at the interruption as he tried to maintain his concentration on flying the craft.

"He didn't mention at all where row nine, plot fourteen actually was, did he?"

"Errr....no." Nikolai said as he eased the controls, manoeuvring the lander past the comparatively huge inter-system boosters of a badly damaged Mandela class light cruiser.

Michael caught the name emblazoned on its aft engine section as they glided past. The Constantine, named after the ancient Roman emperor who ruled almost two thousand years ago. She looked as though she had been in a fight, riddled with blast markings, no doubt damaged beyond repair during the Krenaran war.

"I'm increasing power to the external scanners." Nikolai said, breaking Michael out of his mental history lesson and snapping him back to the present.

"Won't we be detected?"

"It's a risk we'll have to take, we need to find the Liberty somehow."

Michael nodded an agreement as Nikolai keyed in the appropriate controls. After a pause of a few seconds while he frowned at the readout on a tiny display to his right he said, "Okay, I'm picking up numerous power spikes, most small and several fluctuating, all E.D.F or human in origin. Except for one, it's Solarian."

"That must be the Liberties Solarian power core," Michael replied with a smile. "We've found her."

The lander pitched slightly to its right in order to line itself up with this power spike and began to head straight for it, the other landers all following in close formation changed course to match.

After nearly an hour of drifting through fields of scrap and broken hulls, they passed over the hull of an old mining vessel, it read Martinez mining operations co. on the side of it. Then the dark matt black and shining silver hull of the Liberty itself came into view, Michael smiled at the sight of his old ship again.

From the outside at least it looked remarkably well preserved. The fusion cannon was still there, the twin upper torpedo launchers, even the graviton shielding system.

He noticed something immediately though, port-hole lights were lit within the main bridge, someone was over there. The Liberty typically had very few port-hole lights, as light emissions tended to interrupt its stealth abilities, after all lights from port-holes could be detected. The only ones that were typically visible were the bridge lights.

"Nikolai, patch in a communication to the Liberty, I want to know who's home."

"It will break radio silence," Vargev replied.

"We'll be aboard in minutes anyway," Michael frowned.

"Okay, patching you in now, audio only."

"This is lander alpha to Liberty, please respond."

After a pause of a few seconds the slightly garbled communication came back, "lander…..this is Liberty……communications……..under repair."

So the Liberty wasn't as completely untouched as she appeared, it was to be expected, Michael thought. He just hoped her systems hadn't been affected too badly, he needed them at their best. "Liberty, open your port docking hatch to allow us to come aboard."

"…..Haa….opening."

Michael looked at Nikolai, "have they opened it?"

He checked his instruments, "sensors say they have."

"Think you can dock this thing?"

Nikolai shrugged, "Michael I am a ground soldier, landers like this are normally only used by the airborne battalions like the twenty sixth. Just flying the damn thing is hard enough for me, now you want me to dock it as well? especially with the Liberty having a contoured hull."

Michael nodded his understanding, Nikolai was a soldier not a pilot and ships with contoured hulls were notoriously difficult to dock with, that's exactly why the Liberty had one so that trying to board her was difficult. With its graviton shields raised you couldn't even teleport aboard, making the ship damn near impervious to any type of boarding action, unless of course it was someone who had already been trained to dock with the Liberty, someone like Michael.

"Okay, I'll fly her in from here." He said as he moved to swap seats with the stocky Russian, who readily accepted.

Michael was new to variable geometry propulsion craft, yet he picked up the controls pretty quickly, aided by his years of practice flying the Liberty itself, and before that Peregrine fighters at the academy. As some would say he is an 'old stick'.

The Liberties hull was sloped at exactly thirteen degrees from the vertical, meaning he would have to orient the lander at exactly the same angle in order to not collide with the hull when attempting to dock.

Keeping a very close eye on the attitude readout, he applied a tiny amount of thrust to bring the craft into alignment, then manoeuvred the lander so its starboard side hatch and the Liberties own port hatch were in perfect synchronisation.

Using just the power from the lander's port anti-grav impeller he inched the craft sideways, closing the gap between the two docking ports. The lander's small stubby wing overlaid the Liberties hull just a little, but due to the lander's exact alignment with the Liberty it didn't actually touch, casting a tiny shadow over the larger Liberties hull as it edged closer and closer. Then with a 'clunk' the two docking ports met. There was a gap of barely thirty centimetres between the top of the Liberties hull and the bottom of the lander's winglet. Michael secured the hatch then cut all power.

Nikolai was sat open mouthed, in awe of Michael's piloting ability.

"That is how you dock with an undockable ship," he smiled. "Let's go say hi."

Those in the cold main cabin were already chomping at the bit to get out onto the hopefully warmer interior of the warship and had opened the hatch doors already, clambering through onto the definitely warmer yet much darker interior of the Liberty.

Michael took a second to re-familiarise himself with his surroundings, the displays were all intact though some of the interior lights were missing, in their places bundles of bare cabling trailed out from panels that had been opened, yet so far the 'cannibalisation' had been surprisingly minor.

He sniffed at the air and smiled, although he was by definition retired now, happily married to his beloved Kathryn and finally settled, he also knew where his true home lay, and it was here, on this ship out amongst the stars.

He, Nikolai and a contingent of twenty commandoes from the lander began to search their way through the ship, passing the tiny med-bay, once Kathryn's old stomping ground. Now completely empty, bereft, stripped of every single item. It resembled the empty rooms when he first moved into his house, the beds, even the dermal regeneration booth she once used to heal Nikolai's wounds, all was gone. Michael felt a twinge of sadness, though stoically he continued on his way to the bridge.

The ship was eerily quiet, there was not the usual hubbub of officers flitting from duty station to duty station he was so accustomed to seeing when he walked this route hundreds of times as the ship's Captain.

Ultimately Michael came to the elevator stop, "main bridge," he said to the voice interface.

"Destination confirmed," came the reply.

At least this was working, Michael thought as he entered and it quickly sped him to his destination, the elevator doors opened out to what could only be described as ordered chaos, half a dozen naval officers had their heads beneath consoles or trying to repair systems that had been removed.

One man was stood in the centre of the bridge overseeing the repair effort, upon hearing Michael, Nikolai, and several commandoes enter, he turned to face them.

"Captain Michael Alexander, I am Commander Maxwell Thorne your new executive officer for this mission."

E.D.F Chronicles – The Cyberian menace

Thorne was a little older than Michael remembered, stood rigidly upright and greying slightly at the temples. He was a far cry from his former second in command Quinn Kinraid, now the Captain of the Valley-forge. Other than his tenure aboard the Eurinades Michael had only met Thorne once before, at an E.D.F tactical briefing on the Dracos just after the incident at Auriga III. A very rigid, inflexible, by the book officer, who was a little too sure of himself, Michael didn't especially like him then, and he didn't really like him now.

"I hereby transfer command of the Liberty over to you Captain."

"Thank you," Michael nodded. "I hereby receive command, what's our status?"

"We have audio and limited video capability on comms. The med-bay has been completely stripped, and Lieutenant commander Logameier is working on getting long range scanners back online, we have main power up and running and full weapons and defensive systems Captain."

"Good," Michael replied. He was expecting far worse, at least the ship was largely spaceworthy, although they would need those sensors if they were to search for that command cruiser.

Just then Lieutenant commander Logameier walked onto the bridge, "Captain! It's great to see you again!" A wide grin played across his features as he hurried toward Michael and shook his hand vigorously.

"Johnson; Johnson Logameier," Michael smiled as he was reacquainted with his former chief engineer. "How have you been doing?"

"Pretty good actually sir, I got myself a promotion, and was transferred to the Washington class E.D.F.S Richelieu after the Liberty was decommissioned. I'm glad they have given me temporary attachment to the Liberty, it's been a while sir."

"That it has Lieutenant; that it has." Michael nodded, "how long until we are fully operational again?"

"I have repair teams working to restore the cannibalised systems, it will be about two days until we have full system usage again."

Nikolai interrupted, "I can have my commandoes assist the Lieutenant commander's repair teams?"

Logameier nodded, "it would speed up the repair time significantly."

Michael smiled, "take all the men you need, I want this ship ready to depart in one day, the longer we delay the more lives are lost."

"Understood Captain," Logameier replied as he and Nikolai went off to oversee the transfer of his commandoes aboard.

Michael took one last look at the bridge, taking in its familiarity, apart from the obvious missing components it was really just like he left it. Then with a gentle smile he returned to his old ready room, quickly noticing the food synthesiser on the wall was missing, *oh we can't have this! Where will I get my latté.*

Just as he sat at his glass desk, which by the grace of God was still there, the door chime sounded.

"Enter."

Commander Thorne walked into the room, the doors closing gently behind him as he stood in his typical rigid stance directly opposite to him.

"Permission to speak freely sir?" Thorne asked, his eyes piercing, unmoving.

I've been here all of five minutes, and already he's riding my ass, "by all means Commander."

Thorne looked to relax just a little, his eyes lowered, regarding Michael. "I think it is a mistake to have the Commandoes help the repair teams, sir."

Michael raised his eyebrows at this, "really, how so?"

"The commandoes are soldiers sir, they lack the engineering knowledge of our own repair teams sir."

Michael was beginning to quickly grow tired at hearing his derisory attitude, "tell me Commander, if the commandoes need to cross a river quickly during a combat situation, how do they do it?"

"By creating a pontoon bridge, sir." Thorne replied, his eyes began to lose their steely gaze, as he realised the firm ground he thought he was standing on was beginning to shift under his feet.

"And what sort of knowledge would a person require to erect such a bridge, Commander?" Michael asked, his tone pointed, direct.

"Errrm....engineering knowledge sir," Thorne began to shuffle uneasily.

"So they do have engineering knowledge after all," Michael smiled, now confident he was winning this particular clash of wills.

"Errr....yes sir." Thorne continued to squirm.

"Commander, do you know how many people are actually dying out there for every single day we delay?" It was Michael's turn to have the steely gaze.

"No sir."

"The latest figures suggest we are losing three thousand, seven hundred people for every day this conflict continues."

Thorne took a step back, as if staggered by the scale of the bloodshed. Michael took full advantage, "do you want to explain to those three thousand, seven hundred and ten families that their sons or daughters did not return home because we left it an extra day before we set out on our mission?"

Thorne shook his head in alarm, "no sir."

"I should think not, commander. Take your station."

"yes sir, thank you sir." Thorne scurried out of Michael's quarters like a scolded dog.

"Secure that conduit now! Re-route the plasma flow through the secondary phase inhibitors, but don't overload the primary ones or they'll explode!" Mikomi Onuguchi, the Valley-forge's chief engineer barked out orders to his staff. After the battle at Sigma XI he had a litany of damaged systems and sub-systems to work through as the ship limped like a wounded beast through plasma drive.

Admiral Tolaris aboard the Aedris had helped to save the planet from the Cyberian assault although the cost had already been great. Naval reinforcements from Gamma IV, and a few already battered ships that could be spared from the dreadful fighting around Eidolon had just about managed to allow the Valley-forge to make the jump into plasma drive heading for Charlie base in order to get the repairs it badly needed.

The ship had been hit three times in three different sections, the worst was the damage it received to deck twenty six, the forward section of that deck was one of several that housed the main fighter bays. Support crew, technicians, and standby pilots were all present in that section at the time, thirty men had died from exposure from just that single hit.

Luckily the commander flight group, D'mitry Anatoly was monitoring flight operations from the bridge at the time. Onuguchi felt a noticeable pang of sadness, mixed with pride at the flight group's efforts. Despite being almost completely wiped out, they did so defending their ship, sacrificing themselves so that the Valley-forge itself did not suffer a worse fate.

His wrist comm. chimed and not for the first time today, "Commander, report. How are th' repairs coming?" Kinraid asked in his typical deep Irish twang.

"Slowly sir, we took a heck of a beating, we're still limited to plasma factor two right now as the primary phase inhibitors were damaged. If we get a phase variance in the plasma flow through those inhibitors, even a small one, and that variance travels back to either number one or number two plasma cores, then we could blow the ship sky high."

"I understand, when is th' earliest we could get full speed again?"

"I have engineering teams working round the clock as we speak, although I would have to say it would be another five hours at the earliest."

That worried Kinraid, they were operating alone out here without cover, and having to travel very slowly to boot. All of which made them a very tempting target for any Cyberian cruiser that happened to chance upon them. That's why he maintained a full alert status, for the time being at least.

Ian J Smethurst

It was times like this, Kinraid thought. *That really brings it home how challenging being in command could be, men fighting and dying with but a single word, and ultimately their deaths were on your conscience, because they had died following your orders.*

Already he knew he would hate having to write out killed in action reports, before sending them off to their next of kins. These would be the first K.I.A reports he would have to write during his command.

His former superior officer, friend, and mentor Michael Alexander had often said to him filling in those reports never got any easier no matter how many years you spent in that chair. These were your colleagues, friends, and in a way a second family dying for *you*, their Captain. Then you had to inform their parents, wives and husbands exactly how they died. It was one of the hardest rigours of command.

Kinraid did not relish the task one bit.

Looking over the bridge, much of the debris littering the floor had been cleared, though the damage was all too evident, blackened scorched hollows where terminals had been, a great dark wound where the bridge perimeter wall met the roof, the remains of the conduit which had ruptured spectacularly in a violent spray of white hot metal, fire and sparks.

Over the next few hours Quinn Kinraid dared not leave the bridge, he kept the ship at maximum readiness while they crept through plasma drive alert to the slightest hint of a Cyberian attack, especially since they were travelling dangerously close to the frontier worlds – the front line in this bitter war.

Nothing has shown up on sensors, which was one good thing he supposed. Cyberian ships in particular had a huge sensor echo, partly due to their enormous size and the materials they were made up of, they reflected sensor telemetry very easily. Though being damned near impervious to all but the biggest guns they could throw at them, he guessed they didn't really care what kind of sensor echo they put out.

His wrist comm. interrupted his thoughts, "Onuguchi to bridge, we have full plasma drive ability again."

That man is a miracle worker, "Well done Mr. Onuguchi!" Kinraid immediately straightened in his seat, overjoyed. *Now they could get things done* he grinned.

"Lieutenant Jansen," he turned his attention to the young blonde haired woman manning the navigation console. "Maximum plasma drive, now!"

"Yes, sir!" Jansen replied enthusiastically, returning the smile.

The ship suddenly leapt into its maximum speed of plasma factor five.

"What's our new E.T.A to Charlie base, Lieutenant?" Kinraid asked, now that he had full speed available again the last thing he wanted was to dawdle in open space without any kind of fleet cover.

"Three days, fourteen hours sir," She replied.

Well, three days is a long time Kinraid thought, *but better than almost a fortnight at plasma factor two. It'll give Onuguchi time to continue his repairs as well, let's just hope we don't run into any trouble on the way.*

Commander Anizeres's voice then broke through the usual comings and goings of the bridge staff, "Captain I have a secure transmission for you, its origin is Alpha base."

"I'll take it in my quarters," Quinn replied.

It will give me time to get my ass out of that chair, it was starting to get numb anyway. He made his way across the bridge to his private quarters. The doors slid open as he entered, striding across the room he adopted a half standing, half leaning stance on his black polished desk.

"Authorisation Kinraid Alpha Omega one one five, decode and transmit."

The face of Admiral Montrose appeared on the small viewer, time-stamped three days ago. *We're a long way from Alpha base, so the message had to have been transmitted via microwave data carrier, bounced from various bases until it got here. Looks like this ones been doing the rounds,* Quinn thought.

"Play."

"Captain Kinraid, as you are no doubt made aware, we are operating on the possibility that a Cyberian command ship is operating out there somewhere transmitting orders to the other ships, just like a giant server for a network of computers. The Liberty is being brought out of retirement and tasked with locating this command ship, although we are also operating on the very real assumption that this ship will be extremely heavily armed and armoured. The Valley-forge has the most powerful fusion based weaponry we possess. Your orders are, once you have received a signal from the Liberty, to head immediately to the co-ordinates sent by the Liberty and to engage and destroy this threat. Use whatever means are at your disposal. These orders take precedence over any other orders you may have, Montrose out."

Kinraid sat back in his chair, slightly taken aback and rubbing his chin thoughtfully. *If the Liberty has been brought out of retirement, that can mean only one thing. Michael Alexander has been brought out of retirement as well.* The thought filled him with excitement, the Liberty and the Valley-forge fighting side-by-side, he hoped his ship would be ready.

The remaining three day journey to Charlie base went uneventfully, fortunately for the Valley-forge as they were still in no condition to put up much of a fight. The ship announced its presence into normal space in typically loud fashion, a gigantic burst of raw plasma energy as it exited the plasma wake. A ship the sheer size of the Valley-forge always made an impact when it came out of F.T.L travel.

"Okay Jansen, take her in carefully, remember we don't have a lot of room to manoeuvre." Kinraid said looking at her.

"Aye sir, powering up inter-system boosters one quarter power, port and starboard thrusters at my command," she nodded as she focused on the controls in front of her.

The huge block of six different ion engines all lit up in unison a pale blue colour, as power was gently shunted to them.

Carefully, Lieutenant Jansen slowly coerced the mammoth three thousand metre long battleship into one of the six main repair bays of the immense orbital shipyards of Charlie base. Even the giant bays of this mighty installation were only just able to accommodate a ship of such size and majesty as the Valley-forge.

Dozens of inspection lights lit up along the walls as the ship inched its way further inside, people aboard crowded the docking bays and observation booths, struggling to get a glimpse at the huge flagship of the E.D.F, nearly all of them gasped as the inspection lights lit up the damage the ship had taken, like wounds inflicted upon some great beast.

The main docking arm extended outward from the tapered semi-circular prow of the ship, gently connecting with the berthing pod of the bay itself, looking for all the world like a tiny insignificant twig.

"Excellent job Lieutenant," Kinraid smiled.

"Thank you sir," Jansen replied breathing a sigh of relief, manoeuvring such a large and unwieldy ship as this into dock was one of the ultimate tests of a pilot's skill, especially with a ship the size of the Valley-forge there was absolutely no room for error. Literally half a metre remained on either side of the port and starboard laser cannon barrels, the widest point of the ship.

"Secure all stations for docking," Kinraid announced as he made for the elevator, "I'm going t' pay the base commander a visit."

The base commander was, of course, General Georgianos Kalidis. Kinraid had met him before, and found him to be a competent if slightly average commander, although his saving grace was his engineering knowledge, Kalidis was one of the finest engineers in the entire E.D.F hence why he was in charge of the place. Nikolai Vargev though had a different opinion of the man, he hated him, labelling him a coward and very nearly a traitor. Kinraid himself never did quite understand the Colonel's dislike of the man.

As far as he was aware his team worked miracles getting the Liberty repaired enough to go after the Krenaran agent Lathiel a decade ago. Without his help the Liberty would never have cleared orbit, and therefore could not have prevented the assassination attempt on the then president, James Rushfeldt. So in his mind Kinraid had nothing but praise for the man.

Eventually he made it through the labyrinthine corridors and sub-sections of the ship, and through the inter-connecting berthing corridor where the figure of Kalidis stood expectantly waiting flanked by half a dozen of his top engineers.

"Captain Kinraid," he smiled as though one smiling through gritted teeth. "It didn't take you long to break the pride of the fleet did it?"

The Captain handed Kalidis a data navigator containing a full list of the damaged and under repair systems on board. The list was truly impressive, Kalidis perused it thoughtfully, taking his time, making Kinraid stand there like some naughty schoolboy, something the General enjoyed immensely.

"You lost every single one of your fighter cover?"

Kinraid nodded, "If I may General, I don't think you realise just how ferocious the fighting was out there, we were vastly outgunned and outnumbered, we were overwhelmed. If the Solarian fleet hadn't intervened at the last minute we would have lost Sigma XI.

"All excuses Captain," Kalidis retorted not taking his eyes off the list, not even regarding him.

Quinn decided to let the matter drop, Kalidis was just an engineer anyway, what did he know about actual ship combat.

"Command has informed me that they will need the ship repaired and fully re-equipped quickly as you're to head up a task force to engage this command ship, wherever it is. Looking at this you are looking at a minimum of three days repair time, and that's pulling extra shifts, I'll have to take men off repairing other ships to assist. You've given us a heck of a headache here Captain."

Kinraid felt his ire begin to raise and felt like saying – well sorry to interrupt 'your' delicate schedule, but there's a fecking war on!

Instead he simply bit his lip and slowly let the matter drop, although he now realised that Nikolai was right, Kalidis was an asshole.

During the course of the next few days as the repairs went on, the engineering teams of the Valley-forge assisted those sent by Kalidis in the rush to get the ship back to full strength again. Two new wings of Peregrine fighters were added, together with their accompanying pilots from the eighty second and eighty eighth tactical fighter wings.

Everywhere men scrambled to re-attach severed or damaged power couplings, reinforce bulkheads, repair drones operated from within the station scuttled along the ships giant titanium alloy outer hull like tiny metallic spiders, re-sealing the immense melted holes in the Valley-forges hull, all of which was overseen by both Kinraid and Kalidis.

As the work went on, both Solarian ships and E.D.F vessels not already fighting in the front lines began to arrive. The taskforce was forming, including the Faeriath itself, the repairs to the battered vessel largely complete.

Kinraid had never met Televis, his immediate predecessor during his time on the Liberty, although he had heard about him. Michael had spoken often about the former Solarian commander. Kinraid watched with a sense of pride as ships came from far and wide, from half a galaxy away heeding the call to arms.

E.D.F.S Liberty
On-route to Charlie base, Gamma IV.

Exactly as Michael had ordered, the repairs to the Liberty had taken just over a day to complete, and now they were two days into the journey to Charlie base. During that day Michael had learned a great deal of how cannibalised parts of many of the ships lying at the Epsilon-zero one surplus station were used. Logameier had told him that civilian craft were often bought, repaired, and then pressed into service as small freighters or transports for small emerging businesses that lacked the necessary capital to buy newer more expensive craft.

Likewise, some of the systems aboard E.D.F craft were re-used in civilian projects, both legal and illegal. For example the crew quarters block on a Trojan class destroyer would make a good habitation block on another world, or a small hospital, as well as a temporary hideout for would be pirates. Some of the power cores used on ships were also capable, with some modification, of also being used to replace an ageing or failing power supply on a colony world somewhere giving light and power to peoples homes, it was a noble purpose, and it felt right. After all why shouldn't parts of ships that had passed their prime go back to help those communities that had helped to build them in the first place.

After hearing nearly two hours worth of Logameiers sermons on the subject, Michael had very nearly gone from being a true and loyal friend of his chief engineer to nearly throwing him out the nearest access port. He also knew that Cosgreene and Smythe didn't really care about any of that, they simply cared about one thing – getting the money for whatever clandestine uses these 'parts' were being used for.

In a way that realisation had both pleased and angered him in equal measure, as those parts were being used to help the less fortunate in society that indeed felt right, it felt good. Although Cosgreene's unsympathetic and unwilling view to see anything other than how many credits he could make from these unfortunates gave him a nasty taste in his mouth. It painted Cosgreene as a miserly, lecherous kind of man. Which of course he was, however due to his status as a civilian and not a member of an E.D.F organisation, meant that Michael could not touch him.

It would be another ten days before the Liberty reached Gamma IV, a place he knew well, as he had also been there before, commanding this ship during the great battle against the Krenarans, it had damned near killed him too. He remembered the time when he and Nikolai fought against that giant Krenaran brute Alax, his sheer size and power was terrifying to behold. In a way he was glad these Cyberians were smaller, more fragile, though being a completely mechanoid race, they were likely just as physically strong as Alax once was. Not to mention the Cyberians ability to swarm over a target like a plague of locusts, and the devastating effects of their weaponry made them extremely dangerous opponents, that's why the Krenarans could not defeat them, and also why the E.D.F and the Solarians are struggling against them.

Still, the next ten days at least gave Logameier the chance to iron out many of the problems caused by stripping some of the Liberties systems, and since the Liberties former pilot, and the best pilot he had ever known; Eldathar was away fighting with the Solarian fleet. The only other person who had any real flight experience with the Liberties rather unique flight systems was himself. And so far during this mission, he had to fulfill the roles of both pilot and commanding officer.

As the days drew on, he took turns between resting and piloting, putting the ship onto auto-navigate and informing Ensign Mc'arthur to notify him if anything unusual happened.

Ensign Mc'arthur was studying for command officer certification, a kind of competency based test that all crewmembers must take before becoming a fully fledged bridge officer. It was a requirement right across the navy, thus to gain experience he placed Mc'arthur in command of the relief shift, otherwise known as the second watch.

Unfortunately the young Ensign would not get his wish of leading the ship into battle, as the journey was a relatively uneventful one, much to his dismay.

Michael advised him to be careful what he wished for, for those who had seen true battle, real bloodshed being spilled, and the true horror of all-out war, would not wish for it again.

During that temporary lull, the calm before the inevitable storm, Michael's thoughts strayed back to his wife Kathryn. How he missed her, wished he could be there now with her. He dearly hoped she hadn't given birth without him, missing the birth of his second child would be devastating, especially since the first had been killed in the Krenaran war along with his first wife Jana. Two innocent lives snuffed out at a stroke from a single torpedo hit.

Though he had to admit he had always felt an attraction to Kathryn from the moment she came aboard the Liberty, part of the reason why he hadn't done anything about it for such a long time wasn't just down to the fact that he was in command, and totally against regulations for a Captain to pursue a relationship with a crewmember under his command. He was also scared, when the news came of the deaths of Jana and their five year old son Theo, it had shaken him so badly, right down to the very core of his being that in his mind he just could not take the risk of something similar ever happening again, so he made himself unobtainable.

Kathryn was the only woman since then to have broken through that emotional armour he had built around himself, and that was why he had eventually gave into his feelings and allowed himself to fall in love again.

Now it was almost like history was repeating itself, a new nightmare was fast approaching and it threatened to destroy everything he held dear all over again, his love, his happiness. Except that this time he had a chance to stop it before it ever came close to Kathryn and his unborn child, and come hell or high water he was going to take that chance. The Cyberians would not repeat what the Krenarans once did, he would see to that. They would be destroyed before they ever came anywhere near Earth.

After another eight days of travelling at maximum plasma drive, the sensory readout showed they were approaching the Gamma system, Michael dropped the ship out of plasma drive about half a million kilometres away from Gamma IV and proceeded the rest of the way at sub-light speed.

"Captain," Thorne exclaimed. "I'm reading a conglomeration of ships, thirty E.D.F vessels of various classes, five Krenaran, and another thirty Solarian. Sixty five ships altogether, and except for the Solarians and the Krenarans not a single battleship amongst them."

"We'll need every single one of them if we're to succeed," Michael replied staring at the viewscreen.

"Incoming transmission Captain, it's from the Valley-forge," Thorne said as he turned back to his console.

Quinn, Michael thought. "Put it on viewer."

Instantly the image of the arrayed ships changed to the familiar face of Quinn Kinraid, the new commanding officer of that mammoth battleship and Michael's personal friend, a man that he had not seen in over three years.

"Captain Michael Alexander, so they finally thrown you back out into space again."

"Kicking and screaming Quinn, believe me." Michael smiled.

"Well they've got a bloody nerve is all I can say, leaving such a vital mission to a pipsqueak like the Liberty." Quinn smiled in jest.

"We might be a pipsqueak compared to you, but the speed and manoeuvrability of the Liberty can still run rings around you at sub-light speed, and our weapons are powerful enough to cause you some real damage. We can also outrun you at plasma drive as well."

Kinraid nodded in agreement, "that is true of course."

"How are you settling in over there?"

"Truth be told Captain, commanding such a large ship with a crew as big as the Valley-forge's is bloody hard work. In a way I miss the sense of family of a small ship like the Liberty, with a crew of just forty one men all depending on each other for their survival, there is a closeness there which the Valley-forge tends to lack. We have one thousand seven hundred men aboard, I can go weeks without ever seeing some of them at all."

"You'll get used to it, command of a large battleship is a completely different thing to commanding a small destroyer, or a fast attack ship like the Liberty."

"Let's just hope you can find this ship, then us lot can charge in and blow it out of the stars; Kinraid out."

Michael smiled, *here's hoping.*

"Setting new course, bearing zero-eight-five degrees, elevation zero; plasma factor four."

The Liberty shot once more into plasma drive, leaving the giant build up of ships, and Charlie base itself far behind.

Michael plotted a simple straight course along the outermost periphery of the Cyberian attack wave, common sense told him that a ship of such importance to the Cyberians would almost certainly not be risked in the front lines. Instead it would likely be directing things from a distance, following behind the Cyberian advance.

"Set external sensors to maximum resolution, continuous scans, I want to know the instant we pick anything up. Also have all stealth countermeasures set to maximum, we do not want to be detected by these guys."

"Understood," Thorne nodded, "Sir, what will we do if we are detected?"

"Well, we cannot hang in a fight with those things because we'll be spare parts before we even know what hit us, but we *can* outmanoeuvre them, so our best bet is simply to run and hide, cut all power and wait for them to pass us by."

"I understand, it's a little risky though."

"Risky I agree," Michael fixed him with a stern gaze. "This is war Commander, there is always risk. And it's certainly less risky than trying to slug it out with one of those things and be blown back to the stone age. We'll leave the fighting to the Valley-forge and the fleet."

Thorne nodded his understanding and turned back to working furiously at his console, increasing sensors to their maximum settings, and raising the stealth systems to their highest readiness. The power output curve was more noticeable, and if they were detected they would have to cut all power and just drift. Making it very easy for an enemy to pick them up, *but as in all things Michael had an answer,* Thorne thought sarcastically. Except this time he very much doubted he did. *This great Commander, most decorated serving officer in the fleet, was not so great after all, at least not to me.*

They cruised through plasma drive at just over half what the ship was capable of achieving, Michael wanted a slow voyage so as to give the sensors time to pick up even the faintest trace. If they went barrelling along at plasma factor seven, they would already have shot past it before the sensors even had a chance to work out what it was they detected. Michael knew this all too well, the impatient Maxwell Thorne didn't however, and used it as just another excuse to butt-horns with him.

"Captain, if we are travelling along at such a slow rate, surely that raises the death rate on other worlds, as you said yourself any delay costs lives and also allows the Cyberian ships to detect us that much easier."

Michael turned to face him, his tone hard as steel. "You are correct on both counts Commander Thorne, however in order to get the best possible reading from the sensors, we have to travel at a lower speed."

Thorne once again turned away, his mood darkening, he busied himself checking over the constant deluge of sensor data cascading down his display.

Down in the main cargo hold Nikolai was busy briefing his men, with the amount of commandoes aboard it was a tight squeeze to fit them all into the bay, the largest open space on the ship.

"Okay, intel says the Cyberians are fast, very strong, and carry matter convertor weapons similar in function to that used on their ships, just in a hand portable version. They tend to fire a pulse of energy rather than a direct beam, although if that pulse hits any of us, we will be toast instantly. We've seen the effects these weapons have on men and women, and I don't want to be reduced to a pair of smoky boots today, that is not what I came out of retirement for comrades."

"But Colonel, they have the most sophisticated weaponry, they're tougher than us, and they have the numbers to back them up, how can we hope to prevail against such an enemy?"

Several other commandoes muttered their own misgivings in a wave of unrest that seemed to float across the room.

"Settledown!" Vargev shouted over the din.

In an instant a respectful hush fell over the room.

"What's your name soldier?" Vargev asked the commando who had questioned him.

"Weasel, sir."

Vargev smiled, nodding just slightly. "Weasel, that's a good name, the name of a ferocious animal when in combat."

"Yes sir," the commando smiled.

"Let me tell you something Weasel, nobody is tougher than an E.D.F commando; anywhere. Anyone that says otherwise is a liar, we fought Krenarans and won, we fought Dracos and won, and we'll fight these assholes and win too; you hear me soldier!"

"Sir, yes sir!" came the resounding reply.

"Damn right, okay with that out of the way, here are our advantages and how we are going to use them." He looked over the arrayed men making sure their focus was on him. "The Cyberians attack in a swarm, using their numbers to literally roll over their enemies. So we'll form a bottleneck, contain them so they cannot bring their numbers to bear. We'll have disciplined fire teams, if the front rank needs to reload, the second rank steps forward to take their place, maintaining our rate of fire throughout the engagement."

"What about armour, we'll need protection against their weapons?" Another commando spoke up.

"Armour will not help us in this situation, it'll just slow us down, besides if we do get hit no amount of armour will protect us anyway. Their weapons work by converting matter into energy, literally anything it touches, that's including your armour. It's why you get the scorch marks on the sides of buildings and on the ground, it's the energy earthing itself."

The commandoes all silently nodded their understanding.

"I want all men to carry grenades, there will be designated grenade launchers and several fire teams carrying slingshots loaded with armour piercing missiles. I have requested that all men be equipped with E.M.P flash grenades. Being a mechanical race, they will be vulnerable to electro-magnetic bursts; good hunting!"

"Ooragh!" came the familiar roar in return.

For three days the Liberty continued on course without detecting so much as a fragment to indicate any presence of this so called command ship. Come the fourth day, things took a turn for the worse.

"Captain I'm reading something closing on our position, its hull configuration matches that of a Cyberian cruiser."

Well, it took them long enough, Michael thought while studying his sensor map displayed on the screen in-front of his pilot's chair, noticing that an uninhabited system by the name of Prenumbria was less than a light year away. By the looks of it, it had three large gas giants in which to hide in as well.

"I'm changing course, bearing zero-three-five degrees, elevation forty."

The Liberty instantly switched from one plasma tunnel and entered a new one.

"It doesn't seem to be on an intercept course," Thorne replied studying the sensor readouts closely. "It looks like our plasma trail has piqued its curiosity, but our stealth systems have it confused."

"Probably wondering why there is a plasma trail passing by with nothing in it," Michael replied.

"Could be."

"I'm dropping us out of plasma drive and plotting a direct course to Prenumbria VI," Michael said.

Out of the three gas giants Prenumbria VI was the densest, with large polar regions, the interference from the planets magnetosphere should help to shield the ship from their scanners, he just hoped the Liberties hull would stand up to the pressure.

"We're entering the outer layer," Michael announced.

The Liberty descended into a seething mass of deep blue helium and argon gas, cavorting and swirling around its black hull as it sunk deeper into the gas giant.

"Cyberian ship has come out of plasma drive, it'll approach the planet in exactly one minute thirty four seconds at its current speed." Thorne announced.

They're pretty quick too for their size. Michael thought as he carefully manoeuvred the ship into the upper polar region of the planet.

"Cut all power now, except for minimal sensors and the stealth systems."

"Cutting power," Thorne repeated.

The bridge lights went dark, the brilliant electric blue of the indented thrusters on the port and starboard side of the ship flickered out, as did the main Ion engine. The Liberty sat motionless, not daring to move. Even the environmental systems were cut, the whole crew barely breathed as that giant Cyberian cruiser came closer and closer to the planet.

The Liberty was rocked slightly, people were jostled gently in their seats.

"Wha…what the heck was that?" Thorne whispered.

"Just a little turbulence caused by the gases swirling around us, it's okay." Michael whispered back, "just keep your eyes peeled on that ship."

The cruiser seemed to hang in orbit of the planet for several minutes, Michael hoped against hope that it wouldn't detect them.

A flash of inspiration suddenly came to him, turning to Thorne he asked, "Commander, any chance we can initiate a direct link through this interference, to the central computer core on that ship?"

"We can give it a shot, compatibility will be difficult though, it will be like a Japanese man speaking to an American and expecting them to understand one another."

"Try your best, we only have a few more minutes at most."

Thorne typed furiously at his console, eyes straining to see the information sprawling across his screen.

After some more typing, Thorne finally said, "okay we've broken through their data encryption. We're in, but we've triggered a safeguard, we only have a few more seconds before we are locked out of the system."

"Download everything you can from their comm. chatter, we'll go through it later."

"Downloading," Thorne replied.

There was a tense pause for just a few seconds more before Thorne let out a loud sigh, "that's it, I've been locked out of the system, the link's been severed."

"How much did you get?" Michael asked.

"I managed to download three terabytes worth of information, not much." Thorne said with a hint of defeat to his voice.

"It's a start."

Thorne quickly turned back to his screen, noticing his console suddenly coming alive with data and flashing alerts, "Uh-oh, we've certainly attracted their attention now, I'm reading power increases right across the board, looks like they are readying weapons."

"Well," Michael shrugged, "I guess hiding is out of the question, ready our weapons too, raise graviton shields, full power to the main fusion cannon and torpedoes. Maximum power to engines and thrusters, we'll only get one chance."

"Main power coming back online, graviton shields are active and fusion cannon is powering up," Thorne replied.

Michael had a plan, he was going to hit their main sublight engines, hopefully take them out and let the gravity of Prenumbria VI do the rest for him, pulling the other ship down to its eventual destruction.

"Captain, I'm reading something odd over here, the Cyberian ships weapons are powered and they are trying to fire their weapons, but the strength of the beam is being weakened by the planet itself, its not just not strong enough to hit us."

Michael contemplated this for a moment, then the answer hit him like a sledgehammer, *of course! The gases that were swirling all around them were still matter, even if it is in a gaseous form. The gases must be dissipating the beam, even a Cyberian cruiser cannot change all the matter of a gas giant into energy, so the beam gradually weakens so much it disperses.*

"I'm altering our course, keeping us at the same altitude, but I'm moving to a new location within the polar region, I want to come at them from a different angle, one they won't expect."

The Liberty deftly spun around and glided a few kilometres further within the region. A move that Michael hoped would totally confuse their targeting sensors with all the magnetic interference around. No doubt they had locked a fix on their position from triangulating the data-link back to its source.

Now that the Liberty had moved, it would have to try all over again to get another fix on its location, and this time they had no data-link to triangulate back to. The Liberty however still knew where the Cyberian ship was in relation to itself, as the cruiser had stopped motionless above the planet trying to ascertain just where the tiny E.D.F ship was.

Michael had all the time in the world to complete his plan, as he gently pitched the nose upward so that it was now lined up perfectly for its charge.

"Fusion cannon's at full power," Logameier announced.

Michael offered a silent prayer, between thin pressed lips he whispered, "upon the shoulders of giants I stand, on the wings of a bird I soar......now!"

The Liberty shot forward at maximum speed, its thrusters glowing intensely as the gasses swirled about its hull, like a dart through smoke it shot through the outer layer of Prenumbria VI, gradually the Cyberian craft and the stars beyond became visible.

"Fire!" Michael shouted.

The fusion cannon roared its anger, the incandescent blue beam of destruction raced forth, smashing into the Cyberian craft's primary sub-light drive, blasting it wide open in a torrent of flame and shattered debris. The enemy ship desperately tried to get a lock onto it in the brief half-second it was afforded, but to no avail, by the time the enemy craft's weapons had begun to discharge the Liberty had already shot straight past it.

Secondary explosions began to rip through the cruisers devastated engines as the planet's gravity began to inexorably pull the ship down toward it, with its main drive destroyed it futilely attempted to maintain altitude through its thrusters, though the gravity pull was simply too strong. It could not jump into plasma drive to escape either, as it lacked the forward velocity needed to open a stable plasma wake.

The giant craft was doomed, reduced to a slow tortuous descent into oblivion, where eventually the enormous pressure deeper within the gas giant would crush it like a tin can. As it descended it began to turn as if looking up at the Liberty which had by now turned around ready to deal a killer blow with its fusion cannon if necessary. Michael watched the giant craft slowly die, and if any ship he had ever known had hate filled eyes it was that one. It was as though the craft stared up at them, unblinking, uncaring just utterly consumed by hate, hate for the living.

It sent a noticeable chill up his spine.

The pressure began to overcome it, and the Cyberian craft began to slowly buckle and break apart, even armour as thick as this could not withstand gravity itself, and inevitably the craft tore itself apart looking like tiny metallic speckles lost in the depths of an ocean of gas.

"Upon the wings of a bird I soar," Michael repeated more for comfort than anything else as the Liberty spun back around, and leapt into plasma drive to resume its search.

Now safely travelling through the plasma wake Thorne was checking over the communications intercepted between the various Cyberian ships they had managed to download, it wasn't much, but at least it might give them a hint.

"Captain, I'm looking through these messages, and it's like a series of Chinese whispers passed from ship-to-ship, every vessel, drone and soldier is connected to another via data-links, forming one enormous network, that's how they get their instructions. I've been cross-referencing them, and I think I might have found something."

"What is it?" Michael asked from the pilot's chair.

"Well, time and time again one place is showing up in the encoding, Ralchas III."

Michael frowned, he was unfamiliar with the system, "bring it up on a starchart on the main viewer."

The swirling tunnel through space was instead replaced by a shimmering holographic representation of the galaxy, before zooming in and highlighting E.O.C.A territory, displaying a series of squares that showed the various individual sectors. A crosshairs was shown over a tiny system right on the border between the Connaught and Molrav sectors.

"Doesn't seem that important a system, it comes up as lifeless, uninhabited." Thorne mused.

"If you wanted to hide a ship of such importance, and still keep it close enough to remain in contact, what would you choose?" Michael asked.

"Somewhere quiet, out of the way." Thorne smiled suddenly realising, "where nobody would look."

"Exactly, this might be just the place we are looking for, we just need to follow the trail of breadcrumbs." Michael smiled.

"Breadcrumbs?" Thorne asked not really understanding the reference.

"We've stumbled upon a big clue commander, the encoding on those messages all leads back to one place, Ralchas III. Like a trail of breadcrumbs for us to follow."

"Should I notify the fleet sir?"

Michael shook his head, "not yet, it could still be a trap, better to confirm it ourselves first. I'm altering course, bearing one-five-seven, elevation fourteen; destination Ralchas III."

The Liberty swiftly glided out of one plasma tunnel, and entered a completely new one.

"E.T.A approximately seventeen hours," Michael informed the crew. He was trying not to let the excitement of this sudden revelation get to him, but even he had to admit it was pretty hard not to. They might have finally located the one ship that could end all of this.

"Sir, what do we do if we do find something there?" Logameier asked.

"If it's the ship we're looking for – we report its position to the fleet and either hide, or run like hell," Michael grinned.

13. The great battle for E.O.C.A

The Liberty pressed on, following the coded messages it had intercepted, Michael hoped that the encoding was genuine and they weren't being fed disinformation in order to lure them into some kind of trap.

Wait, that's more like organic thinking, he mused. *We are dealing with a machine intelligence here, so the likelihood is that the encoding is actually genuine.*

That at least filled him with some hope, as otherwise at best they would have to abandon the search, and at worst could be blasted into space dust. Neither proposition seemed particularly appealing.

He also hoped that if this ship was detected, the fleet would hurry up and join them, he doubted that that command ship would be alone. One Cyberian cruiser they might be able to deal with, but not two or three, and God knows what weaponry the command ship itself was carrying.

He had sent the order down to the main cargo hold for Nikolai to ready his men, they were all suited up in environment suits ready to storm that ship if need be.

The hours ticked by, the tension grew, the entire crew could feel it, this was their moment it was time to step up or die trying.

"Approaching Ralchas III," Michael's voice cut through the tension like a knife, they would all know whether they were right or not very soon.

A flash of bright light heralded the Liberty dropping out of plasma drive into the midst of the system.

"Anything?" Michael asked.

"Sensors aren't picking up anything yet," Thorne replied as he studied the real-time data flowing like a waterfall through his screen.

Michael sighed, downcast. So it was just a wild goose chase after all, he had been wrong. Ralchas III was only a small system, just three planets circled a small young yellow sun, one of which was a runaway greenhouse planet far too hot to sustain life, and the other two were gas giants, the furthest had a ring system and was comprised of frozen carbon dioxide crystals and ammonium hydroxide gas. It was first discovered by an explorator mission some fifteen years ago, and was passed by pretty quickly.

"You mean there's nothing, no plasma decay, ionisation from sub-light engines, anything whatsoever to assume a ship passed by here recently?"

"Not a peep Captain, the whole system is as barren as a whores bare arse in a leper colony," Thorne replied.

The entirety of the bridge staff chuckled at that, it reminded Michael of something that Kinraid would have come out with. He wondered that even though Kinraid was now commanding that other ship that perhaps he did leave something behind after all. Nevertheless he appreciated the Commanders attempts to ease the tension that was still lying thick in the room.

"Maybe they left?" Logameier offered.

"Unlikely, if they did there would be some trace, plasma residue left over from a decayed plasma drive jump or something," Michael replied. "It doesn't make sense, all the communiqués point to this one system."

"It could be a ruse, trying to lure us away," Thorne ventured.

Michael frowned, thinking hard. *Something wasn't right here he could feel it in his gut, they were missing something. Could they be that sophisticated tactically? Able to plan out foils and countermeasures in order to lure ships away? He doubted it, not with a machine intelligence, they don't usually play guessing games. They were far too direct in their approach for that."*

"Wait a minute," he whispered, more to himself than anyone else. "What if they were doing the exact same thing the Liberty did to mask itself at Prenumbria VI, using the magnetic interferences of one of the gas giants to hide itself from our sensors?"

"Commander, increase the gain on the magnetic spectrometers to filter out any magnetic interference caused by the polar regions of those gas giants and re-scan. Tell me what you see."

"Understood," Thorne replied as he busied himself working the controls, it took a short while for all the interference to clear, then. "I'm picking up nothing above the third planet, holy! Wait a second, there's still a fair bit of interference but I'm sure I've got three targets located above the second planet. My God one of them is huge, it's at least twice the size of the nearby cruisers."

"Put it on the viewer," Michael replied.

The image was hazy and hard to make out, but there it was. The whole crew gasped at the magnitude of the ship looming on the screen, more like a mobile battlestation than a ship. The mid-section was flat like the other cruisers, though much larger. It boasted the same weapon configuration of four matter convertors at the front, except there were two raised sections with the same plethora of communications antennae looking like some parody of fur growing upon it. There were two bulbous pods, one on each side of the ship, each one at least the size of a Cyberian cruiser itself, these two pods contained two more matter convertors each, as well as a swathe of more antennae. The whole thing dwarfed the cruisers accompanying it, and they were not exactly small either, each comparable in size to a Danitza class battleship.

"Sweet Jesus," Michael gasped, "I think we are going to need more ships."

"Errm, Captain. I think they know we have detected them," Thorne said with a notable edge of concern to his voice.

"Why?"

"Their engines are powering up and they are heading this way."

"Send an alert one priority message to the fleet, we have located the command cruiser, I'm bringing us about and initiating an immediate jump into plasma drive," Michael swung his arms hard down on the chair as he said so."

"Alert-one, Alert-one, primary target has been acquired, co-ordinates one-five-seven, elevation fourteen degrees." Thorne hurriedly spoke into his console, he only hoped the message would get there in time. He took another look at the sensor readout in front of him.

"Oh god, they're following us Captain matching our course, they've increased speed to plasma factor seven."

Jesus these things can move, normally big guys like these were slow, Michael thought. "Increasing speed to plasma factor seven. Logameier you had better get to engineering, we are going to need to wring every last drop of juice out of that plasma drive system, we might even need to overcharge it."

"You know how dangerous that is, Captain." Logameier warned.

"If we can't outrun them, all that will be left of us is pieces anyway."

"Good point, I'll be in engineering," Logameier said as he left the bridge.

"They are still gaining, they'll overtake us in eleven minutes," Thorne announced.

"What about the fleet? E.T.A" Michael replied from his chair.

"If they depart now, they'll still be three hours away at maximum speed." Thorne replied, the alarm still evident in his voice.

The Liberty raced through plasma drive desperately trying to outrun them, although right now it was a losing battle as slowly yet inevitably those three Cyberian behemoths crept closer and closer.

Suddenly Thorne's console began to sound a faint beeping, "message incoming in from the Valley-forge, they have received our message and the fleet has departed Charlie base."

"Good, now all we have to do is somehow keep those Cyberian ships busy for three hours, while the fleet gets here."

"Errm, not just three ships Captain," Thorne replied. "I'm reading another twenty Cyberian ships converging on this location, the closest is twenty minutes away."

"Oh wonderful, that's all we need," Michael sighed. "They really don't want us to leave here do they. Time until those three Cyberian ships overtake us?"

"Eight minutes."

Michael patched in a direct comms. line to engineering from the console in front of his chair. "Remember what I said about overcharging the plasma drive Mr. Logameier."

"Errr...yes Captain."

"Do it now."

"I can give you plasma factor seven point six for four minutes, the coils on the main plasma drive ejectors are already overheating. When they blow we'll be flung out of plasma drive entirely."

"I'm well aware of that Lieutenant, Alexander out."

He watched on his console as he nudged the ship's speed up a little further in small increments until it finally read seven point six. He dared not go any faster, he'd blow the ship apart trying.

"Commander," Michael turned toward Thorne, "give me a quick scan of the surrounding area, anything we can hide in, hopefully that should buy us a few more minutes; anything at all."

"Scanning," Thorne replied as he read his display. "There's not much, this part of space is relatively barren. There is a small asteroid field point one five light years away called the Brentt cluster."

"We'll take it, thank god for small mercies. Transfer the co-ordinates to my display and I'll alter course," Michael replied visibly relieved.

As the co-ordinates flashed up on his console, he gingerly altered course to match. Exiting the tunnel they were in, and replacing it with an entirely new one. Michael knew that ships with overcharged engines were highly susceptible to being flung out of plasma drive when making too sudden manoeuvres, similar to a car on ice, it had to be handled extremely carefully.

"We'll reach the asteroid field in six minutes," Thorne said.

Sweet Jesus, Michael thought. *That barely gives us enough time to head inside the field before they're on top of us.*

The minutes seemed to tick by like hours as the Liberty desperately tried to outpace its pursuers. Then it happened, at first it felt like a barely perceptible juddering through the deckplating of the ship, more noticeable at the lower decks nearer to the plasma drive itself. It steadily began to rise in its intensity.

Suddenly a voice disturbed Michael as he watched the ship closing with the field ahead of them. "Logameier to bridge, we got a problem down here. Plasma ejector coils are almost completely shot, they are beginning to collapse under the pressure sir."

"Just one more minute," Michael replied. "We just need to hold on for a little longer." Silently Michael prayed those coils would hold.

"Captain! We don't have another minute! If we keep going at this speed, we'll be flung straight out of plasma drive like a spinning top, quite possibly straight into that asteroid field out there."

Michael let out a final defeated sigh, "alright, I'm dropping her out of plasma drive now." He realised he could not afford the risk of spreading the Liberty like a paté all over that asteroid field.

He ever-so-gently brought the ship out of plasma drive, the half-orb housing the Liberties plasma drive systems was still fizzing and crackling as it threatened to overload, the crackling slowed as the engine began to cool.

"Another few seconds Captain, and we'd all have been toast." Thorne reminded him with a suspicious glint in his eye.

"Thank you Commander, I don't need to be……"

He didn't even have time to finish his sentence before the Cyberian flotilla appeared out of plasma drive directly behind the tiny craft. Immediately drones began to separate off from their parent craft heading straight for the Liberty like a swarm of angry insects.

Michael shunted all the power he could lay his hands on toward the Ion sub-light engine, in a last ditch attempt to reach the haven of the asteroid field and lose their pursuers.

"It will take us another ten minutes to enter that asteroid field fully at sub-light speed, the Cyberian ships will be in range long before then. We are outmanoeuvred and seriously outgunned, the only options we have is to either surrender or fight Captain," Thorne said, studying Michael closely.

"And we all know that the Cyberians rarely take prisoners," deep down Michael knew that Thorne was right, even though trying to attack an enemy of this magnitude was suicide. Even ramming them, he doubted the Liberty was large enough to cause much damage.

They were beaten, and he knew it, for once his gamble had not paid off.

Swinging the little ship around, he saw on the viewer the haze of little specks that were the drones coming for them, he looked upon the massive form of those three ships, each one twenty times the size of the Liberty. He knew in that moment he was looking upon death itself, silent unyielding inexorable death.

"It's been an honour serving with you all," he said. A palpable note of sadness in his voice as he steeled himself ready to make their final stand, ready to die for what they all believed in, for the sanctity of life against those that would destroy it.

"Drones closing to within weapons range," Thorne's voice broke through the silence.

"Going full evasive," Michael replied as he once again accelerated the ship hard to maximum sub-light speed, thrusters blazed intense blue as the ship jinked hard from port to starboard. Knowing full well that if those drones managed to hit the Liberties graviton shields, those giants out there would be able to shoot straight through them and obliterate them all. He couldn't let that happen, but there were just too many of them.

E.D.F Chronicles – The Cyberian menace

He strained against the controls, wringing every last ounce of power from the thrusters, jerking the ship hard one way then another in an insane dance against this plethora of drones. Beads of perspiration began to form on his brow as he fought hard to avoid the mass of tiny fighter sized craft buzzing all around them. Bright bursts of energy exploded all around the ship as it flipped, barrel rolled and jinked its way out of being hit. In the end however, all the aerobatics, the intense manoeuvring was to no avail. The enemy were simply too numerous, hundreds buzzed like a swarm around the lone ship. And inevitably some shots did get through, the shields rippled like frosted glass and in so doing the drones instantly scanned the shield impacts, immediately transmitting that data straight back to their parent ships. They now had the Liberties shield frequency, and despite being at full strength, the ships graviton shields were now utterly useless.

The green energy beams of those deadly matter convertors began to reach out, tracking the fast little ship like a laser light show, everywhere the Liberty tried to manoeuvre those beams would follow, trying to trap it in their deadly web.

Michael had thus far not fired the Liberties weapons, instead concentrating purely on evading their deadly beams. He was also saving his shots for the larger craft and didn't want to waste them by hitting one of the drones that flew hither and thither instead. As the Liberty danced, swooped and soared around those beams Michael finally got his chance, and he immediately launched everything the Liberty had toward this giant command ship, hoping that if he could damage it enough it might cause the other ships to back off a little and allow them to escape.

A flurry of high energy torpedoes raced toward the enemy craft with horrific speed, smashing home in huge explosions carving out deep blackened impact craters in the huge ship's hull. Yet in all the tumult, once the explosions had died down and the debris drifted away, not a single blast had managed to penetrate the immensely thick outer hull of the ship.

Michael was stunned; most other ships would be in pieces after a fusillade like that, yet this ship still stood, and with only a few scratches to show for it. He unleashed the fury of the fusion cannon, the immensely powerful bright blue beam of destruction finally did manage to rip its way through that enemy ship's hull. Though it took time to blast through the thick hull armour, and even then after managing to damage it, it was not enough to seriously affect the gargantuan vessel before the fusion cannon itself ran out of power and shut down, needing to recharge.

Michael gasped an exasperated sigh, "we have thrown everything we have against that thing, and so far only succeeded in giving it a minor scrape."

As Michael finished speaking, an ever so slight lapse in concentration meant that the Liberty just clipped the edge of one of those beams, the Cyberian cruisers had already gleaned knowledge of the ship's shield frequency and had applied it to the output of their own weapons arrays. The matter convertor passed straight through the Liberties shields as if they simply didn't exist. The beam washed over an entire section of the ships hull, dissolving it as it passed, stripping away the outer hull leaving behind exposed decks and support struts beneath. It was as if someone had just opened the ship up to look inside.

The ship shuddered violently as pressurized oxygen inside vented out into space, people clung to stations and chairs in a desperate bid to hold on, others were thrown to the ground. Those that were working in the affected areas were not so lucky, their bodies simply dissolving into nothingness, erased from existence as that deadly beam passed over them, those the beam had failed to touch were simply blown forcefully out into space to die of exposure.

"Hull breach! Decks three and four, port section, emergency bulkheads are in place, there are reports of casualties." Thorne announced as he watched his flickering console.

"How many?" Michael asked cursing himself for his momentary distraction.

"Four people were working in that section, the outer hull has been weakened, structural integrity is down to seventy one percent."

We can't outrun them, we can't outfight them, Michael knew they were way over their head with this, what he needed was a fleet not a lone ship.

"I'm throwing everything we have into the sub-light drive and setting a collision course. At least our sacrifice will soften them up so others can finish what we have started." He offered a small prayer to his un-born child still in his wife's belly, not knowing she had already given birth.

Once I needed to keep the nightmares away, and I was found wanting. Because of that two of the most precious things in my life were taken away from me, my wife Jana and my son Theo. I will not be found wanting again, even if it means my own life I will keep those nightmares away, I hope that one day when you are older you will understand. Please God, protect my child.

The Liberties main Ion engine blazed a bright electric blue for the very last time, the plucky, agile, deadly little ship that had proved such a thorn to the enemies of mankind increased speed, dodging and weaving its way around the myriad of matter convertor beams trying to reduce it to its constituent parts. One final act of defiance, a suicidal charge into the enemy command ship itself.

"Captain wait! We have ships coming in!" The elated voice of Maxwell Thorne cut through the atmosphere, as he read through the telemetry data of an entire fleet dropping out of plasma drive to starboard.

"More Cyberians?" Michael asked, still on course to ram the other ship.

"No, they're Krenarans. I'm reading eighty stealth ships and six command carriers."

A grin played across Michael's features. *Dalvosh must have done it, re-formed what was left of the Krenaran fleet.*

In a typical display of machine intelligence, the three Cyberian cruisers turned all their attention toward this new bigger threat. The drones broke off their harassment of the Liberty, and like a shoal of fish, also turned their attention toward the Krenarans.

Leaving the Liberty completely alone.

Michael pitched the Liberty into a steep climb, barely avoiding the Cyberian command ship's hull to the crescendo of a dozen proximity alarms going off. As it rushed along close to the enemy craft's hull, Michael fired torpedo after torpedo, raking its outer hull in a line of bright explosions.

"Incoming message Captain, it's from the Kralath-kar," Thorne said.

"Looks like you could use some help, Liberty." Came the familiar deep gravely voice of Dalvosh.

"Are you ever a sight for sore eyes," Michael replied. "We have to keep them occupied for another two and a half hours while the rest of the fleet get here, and more Cyberians are on the way."

"We'll give them a good fight." Dalvosh said, his green scales curling up into a grin, exposing sharp teeth.

"It'll be one for the record books; okay let's do this!" Michael grinned.

On his throne-like chair in the dark brooding command centre of the Kralath-kar, Dalvosh barked out his orders. "Stealth ships form up into your attack groups, standard delta-vee attack formation, target the drones leave the bigger ships for us. Command cruisers scramble all fighters and lock H.O.T rockets into attack position. The Cyberians will rue the day they ever clashed blades with a Krenaran."

As though a volcano had just erupted the two fleets set upon one another with such ferocity space became awash with particle cannon beams, torpedoes streaked out toward their targets exploding in bright plumes of flame, like thunder crackers in the greatest fireworks display anyone had ever seen.

Particle cannon fire cut bright fiery swathes through the hundreds of drones that buzzed, jinked, and attacked relentlessly as the larger command cruisers led by the Kralath-kar itself continued to close. The deadly torpedo pods rising almost in unison across all six of the giant craft. Although not quite the size of their Cyberian counterparts they still utterly dwarfed the surrounding stealth ships and Liberty now swooping down for another attack run.

"All torpedoes are locked onto their designated targets, pods are fully extended, we'll be in optimal firing range in one minute."

"Good," Dalvosh replied, his sizeable fists began to clench down around the arms of his chair, this was personal. The Cyberians had effectively destroyed his people, their way of life, taken away their pride and dignity. They had turned the Krenarans from a once powerful empire into a disparate scattered people, wanderers struggling to survive. This would be justice, sweet revenge for what they had done.

All across the Krenaran fleet bursts of light peppered them from the drones energy pulses trying to register their shield frequency. The Kralath-kar itself was the only Krenaran ship to be shielded, and that was only from a bunch of stolen Solarian shield generators salvaged from a destroyed battlecruiser during the war with the humans. A war they would have won if the Solarians hadn't interfered. *It was slightly ironic*, Dalvosh thought. *That they should be fighting for their survival alongside those that were their hated enemy just ten Earth years ago.* They had a bigger enemy now, so Dalvosh had to cast aside past hatreds and revulsions in order to help defeat an enemy that threatened to annihilate them in the here and now.

He watched as one of his cruisers began to list, drifting, its bow drooping as fires burst forth from a dozen breaches in its hull caused by simultaneous attacks from three different matter convertors. Finally as its primary power core ruptured, it blew itself apart in an immense explosion lighting up the entire formation.

"We are at firing range," one of his sub-ordinates said.

"Fire!" Dalvosh screamed at the viewer, slamming down his fists on the chair arms, spitting forth every ounce of hatred he had for these vile machine things.

As one, all five Krenaran vessels unleashed their lethal payload of H.O.T rockets in one furious torrent of fire. The giant warheads far larger than a standard torpedo, raced toward their targets, their contrails blazing out brightly behind them looking like a tightly packed mass of comets. The warheads separated as though in a starburst as their own guidance systems acquired their designated targets.

The drones swiftly altered course, veering this way and that in order to intercept the massive torpedo launch, over seventy torpedoes all raced headlong toward these three ships. Drones rammed themselves against them acting as a screen, sacrificing themselves for the survival of the bigger ships, a myriad of small bright explosions signifying their deaths. Many of these large, slower moving torpedoes did not make it through the mass of drones, and those that did, yet more were stripped into little more than a few floating parts by the Cyberian weapons.

E.D.F Chronicles – The Cyberian menace

Yet out of that giant flurry enough did get through these formidable defences to cause havoc amongst the Cyberian shipping, five warheads smashed through the thick outer hull panels of one of the cruisers, immediately detonating and turning the ship into a charnel inferno, blasting it apart almost instantly. The shockwave its violent demise produced tore apart an entire swathe of drones rushing nearby. Smashed and torn hull plating was thrown out in all directions, crashing violently into nearby Stealth ships and Cyberian craft alike.

Debris slammed into the nearby command ship itself, although very little damage was done, its extraordinarily thick hull even stronger than that of the cruisers surrounding it.

Three more H.O.T rockets tore into a second Cyberian cruiser leaving huge fiery breaches torn and twisted metal flew out from the devastating impacts. Leaving it functional though only barely, ruptures jutted out from the impact sites, fire blazed through several decks. It limped onward, badly wounded and sluggish, providing easy prey for the Liberty diving to the attack.

Michael depressed the fusion cannon control, unleashing the full power of the Liberties most devastating weapon. It tore into the cruiser's already weakened hull, cutting a fire scorched trench from its engines all the way up to its command structure. This last coup-de-grace was too much for the ailing ship and it too burst apart in an equally immense fireball.

He had to throw the Liberty hard from port to starboard, the ship jinked and banked to avoid debris thrown out in its direction.

The shockwave however was unavoidable, slamming into them with all the force of an express train, crewmen were hurled to the floor, consoles ruptured and exploded, the Liberty spun wildly out of control. Blood began to seep down Michael's chin as he inadvertently bit into his lower lip due to the sheer force of the impact.

The initial battle was going well for the Krenarans, the two escorting Cyberian cruisers had been violently obliterated and the command ship itself was damaged though only minor damage from two H.O.T rocket impacts, at least it was something, they could hurt it after all.

The tide though was about to turn, as the first wave of Cyberian reinforcements dropped out of plasma drive directly behind the command cruiser. The shield frequency codes discovered thus far had already been passed on to all these ships as well. With this information already gathered, the reinforcements immediately advanced upon the Krenaran fleet without even waiting to deploy their drones.

Michael managed to regain control of the wayward Liberty, after a short struggle with the control surfaces of his chair.

"Damage report," he announced between breaths, watching the battle playing out on the viewer, the Krenarans had fought well and came within a hairs breadth of destroying that damned command cruiser. Now that reinforcements had arrived however, things were not quite going so well, the momentum of their attack had slowed, and they were slowly being beaten back. In the distance two more stealth ships were caught in the intense laser show of the matter convertors.

Thorne's voice cut through his watchfulness, "there's some minor buckling on the hull where that shockwave hit us, some minor injuries reported but nothing too serious. We were lucky that we were thrown away from the combat instead of into it, we could have easily smashed into one of those other ships out there."

The Krenaran carriers had emptied their H.O.T rocket pods earlier, one weakness was that they took a long time to reload, Michael knew this full well as he watched the fighters now trying to perform the role the carriers did. He also knew that the fighters weapons couldn't possibly harm those ships, they were just not powerful enough. Even the particle cannon and the torpedoes on the Stealth ships were not having much luck trying to get through that thick outer hull, in effect the Krenaran fleet was basically toothless until the carriers were ready to launch their next salvo of H.O.T rockets again.

The Cyberians however took full advantage, silently advancing in their eerie march, uncaring of the damage inflicted upon them, of their losses, as though the grim inexorable approach of death itself. More stealth ships were caught and died, though not in bright blazing fireballs signifying their deaths to the universe, this was a quiet, cold death, simply stripped down until there was nothing left.

Michael began to have serious doubts this Krenaran fleet could hold on for the two hours necessary for backup to arrive.

Having been thrown clear of the combat, he once again shunted power to the Liberties engines and the tiny but deadly ship shot forward to rejoin the combat, diving beneath the spinning wreckage of a half-destroyed stealth ship.

Checking the readout on the status display from the fusion cannon, Michael realised it was up to ninety percent power, still charging. *Damnit, it won't be able to fire in time.*

Looking out at the battle, he quickly realised that with the Cyberians concentrating all their efforts on wiping out the Krenarans, they had a nice free run at that command cruiser. Michael smiled, *this time you won't get away so easily.* He readied both high energy torpedo launchers, and put the ship into a wide barrel roll in order to avoid the occasional flash of a Cyberian weapon, then dived sharply to swoop beneath the giant ships hull, up close it looked enormous, hundreds of antenna stations and empty docking ports for the drones flashed by in a blur of dull steel grey. His target was directly ahead, locking the targeting system onto it, that semi-circular plasma drive system that dwarfed his entire ship.

A couple of drones picked up the movement of the Liberty and began a pursuit, though the Liberty was now at maximum sub-light speed and far out-paced its pursuers.

Michael could see the target rapidly approaching, *Jesus it's big*, he thought. It needed to be, the kind of power it needed to generate to get a ship of this size into plasma drive was well beyond anything the E.D.F could manage.

The Liberty raced along the underside of its hull like a small black swift, nimble, agile and fast. In the space of a split second it was upon them, Michael mashed the torpedo firing control. Two high energy torpedoes shot forth from the Liberties launchers. He didn't hang around to see the detonation, the torpedoes slammed into the plasma drive housing at almost the exact same time the Liberty shot past it.

As the craft raced by, Michael could see the orange fiery glow reflected in the ships hull above them as it lit up, then the almighty flash of the explosion as the plasma drive blew itself apart taking the two drones with it. The Liberty had finally succeeded in damaging this nigh on invincible ship, hitting it hard in the one weak point it had. *Well if we can't destroy this thing, at least it can't run before the other fleet gets here.*

Aboard the Kralath-kar huge cheers erupted as they also witnessed that huge explosion. *The beast was finally wounded now all they had to do was finish it off,* Dalvosh thought. Though by now his fleet was badly mauled itself, three of his six command cruisers lay in blazing ruins, his Stealth ships largely decimated as were the fighters. The Kralath-kar herself was badly damaged after taking several hits from the Cyberian vessels surrounding that accursed command ship. Dead warriors, kinsmen, lay all around him, broken supports littered the floor, flames and smoke billowed out from a devastated systems display monitor.

Although he hated these vile machine creatures, he had to respect them. They were strong, and if there was one thing a Krenaran respected it was strength. Then Dalvosh saw on his flickering viewscreen the ominous green blaze of a matter convertor beam fired straight at them. The outer bridge wall of his ship began to crumple, twist, and buckle as the beam broke down anything it touched into its constituent atoms, converting it into pure energy, the hull crackled and fizzed as raw power flashed before dissipating harmlessly into space, the bridge wall weakened until it was the consistency of paper.

Dalvosh watched in horror, helpless as the beam stripped away at his bridge, dissolving everything it touched. He whispered vehemently one final curse, a last act of defiance.

"Though my body may break, my hatred will remain and whether in this life or the next I shall spit my last breath upon thee!"

Then he spat a gobbet of saliva straight toward the viewer, the spittle never landed as the beam broke through the outer wall instantly devouring everything on the command deck, floors, walls, consoles, Dalvosh's chair and ultimately Dalvosh himself.

The Kralath-kar now out of control, plunged headlong into the ruin of a nearby Krenaran carrier, decimating them both in a tremendous explosion that lit up the entire bedraggled fleet.

Even Michael aboard the Liberty had to shield his eyes, the other Krenaran vessels witnessing the destruction of their flagship began to break formation and scatter, the battle was lost.

The Cyberians did not pursue what pitiful remnants were left of the Krenaran fleet. Their charge, the command cruiser was weakened and unable to jump into plasma drive, stuck at sub-light velocity it would be months or years before it reached the nearest system. The ship that had proven so adept at eluding everyone, Solarians, Krenarans and E.D.F alike was suddenly very vulnerable. It could no longer run or hide, its devastated plasma drive continued to bleed fire and highly charged plasma out into space, making a very noticeable trail if it did decide to move.

For the first time since this whole conflict began, the Cyberians were unsure of themselves, normally known for their fluidity of action, for the ability to transfer data and orders almost instantaneously to every part of their immense war fleet and even individual Cyberian warriors themselves fighting on the ground on more than fifty worlds across space.

Now they simply seemed to huddle together around their damaged command ship, unmoving as if scared, trying to protect their delicate charge, cradling it and waiting for the inevitable final attack that was about to come.

The Liberty, damaged themselves, and in no condition to mount an attack on a fleet as large as this alone, simply took cover in the floating wreckage of the Krenaran ships, clamping itself to the underside of a devastated Krenaran carrier and shutting down all power except minimal power to the sensors.

It was a stalemate; the Liberty would appear as nothing more than wreckage to the Cyberians, yet silently they watched and waited as more Cyberian reinforcements were drafted in, and the command ship desperately trying to repair its destroyed plasma drive before the E.D.F fleet arrived. Even with a crew that did not need to sleep or eat and worked ten times faster than a man,

Michael doubted very much that command ship would be moving again before the cavalry got here.

For the next hour and three quarters, the Liberty remained silently clamped to this wrecked hull, hiding in plain sight and watching as ten more Cyberian cruisers dropped out of plasma drive to render aid to their wounded master.

A massive brilliant flash of light heralded the arrival of the E.D.F fleet together with their Solarian allies, a total of sixty five ships all dropped out of plasma drive together, led by the Valley-forge itself still bearing the scars of the previous engagement it was involved in at Sigma XI, as it had had to leave Charlie base early.

The Cyberian fleet was for once outnumbered, but Michael had seen before that numbers can count for nothing against these guys. The Krenaran fleet had outnumbered them too in the beginning, and look what the Cyberians had done to them.

Cyberian cruisers began to immediately peel off, forming a defensive line between the E.D.F fleet and the command ship.

Michael knew the Liberties time had come, he nodded silently as Thorne gradually brought main power back online, the main engines began to glow their ubiquitous intense blue, growing in intensity all the time. Once main power was up to its optimal level, Michael released the magnetic securing latches anchoring it to this giant piece of floating wreckage and shunted full power to the engines to join up with the E.D.F formation.

"Message incoming from the Valley-forge Captain," Thorne said.

"Put it on the viewer."

Kinraid's face appeared, "good t' have you still with us Captain Alexander, though you don't seem quite as shipshape as ye' left though, a little trouble with the bad guys?" He smiled.

"You don't look so hot yourselves."

"'Tis true, I cannae tell a lie, it's time to end this once and for all." Quinn replied, his voice rousing.

"And the Liberty stands with you."

"Alrighty then, let's get this done!" The Irishman said as he ended the transmission.

Quinn had dropped the Valley-forge out of plasma drive already on alert status, a trick he had picked up from Michael during his time on the Liberty. So the battleship's shields were already at full power, not that it would do them much good. Those huge twin high bore fusion cannons were already fully charged. All he needed was a single shot and that command ship would be history, at least that was what he thought.

He pressed his wrist comm. "Kinraid to commander flight group. Launch all fighters, keep those drones off our back."

"Understood, launching fighters." Anatoly replied.

The twin bay doors opened on either side of the Valley-forge's semi-circular prow once more, no less than twenty four fighters all took flight, the battleship's entire complement. A dozen flew out from the port bay, a dozen from the starboard.

Kinraid watched on the giant holographic viewer as those tiny Peregrines raced forth to intercept the rapidly approaching mass of drones.

"Okay, E.D.F fleet advance behind the fighters, full attack speed and engage once we are through. Remember th' drones are not our target, that command ship is."

"The fleet is responding, they are powering up their engines and moving out," Commander Anizeres replied.

Lieutenant Jansen cut in, "bringing Ion engines up to full power now."

The six huge Ion engines of the Valley-forge utterly dwarfed everything else in the fleet, with a ship of the sheer size and weight of the Valley-forge it took some time for it to accelerate up to its maximum speed, so initially it, and the two Mandela class light cruisers that were escorting it lagged behind the faster elements of the fleet.

The Solarian battlecruisers, easily the fastest swooped to the attack. Their fusion cannons scything through drones in great long swathes. From a distance it looked like great channels of fire cut through the masses. Although as the Solarian ships raced down these fiery lanes, they were repeatedly peppered with the drones energy bursts. Their shield frequencies immediately transmitted to their parent ships.

It was Televis's ship, the Faeriath that would break through first. A dozen more battlecruisers and frigates followed, then came the flagship of the Solarian fleet, the Loganith. *It was time the Cyberians paid for what they had done, paid for the massacre of Orialis and a dozen other worlds since. And paid not just for the terror they had brought to the Solarians, but to the Terrans and the even the Krenarans too,* Televis thought with barely concealed hatred.

"Keep firing!" He shouted from his bridge, "I want them to feel the full wrath of the warhost."

Multiple blue lances of fusion cannon fire slammed into the Cyberian cruisers, flurries of torpedoes streaked toward them detonating in great plumes of fire. Two Cyberian cruisers were already ailing, the damage inflicted by a plethora of fusion cannon hits too much, more torpedoes blasted them apart.

Kinraid looked on, startled at the ferocity of the Solarian attack, at the brutality they were showing. *The Solarians were a normally peaceful race, it was not like*

155

them have they gone mad? Well, if you push a people hard enough, I guess this is what you get.

The Krenarans were faring much worse, those final four command carriers sacrificed their fighter element at the battle of Sigma XI, nor were their sufficient fighters to replace their losses with E.D.F craft at Charlie base. All they had were those H.O.T rockets with which to defend themselves. Kinraid considered that they might get a salvo off, at a pinch two before they bought the farm. Still a salvo of forty eight giant torpedoes heading straight at you was better than nothing.

The Washington class heavy cruisers led the E.D.F contingent, the Missouri and the El-Alamein were at the forefront of the attack, explosions and laser fire lit up the space all around them as their point defence lasers continually blazed away at the waves of drones as the E.D.F fleet tried to push through. Fighters jinked and danced, their own lasers firing repeatedly at targets too numerous to track.

The Liberty was waiting in ambush just behind the lead ships of the fleet, Michael knew they had already obtained their shield frequency from the battle earlier and so did not want to risk his ship early by rushing out first and being cut to ribbons by those matter convertors.

Both the E.D.F and Solarian formations had managed to break through the mass of drones, piercing them in tight, fast, hard-hitting formations rather than try and set up a line of defence like they had had to do around several worlds already. Now it was they who were on the attack, striking hard and fast.

The Washington class ships immediately began pounding the Cyberian cruisers with their archaic yet more effective rotary rail-cannons. Ghandhi and Mandela class vessels continued the assault, firing torpedo after torpedo into those Cyberian ships.

By now four of the Cyberian vessels were ablaze, drifting helplessly, their mighty armoured hulls broken and shattered.

A good start, thought Kinraid. *But by no means enough.*

Then, the Cyberians retaliated.

The Solarian fleet bore the brunt of it, green matter convertor beams lashed out in all directions, criss-crossing each other in elaborate yet deadly lattice effects. The drones had already done their work and the Solarians shields were useless against the assault.

The smaller more agile frigates were able to jink and dodge the worst of it, yet some were still hit, such was the intensity of the fire levelled at them. They span out of control, before crashing into the floating wreckage of the Krenaran fleet earlier.

Worse was to befall the battlecruisers themselves, larger and therefore slightly slower to manoeuvre, several couldn't bank in time running straight through the beams, stripping entire decks, shearing away whole sections of their once resplendent silvery hull. Many were so weakened that they simply crumbled apart.

Televis could only watch in horror as the Loriath, his sister ship jinked hard to avoid one beam yet was caught by another, that tall, proud, beak-like command structure housing the deadly underslung fusion cannon was stripped right down to its internal supports, it listed wildly out of control.

"Hard to starboard!" he shouted, desperately trying to avoid a collision.

The Faeriath shot past, only just missing it as the craft smashed headlong into the ruins of a Krenaran carrier obliterating it in a bright plume of flame.

Televis mourned the loss of such a great ship, and her commander, Atanis, one of the warhost's most respected officers. He would have to grieve later, the fates of three empires lay bound to this one battle.

"Bring us in for an attack run on that command ship." He said as another battlecruiser was literally dissected to pieces. "This ends now."

The Faeriath jinked and rolled, one way then another to avoid the lethal maze of beams, the craft flew over a Cyberian cruiser and then it was revealed to them, their target. The source of so many lives lost amongst his people.

"We have target lock." His tactical officer said, standing at his station to his left.

"This is for Orialis…..Fire!" Televis shouted.

The fusion cannon roared out from the craft, a bright blue beam of destruction slamming headlong into the command cruiser's hull, carving a deep fiery trench, yet still the hull remained un-penetrated.

"What!" Televis cried aloud in exasperation, "how can it be? How can it withstand a direct fusion cannon strike from a battlecruiser, I don't believe it."

Yet it was true, the flames almost immediately died down, leaving a deep blackened, yet still glowing gouge along the upper mid-section of that gigantic craft.

"Torpedoes!" He shouted.

The Faeriath managed to fire just two, before three of the command cruisers eight matter convertors hit home, the beams tore apart the port side crescent wing of the craft, sending it into an uncontrollable spin.

The bridge quickly became a scene of utter desolation, alarms blared out in a crescendo, alerting dead crewmen to the damage the ship had sustained. Fires blazed out of control, circuits flashed and sparked as smoke filled the bridge.

"We've lost flight control!" The panicked pilot said.

E.D.F Chronicles – The Cyberian menace

The image on the viewscreen was spinning so fast it had an almost kaleidoscopic effect. Rooted to his seat, Televis could not make out a single ship in the blur. That was except for the ship dead ahead; another Cyberian cruiser which the Faeriath smashed headlong into before both ships tore themselves apart in an almighty explosion.

Kinraid watched as the battle was going from bad to worse, everywhere ships were dying, broken, fractured hulls lay floating haphazardly like broken toys discarded. Then he saw that Solarian ship in the distance smash into that Cyberian cruiser. Suddenly even though his heart sank at the loss of the ship, it had given him his opening.

There it was, the command ship, revealed to him.

"Lock onto that ship, ready fusion cannons; fire!" Kinraid shouted, if they couldn't destroy it nobody could.

Lights across the ship dimmed noticeably as vast amounts of power was channelled directly from the ships three power cores and shunted to the twin tower block sized high bore fusion cannons once more. The accumulated energy was then unleashed in the form of two immense vivid sapphire blue beams of incredible power, shooting across space and casting everything in a temporary blue glow. The entire battleship was forced backward several metres due to the sheer ferocity of the recoil.

The massive beams smashed headlong into the command ship, wreathing the whole vessel in flame, torn hull plating was thrown out in all directions. The crew cheered as they witnessed the fiery destruction of their nemesis.

The cheers were short lived though, for as the flames died the command ship was still remaining, though badly damaged, an immense jagged rent along the port side of the ship, two of its matter convertors torn apart. Yet still amazingly it had withstood the most powerful weapon the E.D.F possessed.

Kinraid sat open mouthed in shock. *How tough does a ship have to be to withstand a direct hit like that.* He was dumbfounded.

"It'll take another minute for the weapons to build up to full charge again." Iuliov replied.

"Forget it, we won't get another shot."

Kinraid was right, already the Cyberians were turning their attention toward this massive threat, the one ship that could really hurt them. Cyberian cruisers began to peel off to engage the Valley-forge.

The battleship itself was a colossal craft, and Kinraid knew full well that he would not be able to avoid those Cyberian weapons if they hit.

Commander Anizeres broke through the tense silence, "incoming message Captain, it's from the Liberty."

Quinn frowned in puzzlement, *what could they possibly do now?* "Put them through."

Michael appeared on the screen. "Quinn, we are going to attempt to land in the breach you've just made, deploy our commandoes and take this thing out internally. It's our only shot."

With barely a third of the fleet remaining, and many of them already badly damaged he was in no position to mount an argument.

"Okay," Kinraid nodded. "We'll try to cover you as much as we can."

"We'd appreciate the help, Liberty out."

Michael immediately pressed his wrist comm. "Nikolai have your commandoes ready, we're going in."

"About goddamn time," Vargev replied hefting his armschlager.

"How are we going to get those commandoes over there?" Thorne asked.

"We're going to land in that breach," Michael replied, nodding toward the massive open rent in the side of the Cyberian ship.

"What? Are you crazy! Even if we somehow manage to get through those beams, we'll never get close enough."

"It's our only chance Commander! Either follow my orders or leave the bridge!" Michael shot back, he was deadly serious and tired of arguing with this so called Commander, he would remove him if necessary.

Thorne quickly realised that he had overstepped the mark and backed down. "That will not be necessary sir."

"Good, I want maximum power to the thrusters." Michael knew that traversing that net of deadly beams would be tricky, especially with his shields as good as useless. He wished Eldathar were here right now, but the reality was he wasn't, and so it fell to him.

Between them and that command ship, there were some fourteen matter convertor beams, all moving, tracking along the trajectories of over ships, firing and then stopping, not to mention the myriad of floating wreckage and half-destroyed ships. The battle was beginning to wane, the E.D.F/Solarian fleet was almost spent, it was now or never.

Michael bit the bullet and accelerated the Liberty hard.

Just as he did so another fleet arrived, completely out of the blue, their black crescent shaped hulls could mean only one thing; the Dracos were here.

Twenty ships had dropped out of plasma drive led by the Blade of Rhovanion. Michael knew from experience that the Dracos only ever served themselves, so which side of the fence would they fall on this time? Would they side with what was left of the E.D.F/Solarian fleet trying to fight for the right of all life to exist, or would they simply side with the strongest in a grab for power themselves which were the Cyberians.

E.D.F Chronicles – The Cyberian menace

Surely they must know that the Cyberians cannot be bargained or reasoned with, to them they were just numbers, statistics to be eradicated until that number reached zero, there were no emotions involved.

Very quickly he got his answer as the Dracos flotilla charged headlong into the fray, their laser lances and dark matter torpedoes blasting deep craters and gouges into several nearby cruisers.

This new attack seemed to give the weakened E.D.F and Solarian forces a much needed boost as they regrouped and redoubled their attacks. Eight Cyberian cruisers lay drifting in flames as the Dracos and Solarian fleets, once hated enemies, fought side-by-side for the first time in three hundred years, against a foe that threatened them all with extinction.

The charge had certainly gotten the Cyberian's attention as their weapons now trained themselves on the onrushing Dracos ships instead. Michael thanked God once again for small mercies and began his run.

The tiny ship dodged and weaved, hugging close to the hulls of the Cyberian craft so it would be harder to get a fix on them, the ship jinked and zig-zagged, soared high over the hull of one ship, then plunged deep under another, all the while keeping as tight as it possibly could. The blast of a torpedo impact from a ghandhi class destroyer slammed into the cruiser's hull, the impact rocking the Liberty and bathing it in flame as it raced past.

Nikolai formed up his men near the port side hatch, all had donned breathing apparatus and readied their weapons for the final assault. They would have to fight their way to the ships power core where they planned to use demo. charges to blow this ship to high heaven. It was a high risk mission, and a long way to that power core, secretly he doubted many of them would survive, but the fate of humanity rested upon them and the most elite fighting unit in the E.D.F would not let them down.

The ship continued to bank and twist to avoid the fusillade of fire crossing their path, Michael strained at the controls, his forehead creased in concentration, perspiration beading his brow. He knew that if he hit any of those beams they were done for, the Liberty would likely not survive a second hit. Even a slight mistake on his part could ruin everything, the floating wreckage was becoming increasingly problematic as well, as it occasionally drifted across their path. Several times he had to bank hard to avoid a Cyberian weapon, and then squeeze under a large piece of floating hull plating or part of a drifting ship to avoid ploughing straight into it.

The agile little craft raced along the upper hull of the command cruiser in a blur of matt black hull and silver panels, then came to a dead stop right above the huge breach. The ragged edges of which were still glowing a bright amber due to the immense heat generated from the Valley-forges fusion cannons.

160

"Deploy landing legs," Michael said as another blast slammed into the cruiser illuminating the Liberties dark hull in its fiery glow.

"Landing legs extended," Thorne replied.

"Okay easy does it, reducing main engines to five percent power." Michael whispered as he concentrated hard. At this distance he realised that the breach was easily large enough to accommodate the Liberty, the devastating power of those guns had carved out a three hundred metre long gouge in the ships hull and just over a hundred and fifty metres deep.

Any other ship would have been destroyed instantly, but not this one. Michael had to edge the ship in sideways so as to avoid crashing the Liberties frontal section and the barrel of the fusion cannon into the badly scorched interior around the edges of the breach.

The ship gently eased itself onto its three sets of landing legs, crushing several support girders jutting out from the wrecked floor, jets of gas vented off to equalise the weight of the ship.

"Commander, extended our shields out to seal the breach around the aft and starboard side of the ship. Then flood the area with carbon dioxide from the waste gas reclamators."

Thorne understood what the Captain was attempting, if the commandoes opened that hatch straight away, the vacuum of space would cause the blood in their veins to boil, as every bodily fluid would want to rush out to fill the vacuum. The Captain was creating a miniature 'environment' within the shields into which the commandoes could exit safely.

"Extending shields, we only have enough power to extend them for a few minutes." Thorne cast a warning glance over to Michael.

"That's all we'll need."

Carbon dioxide from within two three metre wide tanks on deck four was then pumped out and re-directed to a small exhaust port on the port side of the ship, seeping out like a fog to fill up the space and cancel out the vacuum effect.

Michael then released the hatch and touched his wrist comm. "Nikolai go!"

"Commandoes green light has been given, move!"

Nikolai released the hatch with a whoosh of escaping air, then pushed off into the fog shrouded breach. The other commandoes all surged out behind him, floating weightlessly. Even donning environment suits the biting cold quickly began to take its toll, as frost from quickly freezing carbon dioxide began to form on the eye pieces of Nikolai's breathing gear, his fingers began to feel numb. This vast ragged tear in the side of an even vaster ship occasionally flashed with blues, greens, and vivid violet from weapons fire, with the occasional flash of bright orange from explosions all around. Twisted debris and wreckage lay strewn across what resembled a badly crumpled deck floor, Vargev shook his hand to get some blood flowing again and some feeling back.

After what seemed like an eternity he reached a dull grey bulkhead, quickly pulling out a magnetic breaching charge from his webbing, he activated it and clamped it to the door. He knew he was already feeling the effects of the extreme cold, his mind felt foggy, his touch unsure.

14 Storming the command ship.

Half a dozen commandoes had already succumbed to the intense cold, their freezing bodies floating aimlessly before striking the Liberties shields in a tiny colourless ripple effect. It was regrettable but acceptable losses. Nikolai hated losing any of his men in combat, but also knew that sooner or later it was inevitable.

With a thunderous boom and spray of sparks and shrapnel, the bulkhead exploded open. Nikolai and his commandoes surged inside to be greeted with a couple of Cyberian sentries right on the other side of the bulkhead, Vargev slammed the butt of his Armschlager down with such force that it smashed open the head of the robotic warrior in a shower of sparks. The machine crumpled at his feet as he levelled his weapon and opened fire on the other. A storm of bullets slammed into it pitching it backward and smashing it into a panel where it remained motionless. The Russian strode up to it, calmly levelled his weapon, and fired blasting its cranium to pieces just in case it wasn't playing dead.

Once inside the command ship, Nikolai and the other commandoes quickly realised that it was a good deal warmer than it was outside, although still cold, it wasn't quite as cold. In fact it was twenty degrees below freezing, the perfect temperature in which machines operate at peak efficiency. Vargev was of course used to this kind of temperature, after all it was not too dissimilar to the temperatures at his home in Volgograd this time of year.

"Commandoes form up into your fire teams just as we planned," Vargev said into the mic. attachment within his breathing mask.

The troops quickly pushed forward and formed up into three distinct fire groups. It was a tight squeeze, those behind would struggle to replace the ones that would have to reload in front, and until they fanned out into a larger corridor they would have to make the best of it.

They came to a 'T' junction at the end of this corridor, either side of the adjoining corridor gently sloped around a blind corner as though it was semi-circular.

Nikolai thought the internal structure a little odd, a machine species would not normally use curves and bends in construction, normally they would be rigid, grid-like, to use gentle curves and bends in a large scale construction such as this requires a degree of artisanship almost artistry which a machine intelligence could never aspire to.

There was a lit up display of the deck they were on, attached half-way up a far wall. Though much of it was written in a strange form of machine code which Nikolai could not comprehend, there was also a small hole in the wall with a metallic circle around it. He surmised that it could be some kind of data interface, those onboard simply plugged themselves into the ship to access any information about it.

The whole ship seemed to give off an air of immense age, the interior wasn't shining, new and resplendent as new metal often was. Instead it was faded, dull and pitted with age, it made Nikolai wonder just how old this ship really was.

He ordered his men to corner this position as he consulted the deckplan, commandoes fanned out as he did so. If he was looking at this right, the actual power core was four hundred metres from where they stood. His heart sank, four hundred metres was a heck of a lot of ground to cover in a ship full of hostiles. They would have to fight their way all the way to the core, before attaching the demo. charges to it.

The familiar low pitched rattle of Armschlager fire snapped him back to the present. *Here they come.* Vargev chanced a brief glance around both corners, his eyes widened in shock, it was like a living wall of metal approaching, silent, unyielding. Already several of their number lay in broken heaps, yet heedless they just swept over the fallen, advancing despite the hail of gunfire.

"Commandoes advance!" Nikolai shouted over the roar of weapons fire.

Heavy calibre slugs tore into the legions of machine warriors, dozens upon dozens fell, armour piercing rounds shredding through them. The mechanical warriors were being pushed back, though slowly, it seemed that there was no end to them. Several of the Commandoes were hit in return, their bodies instantly atomised, despite the mounting casualties and the near impossible odds, the E.D.F troops pressed on as best as they could.

"Second rank, ready grenades!" Nikolai shouted as he downed another warrior, the heavy machine gun bucking and swaying as round after round slammed into it, even with armour piercing ammunition it was still tough going.

He had advised that his men carry the new electro mag. pulse flash bangs, they should disable several in a burst. He didn't want to waste them so early but it was increasingly looking like they had no choice, there were just too many of them.

Four of the flashbangs were hurled through the hail of gunfire toward them, exploding in bright flashes of energy. Twenty Cyberians collapsed at a stroke as the powerful electro-magnetic pulse given off shorted out the delicate electronics within.

"Forward!" Vargev screamed, not wanting to give these technological nightmares an inch; through a storm of bullets the big Russian charged at the now retreating Cyberians, gunning several of them down himself.

The accompanying commandoes all followed his lead, charging along with him. They had captured this long semi-circular corridor for now, but at the cost of fifteen of his own men. The casualties were beginning to tell already, he had lost over twenty of his men so far and gained just forty metres.

****

Michael knew the Liberty could not stay here for long, they would soon be detected, and the Valley-forge together with what remained of the Krenaran, Dracos and Solarian ships were preparing for another attack.

"How long until we are ready to fire again?" Kinaid asked for a second time.

"Another ten seconds," Lieutenant Iuliov said.

"Captain, I've got some unusual activity on the sensors," Anizeres said frowning.

"What kind of activity?"

"It's the drones sir, they've changed course. They are now moving en-masse toward us."

"Ready all point defence lasers, target those drones," Kinraid replied.

"Aye sir," Iuliov nodded.

Quinn suspected the Cyberians were largely fighting the Dracos and Solarians, and that the E.D.F fleet was virtually toast, there were only four ships left capable of fighting, not including the Liberty and the Valley-forge. Yet his ship was still a massive threat to that command cruiser, they barely survived the first shot from the Valley-forge's guns, they definitely would not survive another. So Kinraid realised the Cyberians must have given the drones new instructions, to smash themselves against those guns.

"How many are incoming?" Quinn asked.

"Over one hundred of them sir," Anizeres replied, the strain in her voice almost palpable, she was wondering the same as everyone else; were they going to live through this.

Jesus, Kinraid thought. It was a tactic that was going to work too, the Valley-forges point defence lasers, although sophisticated, could never keep that many away. The fighters were already engaged with a separate batch of drones. Quinn could do nothing but hope the damage would not be too severe.

"All hands brace for impact!" He shouted.

The drone swarm came in fast, the fusillade of short range laser fire from the Valley-forges turrets lit up the space around the vessel in bright orange flashes. Dozens were caught in the intense barrage, turrets were firing so fast they threatened to overheat. Kinraid watched with awe at the sheer number of explosions surrounding his ship, laser fire was everywhere, drones spun out of control and exploded as they were hit, others collided into each other to avoid the maelstrom. The intensity of the firefight was breathtaking, although in the end Kinraid was right, they could not keep all of them away, several did make it through the battleship's formidable defences, ramming themselves at full speed into the ships main guns.

Although the Valley-forge was near four thousand metres in length, and a drone the same size as a fifteen metre Peregrine fighter, enough of them ramming into the ship could still cause severe damage, and it did. It was death by a thousand stings. The drones dashed themselves in suicide runs against the gun barrels themselves, smashing through the hull and exploding in bright plumes of flame. The carnage was extreme as men and women were simply blasted down corridors, others were horribly scarred and burned looking like charred meat, bulkheads collapsed as fire swept through several decks cooking crewmen alive where they stood or blasting them out into the cold depths of space.

"Damage report!" Kinraid roared over the crescendo of alarms ear splitting explosions, and shattering of displays.

"Both weapons have been totally destroyed, we have hull breaches across decks twelve, thirteen and fourteen, heavy casualties reported. Structural integrity at fifty six percent and fires are raging across all three decks, fire suppression systems are keeping them contained for now." Anizeres replied, her tone cool as ice absolutely focused on her display. Her auburn hair told another story, matted, loose, and blood-flecked from a number of small nicks from flying debris.

"Damn it!" Kinraid shouted in frustration. "It looks like we won't be able to finish off that thing after all." The ships port and starboard high power laser batteries had already proved to be ineffective against even a standard cruiser, against that command ship they might as well get out and tickle it.

With a sigh, Kinraid realised there was nothing else they could do, it was all up to the Liberty now.

****

Vargev and his surviving commandoes pressed on as best they could. Metallic bodies lay all about them as they fought shin-deep in a sea of destroyed Cyberians, yet still they came on even through the hail of bullets, grenades, and slingshot missiles levelled at them. The commandoes were making ground, but slowly, and vastly outnumbered at every turn. So far they had managed to make it three hundred metres inside this labyrinthine vessel. The cost had been high, eighty of his men had now perished in intense close quarter firefights.

Nikolai fell back momentarily to reload his Armschlager for the third time, he had just one more clip left. Many of his men were running low on ammunition now.

Slamming another clip into the magazine holder, he rejoined the combat just as another commando was hit and instantly vaporised right in front of him, he didn't even have time to scream.

The Armschlager bucked and roared as he poured fire into the almost solid wall of metallic Cyberian warriors not ten metres ahead of him. The flashes of their weapons almost blinding him in their intensity, the other commandoes used whatever cover they could, there wasn't much, which made these corridors the perfect killing field. Some took to diving into the robotic wreckage, though a few found out all too late that not all of the wreckage was truly destroyed, as evidenced by the sickening crunch of a neck snapping, or the screams of a soldier having his eyes gouged out of their sockets.

The grizzled Russian continued to plough on through the debris, spraying the enemy with bullets as easily as he watered flowers in his garden back in the motherland, the roar of a slingshot missile temporarily deafening him as it shot by close to his head, exploding amongst the tide of Cyberian warriors blasting another dozen of them into razor sharp fragments.

Nikolai was bleeding from the cheek, arm and thigh from several shrapnel hits, that missile exploded just a little too close. In this kind of close quarters combat against this kind of enemy, it was impossible not to be hit by flying debris.

Vargev had never been in a true meat grinder mission before, sure he had fought in more than his fair share of pitched battles, but nothing like this. This was wholesale slaughter, nothing less. Two opposing sides slaughtering each other until nothing remained but dead bodies for the crows to pick over.

He began to realise as he gunned down another swathe of Cyberian warriors, that he might not make it out of here alive, that there was no returning home from this. He and his battered men trudged wearily onward wading through the tide of debris, deafening sound of battle and intermingled screams of dying men. Just putting one tired foot in front of another and hoping to hell you weren't one of the unlucky bastards that got hit.

At a snails pace they managed to make it through the next eighty metres of corridor and passageways, all the while fighting through hordes of metal warriors, there were just five men who made it the whole distance to the actual power core chamber itself, and Nikolai was one of them.

They entered a massive circular room, almost eighty metres in diameter, entrances were at various intervals, the floor like the majority of the ship was a bare metal mesh. Nikolai and his remaining men rushed to seal the chamber off. Still, several Cyberians poured in after them, after a short burst of intense gunfire, and the last couple of E.M.P flashbangs, the room was clear.

"Let's get the charges set," Vargev said to his men.

In the centre of this vast room were three gigantic power cores, although the energy they contained was unlike anything the Colonel had ever seen before. They looked like three huge tanks extending upward as far as the eye could see, the energy within glowed a bright luminescent blue, swirling with equally bright greens and purples shifting and moving in and out of phase. It felt a shame to end this mesmerising light show that coated the entire room in its brilliance, though in the end he knew what he had to do, the survival of his race depended upon it.

Taking out the demo. charge from his backpack, he clamped it to the side of the core closest to him. The surface felt cool to the touch, though he could only imagine the kind of temperature inside the thing. He watched as the other commandoes attached their charges as well, quickly synchronising the timer on the detonator to the other explosives, in this way if any of the others were killed, all it took was one man who still lived to explode all the charges together.

As fate would have it, the commandoes weren't that lucky, the Cyberians had learned of their plan and a swathe of warriors burst through three different entrances. Within the space of a heartbeat over one hundred Cyberians poured into the room, the other four commandoes were hit almost immediately, atomised on the spot by the sheer ferocity of fire from the Cyberian weapons.

Nikolai, through some miracle had managed to dodge the majority of the Cyberian weapons fire that came his way, that was except for one single shot that just clipped him in the left thigh. It was enough, his entire left leg vaporised, erased from existence. He slumped down against the side of the power core itself, breathing heavily. The pain was unlike anything he had ever known, an intense fire coursing through his body, there was no blood, just a ragged cauterised stump where his leg had once been.

He wanted so badly to scream out in pain, but the adrenaline coursing through his body and his own indomitable pride would never allow that. He was Colonel Nikolai Vargev, never would he give them the satisfaction of hearing his scream.

He simply sat there, the Armschlager clasped loosely in his left hand, the detonator in his right. As the Cyberians slowly, silently began to approach, he lowered his weapon to the deck, pulled out one of his traditional thick cigars from a pouch on his webbing, took out his lighter and lit it gently, taking a long slow drag and savouring the first puff, he waited.

The Cyberians edged closer, levelling their weapons at this lone wounded soldier, Vargev took one final long puff on his cigar, looked up at them with hollow eyes, calmly accepting his fate, and in one final act of defiance he spat.

"Fuck you!"

Then pressed his detonator.

All five charges exploded simultaneously, the giant tanks fractured, energy crackled around the room as the pent up power was released before exploding in one immense all encompassing fireball. Nikolai was atomised instantly, as were the surrounding Cyberians.

The energy release was devastating, expanding uncontrollably throughout the ship. Explosions tore through the internal structure, bringing down entire decks, ripping through everything they touched. Bulkheads and supports were blasted apart by the sheer force of the explosions.

"Captain, I am no longer reading any lifesigns over there," Thorne announced. "I'm also reading a massive energy wave, it's completely off the scale, the internal structure of the ship is collapsing."

"He did it!" Michael shouted, as he eyed the viewer intently. "Sacrificed himself to destroy the ship. I'm closing the hatch, revert all shields to normal," he said as he worked furiously at the control panel in front of him.

"Shields reverting to normal configuration," Thorne replied with a smile, they had finally done it.

"Increase power to thrusters give me everything you've got, if we're not out of here in ten seconds we're all toast." Michael strained hard at the controls, shunting power to the gravitic engines so that the ship seemed to levitate a few metres off the wreckage of the breach. Explosions continued to rip through the stricken Cyberian command cruiser as the Liberty desperately tried to get some distance away from it.

The landing legs raised upward and secreted themselves within the hidden panels on the underside of the ship.

"Come on!" Michael shouted in desperation as he pressed hard on the main engine control in his right hand.

Kinraid watched from his battered bridge the slow disintegration of the command cruiser, an almighty explosion blasted the rear half of the vessel completely away. He hoped against all hope that the Liberty would get clear in time, *come on Michael get the hell out of there.*

Then, in one final gigantic explosion the rest of the ship blew itself to pieces, taking two nearby Cyberian cruisers with it, the bridge staff shielded their eyes to avoid being blinded, the brilliance of the explosion lit up the entire fleet. The shockwave was huge; the Liberty nowhere to be seen.

As the massive explosion died down, Kinraid's heart sank as he looked on fearfully, his friend and former Captain, everyone on that most famous of ships was gone.

As the shockwave expanded, something emerged, a tiny, faint, dark speck trailing smoke.

"Magnify that area!" Kinraid ordered, leaning forward pensively on his seat.

It was the Liberty, though badly damaged they had made it after all.

Michael's face appeared on the viewscreen, "Did ya miss me!"

"You lucky son of a bitch!" Kinraid replied grinning.

"Luck had nothing to do with it, we got pretty singed back there, but more or less we're okay."

As the tattered remains of the fleet slowly converged ready for the return trip to Charlie base for some much needed repairs, the remaining Cyberian ships simply stayed where they were, motionless, as if stuck in some sort of suspended animation, only the drones moved, milling about in confusion.

"What are they doing?" Thorne asked watching the viewer.

"Nothing really, they're confused, with the command ship destroyed the entire network has collapsed so nobody is getting any information through anymore; the orders have stopped."

Right across worlds spanning half the galaxy it was the same, Cyberian warriors attacking colonies in E.O.C.A and Solarian space simply stopped, shutting themselves down, drones fell from the sky. The people of those war-torn worlds looked on in disbelief, was the war really over?

It was, once again the spirit of humanity, aided by alien allies across the galaxy had prevailed, mankind's right to exist had been confirmed, although the cost had been high, millions of lives had been cruelly snuffed out across a hundred worlds.

Michael's personal cost had also been high, missing the birth of his second child, although this time he had succeeded in what he had set out to do, this time he had indeed kept the nightmares away.

The Liberty and the Valley-forge cruised side by side on their way home, both badly damaged and in dire need of repair, two ships very different yet both fighting for the same thing, the protection of humanity.

Far in the distance a pulsar shone out brightly, its light like a beacon, Michael wondered. *Despite the hardship, despite everything they had fought through, mankind would go on. Just like that pulsar shining brightly out into the depths of space, they were the eternal flame.*

That thought made him smile, gave him hope. This is Michael Alexander, Captain of the E.D.F.S Liberty signing off for the last time.

The Valley-forge and the Liberty continued to cruise side-by-side toward the light of that pulsar, toward the eternal flame.

The end.

E.D.F Chronicles – The Cyberian menace
Epilogue

Volgograd, Earth
One month later.

A chill breeze blew through the Szaika cemetery on the eastern outskirts of the city, disturbing the autumn leaf litter that rustled in the wake of the wind.

Michael stood silent, head bowed. A small gathering had arrived, close family and friends from all over Russia, a small contingent of E.D.F commandoes were also present, clad in their finest mess outfits. The bright scarlet red of their overcoats made them stand out sharply compared to the more demure, utilitarian nature of the typical Russian civilians gathered. They were all stood rigidly to attention, weapons at their sides, the sun glinting off polished bayonets.

An aged Russian orthodox priest read out the eulogy, and an interpreter was standing next to them for the benefit of those who were not from Russia.

"We are gathered here today," began the interpreter after a small pause. "To witness the burial of Nikolai Vargev, a proud man, strong and noble, true patriot of Russia and a great soldier who gave his own life to enable others of the galaxy to live in freedom and in peace."

The coffin was slowly carried forward, hand carved and polished, borne aloft by four more commandoes hand picked from those who had been the closest to him. His most trusted comrades, each one of them having shed blood with him across a dozen different worlds.

The coffin was draped with a white flag depicting the symbol of the E.D.F commandoes, of twin crossed swords overlaid with a planet in the centre and a large wreath surrounding it. A large number 1 was emblazoned within this planet, denoting his unit number.

The hymn of the Tsar's was playing in the background by a lone bugler as the coffin was slowly respectfully carried on its way to the allotted burial site.

The solemn song played with the utmost of reverence and care gave the whole procession an ethereal quality. Michael was still scarcely able to believe Nikolai, his great friend and comrade, was gone.

In the distance a black crow cawed as it neared its nest within a copse of trees, rustling and swaying gently in the breeze.

The Russian cold was biting, even Michael in his thick fur lined trench-coat shivered. He couldn't imagine how the Commandoes were holding up in their thinner mess uniforms, their features betraying no hint of discomfort, just pure stoic professionalism.

The coffin was slowly, gently lowered into the freshly dug allotment, the coffin itself was empty of course. After Nikolai spectacularly blew himself up in order to destroy that command ship, there was not a scrap left of him, nothing to put into a coffin at any rate.

The pastor nodded to Michael to begin his part of the eulogy.

"My great friend Nikolai Vargev," he paused slightly as he felt a slight tightening in his throat. "It was fate that brought us together, when the both of us happened to be marooned on Agemman at the beginning of the Krenaran war. I was stranded as my ship was destroyed in orbit, and you were leading a training exercise at the time of the attack. In the beginning things were difficult, neither of us knew or trusted each other, yet through the fires, the loss, the pain and bloodshed a great friendship was formed, a friendship forged in the fires of battle."

His voice began to crack ever so slightly, his lip began to quiver just a little bit, a tear threatened to roll down his cheek, yet despite the immense pain and loss of losing the closest friend he had ever known, he soldiered on.

"You have been the greatest friend I have ever known, you have taught me and helped me through so much in my own life, without your support and help I doubt I would be standing here today."

Slowly almost painfully, he knelt down and cast a holly wreath atop the coffin, the tear finally gave way, dripping onto the flag.

"Goodbye, old….friend," he whispered voice cracked with emotion.

Each of the assemblage then took a turn to cast a handful of earth onto the grave as a mark of respect.

The pastor began his final sermon.

"And now we commit the body of Nikolai Vargev, beloved son of Russia to the earth, ashes to ashes, earth to earth, dust to dust."

A two minute silence ensued, everyone stood over the grave, heads bowed in respect to such a great man. The silence was total, eerie, the only thing even daring to make a sound was that faint rustling of leaves in the distance and the gentle swaying of trees.

A swift shuffle of arms broke the silence as the eight strong commando contingent hefted their weapons, barrels pointing proudly into the air, and fired three quick volleys. The crack of gunfire echoed loudly around the cemetery, disturbing birds from trees, scaring wildlife. This final act of reverence seemed to hammer home the fact that Nikolai was really gone.

Once the proceedings were over, and the gathering had stopped to pay their respects. Michael thanked the pastor for his kind words then left the gathering, he didn't feel like lingering around, the pain was bad enough already.

E.D.F Chronicles – The Cyberian menace

He made for the hotel room he had booked for the night, while in the somewhat dilapidated cab he did not utter a single word, lost in grief as he remembered the times they had shared, both good and bad. He went to bed alone that night, staring at the bedside lamp, remembering, and keenly missing Kathryn's comforting embrace, her warmth he needed so badly right now. Though he understood why she couldn't be there, she had to take care of tiny Richard, just over a month old himself.

Michael gently rested his head onto his pillow, a final tear rolled its way down his cheek, a tear for his long lost friend and comrade.

Early next morning he bade a silent farewell to Nikolai, and to Russia one final time, and boarded the flight back home. Four hours later he touched down at Denver international airport via hypersonic jet transport, where Kathryn was waiting for him, smiling, and with the baby in his new pram.

He smiled and embraced her tightly, he had missed her so much during the emotional turmoil of the funeral.

"I still can't believe he's gone," Michael said shaking his head.

Kathryn looked at him, "he died as he would have wanted to, a warrior's death and a hero. Sacrificing himself to destroy his enemy, saving us all in the process, that sounds a lot like Nikolai to me." Kathryn replied nodding.

"You're right," Michael smiled, "he died with a weapon in his hand fighting his enemy, somehow I didn't think Nikolai was the type to just retire quietly with his pipe and slippers, relaxing in front of the fire; just not his style."

Kathryn smirked, "you know, you and him have a lot more in common than you both realise."

They clambered back into their car and began the long journey back to the Aspen foothills, to their home.

***

Shortly after the funeral, Michael officially retired once again, for good this time. Although still haunted to a degree due to the tragic losses of his first wife and son, at least he had found a new happiness with his second wife Kathryn, three years later they had a second child, a daughter called Anna.

Twenty years later, Michael now sixty seven developed aggressive pancreatic cancer, which spread into his liver and bowel. The doctors gave him only three months to live, yet he fought for a full year finally passing away in 2099. Living just long enough to witness Anna's years through the E.D.F academy, and then being accepted as chief pilot aboard the brand new Venture class torpedo destroyer. Despite his frailty Michael demanded to be present at the inauguration ceremony where he gave the order to get underway one last time. A proud father in command, and an equally proud daughter at the controls; Michael Alexander passed away just three days after that ceremony.

Richard Alexander, his eldest son went on to teach theoretical propulsion design at the institute of advanced avionics at Sigma XI, authoring several papers in his field.

Kathryn Alexander, after being widowed by Michael never re-married, instead she watched her son and daughter progress, a proud mother who still worked occasionally as a relief nurse at Aspen general hospital. Happy that Michael's legacy was being carried on by his offspring.

Quinn Kinraid went on to command the Valley-forge for another ten years while it remained flagship of the E.D.F fleet, his work helped facilitate a stable empire for the Krenarans once more, though a shadow compared to what it once was, the Krenaran people were nevertheless overjoyed that they had a least some part of what they possessed all those years ago, were not destined to die a slow death as nomads and wanderers, and had begun to repair the damage wrought upon them by the Cyberian advance through their space. His work led to the first true lasting peace between the two empires, finally earning the Krenarans respect in the process.

Johnson Logameier retired shortly after the Cyberian war, using the proceeds to found his own bulk freighter company. Starting with a single ship, a 'fixer upper' he called it, he went on to acquire several more and his company grew to rival some of the largest freight transporters, doing great trade ferrying goods back and forth from the Solarian empire.

Kerulithar continued his efforts to re-unify the Solarian and Dracos empires, re-doubling his efforts after the Cyberian conflict. Since the two races had fought side-by-side for the first time in over three centuries, however the Dracos realising that the Cyberian threat had ended returned to their isolationist ways, although they had a new homeworld, one of the planets ceded to them that was scoured of life by the Cyberians. Though Kerulithar doggedly kept a dialogue open for years afterward.

With the Cyberians defeated, the last major threat to the galaxy was gone, E.O.C.A set to repairing the damage done to its worlds with gusto as peace blossomed for many years between the various empires. The Solarians, badly hurt by the catastrophic damage inflicted upon them by the Cyberian advance, began to enter into a period of slow decline, their power and influence waning. The Solarian empire had passed the torch to mankind who thrived following the re-building of the shattered frontier worlds, eventually superceding them as the foremost race in the galaxy.

Thus, mankind, emerging blindly into the galactic void all those years ago prior to the Krenaran war, had realised the potential the Solarian people always knew it possessed. Embarking in a new golden age of mutual trade, peace, and co-operation between all empires of the galaxy.

Here ends the fourth and final part of the E.D.F saga.

About the author

Ian J. Smethurst is the author of the popular E.D.F chronicles series of novels, now in its fourth and final instalment.

Born in Cheshire, England in 1981, to a traditional family, Ian's mother is a housewife and his father worked in industry and Heavy goods vehicle driving, though now happily retired.

Ian developed an affinity for science fiction and fantasy at a very early age, and was reading various adult fantasy and SF novels from the age of 8. The phenomenon that was Star trek, Star wars, and various Sci-Fi shows came to his attention during his early years in high school, and it was here where Ian's creative writing really began to take root.

His school soon picked up on Ian's latent talent, and would encourage it by giving him the occasional creative writing exercise to complete, and he always loved doing these, excelling at them. His teachers noted that one of his main strengths was in fact creative writing, possessing of a boundless imagination and a vocabulary far in excess of his years which shows through in his writing.

As Ian grew older and the world of work beckoned, his writing began to wane, although the ideas were still there bubbling under the surface. It was during this time when he first began to come up with the idea for E.D.F chronicles, which would linger in the back of his mind for almost a decade.

Finally, in 2007, after much upheaval in his personal life, he took up the pen and began writing seriously, completing the first draft of E.D.F chronicles : The Krenaran massacre in just three months while spending some time out in Bulgaria with family; although it took almost 2 years for it to become a fully written manuscript.

Having now completed the fourth and final novel in his much loved E.D.F Chronicles series which he describes as being a labour of love and his greatest achievement to date, he is hard at work penning a new series the Jack Stone novels, a series of mystery novels set in the Solar system of a distant future, the first of which Aurora Centralis is due for release autumn 2016.

Ian is also a keen historian and was shortlisted for the 2008 writers reign short story contest, with 'Just ten pounds' a contemporary story telling the dangers of knife crime within modern day Britain, and longlisted in the 2011 writers review short story competition with the fantasy ghost story 'nightwhisper'.

Forthcoming works

Aurora Centralis
A Jack Stone Novel

When a mysterious and deadly new drug begins to flood the streets of New York threatening a full blown epidemic. Detective Jack Stone of the systems police must try to track down the source of the shipments and the criminals behind it. For a washed up has-been Detective like Stone, it's the case of a lifetime. Although the places his investigation takes him will be beyond his wildest imaginings, and the forces at work more dangerous than even he realizes in the first of the Jack Stone novels.

Out Summer 2017